Dear Reader:

Years ago, when I was a baby writer with only a few books under my belt, I wrote *Kiss of a Dark Moon,* my second paranormal romance (*Marked by Moonlight* was the first). Like most stories I've written over the years, *Kiss of a Dark Moon* features two protagonists falling in love while battling impossible odds in a fantastical world.

This story captures my profound love of the romance genre . . . and the attitudes and trends that were so popular at the time: werewolves, vampires, witches, fae, and alpha heroes—oh my! Many things have changed over the years (no more answering machines—ha!)—particularly my own style and experiences as a writer. And yet the core story of love and hope amid darkness holds true within these pages. It's what keeps bringing me back to this genre.

I continue to feel only great joy and gratitude to Simon & Schuster for publishing this book then . . . and now again. It's a humbling experience to see the journey of Kit and Rafe return for a new generation of readers.

If you're new to *Kiss of a Dark Moon,* I hope you enjoy this beautiful new edition. If you're an old friend, welcome back!

Happy reading,
Sophie Jordan

# Kiss
## OF A
# Dark Moon

## SOPHIE JORDAN

**G**

**Gallery Books**

New York   Amsterdam/Antwerp   London
Toronto   Sydney/Melbourne   New Delhi

# G

Gallery Books
An Imprint of Simon & Schuster, LLC
1230 Avenue of the Americas
New York, NY 10020

This book is a work of fiction. Any references to historical events, real people,
or real places are used fictitiously. Other names, characters, places, and events
are products of the author's imagination, and any resemblance to actual
events or places or persons, living or dead, is entirely coincidental.

This Gallery Books trade paperback edition May 2026

GALLERY BOOKS and colophon are registered trademarks of Simon & Schuster, LLC

For information about special discounts for bulk purchases, please contact Simon &
Schuster Special Sales at 1-866-506-1949 or business@simonandschuster.com.

The Simon & Schuster Speakers Bureau can bring authors to your live event.
For more information or to book an event, contact the Simon & Schuster Speakers
Bureau at 1-866-248-3049 or visit our website at www.simonspeakers.com.

Manufactured in the United States of America

10  9  8  7  6  5  4  3  2  1

Library of Congress Cataloging-in-Publication Data is available.

ISBN 978-1-6680-7503-6
ISBN 978-1-4165-7987-8 (ebook)

 Scan here to get book recommendations,
exclusive offers, and more delivered to your inbox.

*For the little prince in my life—*
*you've been a hero from day one*

# PROLOGUE

AD 70

Fire licked the night sky, shading the air an eerie blood-red glow. The moon, awash in the same red, followed their movements, a great eye staring down at them as they raced through the village, their feet pounding out a trampled path of mud and snow.

*Blood moon.*

They shoved past the gawking, mesmerized villagers. The flames from the burning fortress cast their faces a demonic red. With stricken expressions the peasants watched flame and smoke devour the fortress atop the hill. Watched instead of running. As they should have. As he did.

His lungs constricted, the cold air a freezing burn in his too-tight chest. Despite the wintry air, his mother's hand felt hot, slippery with sweat around his. Her breath gusted from her blue-tinged lips in loud pants, clouding the air before them.

She pulled him along, her voice frenzied, "Don't stop, Christophe! Don't look back!"

They ran. Fleeing the blood, the mayhem, the beast that

nothing could stop. Not swords. Not the battle-axes of armed knights. Not fire. Nothing.

Choking on smoke-laden air, he worked to keep up with her long strides. He tripped over a gnarled root and fell, losing her hand.

Sprawled on the hard, frozen earth, Christophe could not stop himself. He had to see. Had to look. Throat tight, he looked over his shoulder, feeling like Lot's wife turning for a final glimpse of the damned Sodom.

Even after all that had happened, all he had seen, a gasp ripped from his lips at the sight of his home, writhing in a nest of flames, of the great plume of smoke rising, twisting like a black serpent to kiss the moon.

Even with the parapets engulfed in flame, he made out one figure there, running madly to and fro, screaming a terrible howl that shook the skies. Its large talonlike hands clawed the air.

Not a man. A beast as large as a bear, black hair covering most of its huge frame. The animal had torn Christophe's three eldest brothers apart limb from limb, devouring them until only bloodied masses remained that bore no resemblance to men.

A shrill keening bled into the whistling wind. Christophe scanned the tree-crowded hills, searching for the source, and finding her. A tattered gray cloak whipped around her on a wind of smoke and death. Her ink-black hair flew behind her, a demon's banner amid the white of winter.

The lovely face that had weaved spells about many a man twisted with triumph at the macabre scene. A face he would not forget. A face that should have been blank with death. Entombed beneath earth and stone per his father's edict.

The sorceress stood on a snowcapped rise facing the castle, one slender arm lifted on the wind, a long finger pointing accusingly at the smoldering castle. Her lips peeled back from her teeth in a semblance of a smile, her words a gleeful shriek—a terrible mantra that fell from her mouth again and again and again.

"Curse you, Étienne Marshan! You and your line shall know only hell's hunger."

"*Tresa.*" Her name dropped from his mouth, heavy as a stone sinking through water.

"Burn! Burn! Burn!" she shrieked.

Horrified, he looked back to the fortress, watching as the monstrous creature, fire licking up its great body, jumped from the flaming ramparts and into the moat below. Holding his breath, Christophe prayed the beast had perished. A long moment passed before a large dark-furred head rose from the flame-cast waters and swam for shore.

*His father lived.*

He snapped his gaze back to the rise, searching for the witch who had wrought such evil—but she was gone.

Only her curse remained.

And he. The last of his father's line. *The last Marshan.*

"Not the last," Christophe swore, stumbling over muddied snow. "By God or hell, I'll not be the last."

# 1

Kit's attention strayed from the man sitting across from her. Her gaze flitted over the dimly lit bar and restaurant. Only eight o'clock and the place was busy, every table full. The tiny hairs along her nape stood on end, and she shivered as she assessed her surroundings. Her gaze roamed the dance floor, the tables, then back to the bar, checking each and every face, looking, searching for the source of her unease.

Her date's voice faded to a distant buzz. The music from the band playing onstage subsided to a dull throbbing of drums and guitars, the singer's voice lost entirely as Kit scanned the room. Awareness tightened the skin on her face, made her ears burn and cheeks tingle.

She knew what she was looking for. It had always been so with her—this intuition, the deep sense of knowing. When it came to detecting lycans, her radar was dead on. Even better than her brother's. At least, he claimed this.

Her gaze lit on them then. Three of them sat at the bar, the drinks in their hands untouched as their silver eyes surveyed the room, searching for something besides alcohol to quench their appetites. Four days until the full moon, and they were hungry. Starving. They looked haggard, features drawn and tight. Their bunched muscles corded and flexed beneath their shirts. Even from across the room she sensed their impatience, their desperate hunger.

The closer the full moon, the more dangerous they became. Some hunters refused to hunt altogether so close to moonrise. Not Kit. Those hunters played it safe. Cowards, in her book, disappearing when mankind most needed protection.

They flirted with a waitress, their smiles seductive, enticing, as alluring as fire to a moth. And just as deadly. The girl preened at their attention, clearly flattered, unaware of the dangerous spell they were weaving.

Kit's eyes narrowed as one of them lifted a hand and ran it down the waitress's shoulder in a leisurely stroke. Kit read the threat behind that caress, the barely checked hunger. Hungry in the way a beast covets its prey.

They may not be able to satisfy their blood hunger until shifted, but there were other ways to unleash their aggression, to sate their lust until moonrise. The way their feral gazes followed the young waitress as she moved off, Kit knew the unsuspecting female had just become a candidate for their dark appetites. If she didn't do something, the waitress would be tonight's victim.

"Hello."

Kit snapped her attention back to her date. "Sorry," she murmured, setting her drink down on the table and gathering up her purse. "Would you excuse me? I need to use the ladies' room."

Dan nodded, his soft brown eyes clouding with doubt. He was probably wondering what kind of woman he had agreed to meet for drinks tonight that she needed to dive into the restroom five minutes after saying hello.

She wound her way around tables and waiters, the heels of her boots silent on the carpet as she slipped a hand inside her purse and removed a small bottle of vanilla body spray. She had learned long ago that sweet scents such as vanilla and cinnamon worked best in attracting lycans. With a quick spritz at her throat, she dropped the bottle back in her purse.

Her heart hammering, she cut a path their way. Pasting a smile on her face, she squeezed between two of them, taking special care to brush against them. Physical contact was important. Anything to make herself noticeable.

One of them, the most striking of the trio, with dark hair and tanned skin, leaned forward on his barstool. She slid him a speculative glance, her smile inviting as she asked the bartender to break a twenty.

"Thanks," she murmured, accepting her money and pushing herself off from the bar. She tossed a saucy glance over her shoulder as she sauntered away, catching sight of the dark one's nearly imperceptible nod to his companions. The movement was slight, but enough. Enough for Kit. The trap had been set. Her brother did not approve of her tactics, but they worked for her. The soulless bastards never expected a woman to fight back. Much less pack silver.

Inhaling, she headed toward the winding iron staircase that led to the restaurant's bottom floor, knowing that the three would follow.

Three. Not an advisable number to take on alone. But then, Kit was accustomed to doing things alone.

◗ ◗ ● ◖ ◖ ◖

Leaning forward, Rafe Santiago glanced through the windshield. Fingers of red and gold clawed at the graying sky. He inhaled deeply, lowering his gaze back to the building he had been watching for the last half hour. Watching and waiting. Time was running out. Blood already laced the air, rich and pungent as freshly tilled earth.

The bar's front door swung open. A woman stepped out. Petite, with a mass of short blond waves, she headed down the sidewalk alone, her short strides quick in sexy black boots. "Fuck-me boots." The kind a man liked to imagine wrapped around his waist.

His gaze shot to the seat next to him, to the file there that he had memorized. The photograph within was black-and-white and not the best quality, but he would have recognized her anywhere. He recognized her now. Kit March. Rogue lycan hunter. He grimaced. Or huntress. Whatever he called her, it didn't change the situation. He'd been sent to terminate her.

A quick glance at the night sky through his windshield brought forth a frown.

Four days until the full moon, and the beasts ran restless, almost as dangerous as when the moon beamed brightly overhead, engorged against a dark sky. He'd observed such nights before. Countless times. He knew what was to come, the carnage that resulted when hell's foot soldiers were granted free roam, their lust for blood and flesh at its zenith.

It happened all the time. Unsolved murders around the world spoke to that. Mysterious catastrophes throughout history held no mystery for him. Lycan archivists had documented the truth. Villages sacked. Cities razed. The Siege of Jerusalem in 1099. Jamestown. The riverboat *Sultana*. He knew the truth behind those tragedies. Knew the blame went to lycans.

He assessed his surroundings, his nostrils flaring. Almost as though his thoughts had called them forth, the door to the bar swung open again and *they* emerged.

Three big bastards stepped out into the warm dusk. Even across the street's distance, their eyes glowed a familiar silver. Pack creatures. Bold and deadly. Confident in their power, they had not bothered to don colored contacts as some lycans did, wary of any one of the dozen hunters in the city detecting them.

They stood still as stone for a moment, not speaking as they lifted their faces to the air, no doubt catching the scent of the female who had gone ahead of them. In moments, they were moving, fast as wind, following her with avid, feral eyes as she turned into an alleyway.

Little fool likely had no idea there were three beasts on her tail. She would be overpowered in an instant.

Rafe opened his car door and stepped into the humid night. He treaded silently after them, his strides quick. He couldn't let them get to her first. *If she were attacked . . .*

He blinked hard, refusing to contemplate the prospect. He would not allow that to happen.

For all their sakes.

Quickening his pace, he approached the alley, the sweet scent of vanilla teasing his nose as he followed in Kit March's wake, another predator set loose on the night.

# 2

Kit scanned ahead of her, her nerves stretched taut as wire as she turned down an alley three blocks away from the bar she had just quit.

The steps behind her were undetectable amid the busy city sounds, but she knew they were there nonetheless. Just behind her. She had baited her trap. If she knew how to do one thing well, it was get their attention. After all these years, it had become instinctual to her.

She imagined the sour heat of their breath on her neck and wiped one sweaty palm against her skirt. Her pulse thrummed hotly at her throat and she fought to steady it, knowing they could sense her adrenaline. Smell it like smoke on the air. She didn't want them to detect her unease.

A quick glance up revealed a sun-streaked horizon battling the murk of impending night. Dusk. The hunting hour.

She cursed to herself when she thought of the date whom she'd left behind at the bar, sitting alone now with his glass of Chardonnay as she strolled between the twin brick walls of a shadow-shrouded alley, grade-A scum hot on her heels.

Lately the loneliness had gotten to her, and she let her friend Gus set her up with his next door neighbor's son.

Loneliness. That growing ache for a connection, like the kind her brother had found with his wife, the kind the whole world seemed capable of finding, except for her. Why should her determination to hunt and destroy lycans preclude her from leading a normal life? From finding intimacy with another human being? Her brother was able to combine both worlds. She vowed to do the same.

Whether she could find that with Dan remained to be seen. He seemed like a decent guy. At least from what she could tell after five minutes. They hadn't made it very far past introductions when she had sensed their presence.

The heels of her boots clicked sharply over the broken concrete. In the cavernlike depths of the alley, the heavy tread of their steps rose over the night, and she knew it was time to make her move. Time to show them they'd picked the wrong woman.

A hot gust of air expelled from her lips as she began to dig through her purse. Nearing a Dumpster, she slowed her steps, feigning ignorance of the three dark shapes closing in behind her.

She tensed for the fight.

*Bring it, scumbags.*

Slipping one hand inside her purse, she wrapped her fingers around her gun. The cold metal felt reassuring in her hand as she flicked off the safety. Her lips moved, silently, feverishly, as she issued a quick prayer. The same prayer she always muttered. A silent plea that they not suspect, not realize *who* she was—*what* she was—until it was too late.

Faking a little stumble, she hunkered down low and reached for her boot, as though her heel had come loose. Dropping her purse, she pulled her gun free and whirled around in time to see them lunge, teeth bared in a hiss, eyes glowing a preternatural silver.

She fired. One spun from the bullet to his chest and landed with a hard thud. Caught off guard, the other two stopped, looking in shock from her to the corpse at their feet.

Without blinking, she used her advantage and fired again, dropping another one. They'd obviously never expected a woman to be armed, to fight back. It had never crossed their minds that she could be a viable threat, an actual lycan hunter. Feed and fornicate: nothing else filled their heads. To them, she was merely fresh meat.

Forgetting his comrades, the remaining lycan charged her with the speed known to his cursed species. He launched himself at her, a dark blur in the air. Before she could squeeze out a third shot, he knocked the gun from her hand. It skittered across the filth-covered pavement. Out of reach. He struck her a brutal blow, and her head snapped back, sharp pain exploding in her cheek. She staggered, the coppery taste of blood filling her mouth.

Her breath escaped in a hiss of pain. Recovering her balance, she spat out a mouthful of blood and put her training to use. She spun around and delivered a back kick to his head, gratified at the sharp snap of his neck. A diversionary tactic. She could never hope to outfight a lycan. No mortal could. She only hoped to buy enough time to reach her gun.

As he staggered back from her kick, she spun on her heels and dashed toward her weapon. A hard hand clamped around her ankle. She was slammed to the ground with a cry, inches from her weapon.

He dragged her back over loose gravel and jagged concrete. Grunting, she clawed for a handhold, straining toward her gun. Ignoring the sting of her palms, she flipped onto her back and kicked the lycan squarely in the face with the heel of her boot. Once. Twice.

Blood gushed from his nose as he grappled for her flailing feet.

Still kicking, she stretched an arm behind her, groping for her weapon.

"Need some help?"

Kit looked up at the sound of the thick, gravelly voice. A stranger stood just beyond them, his face in shadow. Light poured from the mouth of the alley, surrounding him, limning his large physique. Great. Just what she needed. Some civilian to worry about.

The lycan looked, too, growling at the new arrival. She took advantage of the distraction, grinding her heel in his eye.

The beast howled and released her ankle.

"Get the hell out of here," she spit out, shooting across the remaining distance for her gun.

"And miss the show?" the dark voice rumbled over the air.

Turning, she fired as the creature came at her again, growling fierce curses, his face a gory mess. Blood sprayed her boots and legs.

The lycan collapsed at her feet. Without hesitating, she kicked the heavy weight away and snatched her weapon from the ground. For a moment she watched the lycan's silver eyes fade, recede to a very mortal—very *dead*—brown. Just another corpse, another homicide for HPD to chalk up to the ever-increasing crime rate.

"Impressive."

Chest heaving with serrated breaths, she rose to her feet and faced the stranger, knowing that her first guess had been wrong.

Not a civilian. Another hunter.

Dread filled her as she lifted her gaze to the man. Most of the agents in the area knew her—or *of* her. And most objected, buying into NODEAL's policy prohibiting female hunters. No doubt this guy worked for NODEAL, the National Organization Against Ancient and Evolving Lycanthropes.

Great. Cooper would hear all about tonight. Specifically, the three-to-one odds. And that meant Gideon would, too. They would tear her a new one for taking such risks. She'd been in bad jams before—and had always made her kills. She would just remind Cooper and Gideon of that very thing.

Brushing loose gravel from her stinging palms, she trained her gaze on the dark figure. Demon-dark eyes gleamed out from his shadowed features. He stepped closer, bringing his face out of shadow. She sucked in a breath.

Inky lashes much too long for any man to possess framed those dark eyes, which watched her intently, making her suddenly self-conscious. Annoying. She normally didn't get self-conscious.

Scooping up her purse, she shoved her gun into it. "You don't need to be here. As you can see, I have it under control."

"Right," he replied, his well-carved lips twisting. A hint of an accent, rich and throaty, laced his voice, the origin indecipherable to her ears.

Eyeing him warily, she fished her cell phone out of her purse and left a quick message on Cooper's voicemail, supplying the location, time, and body count. Even officially unsanctioned to hunt, she gave him a status report after every kill. He was a stickler for keeping their database up-to-date. A single lycan kill couldn't go unrecorded.

The agent continued to watch her, his dark gaze oddly intent. Dropping her phone into her purse, she tossed out "Thanks again."

Turning, she strode away even as she felt his stare drilling into her back. Stepping onto the sidewalk, she glanced regretfully at the door of the bar, then back down at herself. She was splattered in blood; her palms and knees a scraped mess. Resuming her date was out of the question. If Dan was even still waiting. She grimaced. Another botched attempt at a love life.

Watching for cars, she crossed the street, heels clicking, eager to put as much distance as possible between herself and the other hunter.

At her vehicle, she fumbled for her keys, imagining that those sinfully dark eyes were still trained on her, burning through her, making her hot and cold at the same time. He *was* handsome. Understandable that she might lose her composure a bit. The skin at her nape prickled and feathered with unease.

Finding her keys, she noticed that her hand shook. Adrenaline loss, she reasoned, pushing the unlock button. Certainly it had nothing to do with the lycan hunter.

"Where I come from we do not have female hunters."

Spinning around, Kit pressed her back against her car, surprised at how close he stood, caging her in. She must be slipping. She had not even heard him move in behind her.

"Hey, back off." Her hand moved to the bulk of her purse at her side, ready to pull out her gun.

He dipped his face close to her neck. His warm breath misted her neck. "Little girls who smell of vanilla get gobbled up."

"Is that a fact?" She tried to sound calm even as her heart raced. "And where are you from?"

His mouth lifted in an ominous smile that did strange things to her insides, but he did not answer, only stepped closer.

Kit's mouth went dry. Unsure how to respond, she watched his lips lose their smile as he leaned in, his face ruthless and unforgiving, beautiful as any marble sculpture. Those dark eyes of his dropped to her mouth, and her belly tightened. Mesmerized, she couldn't move.

Every instinct said that he was going to kiss her, and a part of her began to suspect she was stupid enough to let him—until she felt the cold steel of a gun against her ribs.

# 3

Kit's pulse jackknifed against her throat. "Who are you?"

"Rafe Santiago."

"Rafe," she echoed, trying to appear calm at the feel of the gun in her side. "Never heard of you."

"But you've heard of EFLA." It was more a statement than a question.

"Yeah." She swallowed back the immediate foul taste that rose in her throat.

The European Federation of Lycan Agents was hard-core. More rigid than NODEAL, its American counterpart.

So he was one of them. She saw it in the cold determination of his gaze, dark as fathomless waters. An EFLA agent. Ruthless in his resolve to hunt lycans and uphold the codes of his organization. Codes that condemned *her* and all she did. All she stood for. "You're with EFLA."

EFLA did not tolerate female hunters in its ranks—or rogue agents of any kind. And by definition, she was both. Cooper had once told her that EFLA would have killed her at the first rumor of her activities. Her and Gideon.

"Your guess would be correct," he replied in an exotic accent that made her think of warm vineyards and dark seas. Deceptive that such a cold-blooded killer—only cold-blooded killers could work for EFLA—should possess a voice like that. Deceptive and dangerous.

She glanced down at the gun trained on her. "Why bother distracting that lycan from his fun with me, then?" Considering what he was—what *she* was—he could have justified finishing off both of them.

A corner of his mouth turned up. "I'm not a sadist."

"Just a killer," she shot back, darting a pointed glance to the gun he held on her.

Something flashed in his eyes. The glassy cold there shuddered like a flame flickering in the wind, letting in a spark of emotion. Then, just like that, it was gone. Cold calculation returned to his gaze. His throaty, exotic voice rolled over her like a drag of silk on naked flesh. "Well, we're both killers, aren't we?"

She snorted. "Somehow I don't think we're the same."

His gaze skimmed her, slowly sliding up the length of her boots and stopping again on her face. "No. We are not."

She drew a deep breath and tried not to feel stripped, vulnerable and exposed under his stare. "So what's next?" She held herself tense, poised for a fight. "Are you going to shoot me?"

"Would it be so easy?"

"You can find out." She tensed.

His lips twitched. Moments passed. The sound of cars rushing along the nearby interstate hummed over the air. She held her breath, debating her next move, staring into his eyes, trying to read him, to determine how far he would carry out his duties to EFLA.

He eased his gun off her. Cocking a brow, he stepped back and discreetly tucked the gun beneath his jacket.

"We're not alike," she continued. "I kill only things that need killing. Monsters." She shot a pointed glare in the direction of the gun he had tucked away. "Not humans. Especially humans who destroy lycans."

"Even humans require killing now and then. When justified. NODEAL would agree with that. Just ask your brother. And his wife."

So he knew about Gideon and Claire. Knew that she had been infected by a lycan and that Gideon had failed to kill her, as NODEAL required. He must also know that Gideon had saved Claire.

"You see how I roll." She waved a hand to the alley were the three corpses lay rotting. "You think I give a rat's ass for NODEAL's policies?"

His lips twitched as though he wanted to laugh. But his expression didn't change; it remained stony as ever.

His words replayed themselves in her head. *When justified.* She stared hard at his face. The impenetrable mask didn't crack. Not a lash blinked over those liquid dark eyes. Was he implying that killing her would be justifiable? Because she dared to hunt lycans? Why should it matter so much to NODEAL or EFLA who performed the messy task of killing the bloodthirsty creatures, as long as it got done?

"Maybe you should reconsider how you play the game. I don't go jamming guns into innocent people," she continued. "Especially if they're dedicated to the same cause I am."

With a tilt of his dark head, he stepped close again, too close. "And are you so innocent?"

She tried to speak, but whatever words she thought to say were trapped in her throat.

Clearly he did not consider her a legitimate hunter. Like all the rest. NODEAL or EFLA, it made little difference. They didn't respect her. Didn't consider her one of them. Sexist bastards. You'd think they would be happy to have another hunter working the streets.

The size and strength of the lycan packs were only growing worldwide. Fortunately they didn't infect indiscriminately. But they bred—and fed, as the rising number of missing persons and unsolved murders each year attested. Every lycan dead made only a tiny dent in the lycan threat against humanity.

Their behavior had grown bolder over the last decade. Kit harbored suspicions; she feared they were no longer satisfied with discreetly existing among the human population. The packs were becoming organized, perhaps even forging alliances. Mankind could be on the brink of war with a species whose very existence they'd chalked up to myth.

Area NODEAL agents knew that Kit hunted the same streets they did—officially unsanctioned, true. But they knew Cooper condoned her activities. And they steered clear of her because of that. None of the three dozen agents comprising the Houston NODEAL division would ever dare pull a gun on her.

But the man before her was different. He didn't answer to Cooper. NODEAL, with its bureaucracy and codes, was bad enough. EFLA was another animal entirely. Staring at the imposing man before her only confirmed that. Everything about him screamed danger. Warned her to get far away from him.

His dark eyes glinted with light, slid over her slowly, thoroughly. "You think yourself as dedicated to hunting lycans as I am? As capable?"

"I don't know anything about you," she hedged.

"But you know about EFLA."

She gave a jerky nod.

He lifted one shoulder. "Then you know all you need to know about me."

"Enough," she agreed. Enough to know she should not stand

here talking to him another minute. For whatever reason, he had not shot her. But that didn't mean he wouldn't.

His gaze roamed over her, like a deadly serpent slithering through grass. "Where's your brother?"

The question startled her, telling her right away that he knew her. Or rather *of* her. This was no chance meeting.

The tiny hairs on her nape prickled. "Why?" she demanded, unease tripping down her spine, urging her to flee from this man who seemed to know everything about her.

Except she never ran from a fight. Especially from some hunter out of the Dark Ages who didn't believe women could hunt lycans— and that any who dared to should be benched. Permanently.

Her fingers curled into a fist at her side. "Why do you want to know about my brother?" She fought back the worry from her voice. It would do no good to sound concerned, to reveal that he had rattled her.

Officially, Gideon had quit NODEAL two years ago. Unofficially, he still hunted. But he hunted his way. More often performing rescue missions than the strict killing sprees of his past. He no longer relished the hunt, the kill. Meeting Claire had changed that. Changed him. He focused on saving lives rather than terminating lycans. Another reason for the growing gulf between them. That and his marriage. He had found someone with whom to share his life. Someone who fulfilled him more than the taste of revenge ever had.

He'd gone soft. Something Kit vowed would never happen to her. She would never forget her goal in life: To rid the world of lycans. To make them pay.

"He's quite the legend. Perhaps I only want to meet him."

She narrowed her gaze on him. "Why are you really here? Aren't there enough lycans to hunt on your continent?"

He cocked his head to the side. "Of course. Though I must say

you Americans could use some of EFLA's talent. Lycans are growing at an alarming rate here."

"So you want to help us out, is that it?"

"I'm just . . . visiting."

Kit snorted. Visiting. Right. She didn't believe in coincidence.
Or that he was out for her brother's autograph. This was no random meeting. In her line of work, random didn't exist.

"Visiting," she echoed, her hand moving for the car door's handle. "So instead of touring the Space Center, you decide to troll the
streets for lycans? Coincidentally the same lycans I'm hunting?"

He smiled, transforming his face in the process. She no longer
stared at a face carved of stone, rigid and imposing in its male
beauty. He now looked human. Approachable. Something in her
chest tightened, twisted at the sight.

"I'm not interested in tourist activities, Katherine."

She flinched. No one called her Katherine. At least she didn't
remember anyone ever calling her that. There was a time in her
life where her memories were dim. Before the age of eight. Before
her parents died. The harder she tried to remember those days, the
more elusive they were, running ahead of her, fast as smoke on the
wind, forever beyond her reach.

"How do you know my name?" she demanded.

"I know a lot about you. And your brother. It's my job to know
such things."

Her lungs contracted as she remembered all Cooper had ever
told her about EFLA—things that made NODEAL look about as
fierce as a hall monitor in junior high. Was he here to investigate
her? And Gideon? Did he know about her brother's alliance with
Darius?" A shiver rolled down her spine. That could be bad. Very
bad. "What do you want?"

"I wanted to meet you."

Her fingers tightened around the door handle. Still, she could not retreat. Curiosity outweighed her trepidation. "How do you know about me?"

"A female agent? Come, Katherine—"

"Kit," she broke in.

"Kit." He nodded once. "EFLA has known about you for a while. We've been following your activities with great interest. We've documented every kill you've ever made. Impressive. We're amazed you're still alive."

Was he here to remedy that?

"Well, now you've met me." Lifting the handle, she opened her car door.

"Maybe we could go somewhere. We must talk—"

"I don't see what we could possibly have to say to one another." Sliding into the driver's seat, she tried to shut the door.

His hand caught it. Glaring at the tanned, elegant fingers, she tried to tug the door shut, grunting from the effort.

"How about that NODEAL is a thing of the past. And Cooper is on his way out."

She ceased tugging on the door and stared at him in alarm. Her palm grew sweaty where it clutched the door's arm rest. Her job—hunting in relative freedom—depended on Cooper's looking the other way. Without Cooper, NODEAL might actually stop her from hunting. Or try to, anyway.

"I thought that might get your attention."

"What are you talking about?"

"It's been in the works for some time now. EFLA and NODEAL are merging." He paused, adding, "With EFLA at the helm."

"Shit," she muttered, her heart squeezing painfully in her chest, as though an invisible fist had grabbed hold of it. All her hopes of being a paid, sanctioned agent vanished at his announcement.

"Your fun is over."

"It was never fun to me, never a game," she snapped, thinking of her parents, thinking of all she had lost because of the soulless fiends walking the earth.

Heart racing, she knew she had to go. Had to talk to Cooper. Had to get in contact with her brother. With another grunt of effort, she managed to slam the door.

"Thanks for the information," she said through the window, her words ringing hollowly.

"They sent me for you."

Her fingers stilled around her keys. Her mind reeled. Still, she did not look his way again, avoided drowning in the fathomless pools of his eyes. Dark puddles without reflection. The eyes of a killer. An assassin. *Her* assassin. Not at this moment, perhaps. But eventually.

She stared straight ahead. He continued talking, his voice loud and clear through the window's glass. Undeniable. "I'm here to stop you."

She swallowed through her suddenly too tight throat. "And my brother?"

"Him, too. Where is he, Kit?"

So he knew Gideon was out of town, but evidently not where. A shaky breath shuddered past her lips: mingled relief and gratitude that Gideon and Claire had chosen now to take a vacation.

Gideon's absence was probably the only reason this man wasn't bothering to kill her now. He needed her to get to Gideon. It was not an advantage she was about to give up.

"You expect me to offer him up to you?" She turned the key in the ignition. The engine of her VW purred to life. "Sorry. You're going to have to work a little harder for your kill."

She slid the gear into reverse and turned, locking gazes with him through the glass, knowing that while he wouldn't stop her from leaving, he also wouldn't stop. They would meet again. EFLA was that way. Relentless.

"Keep away from me," she added, "Or you'll regret it."

He gave a small nod of acknowledgment, well-shaped lips curving in a humorless smile. "I look forward to the next time we meet."

His blasé attitude struck a nerve. Did he think her weak? Easy to kill? Because she was a woman? Familiar indignation spiraled through her.

"Go ahead. Underestimate me. It will be your mistake."

His smile deepened, grooves forming in the planes of his cheeks. The bastard was too handsome for his own good.

Easing her foot off the brake, she pressed down on the gas pedal and drove away.

# 4

Darkness had fallen by the time she pulled into her brother's driveway. Locusts sang, their calls strident and insistent on the warm night. She let herself in with the spare key Gideon had given her, looking over her shoulder and searching the shadows as she unlocked the front door. Her feet shifted in place on the porch, the wood creaking beneath her.

Flipping on the light switch, she hesitated at the edge of the living room, her gaze sweeping the tidy room, almost expecting someone to jump out at her. It wouldn't hurt to be extra cautious. There could be other EFLA agents in town besides Rafe Santiago.

Shaking off her stillness, she locked the door and punched in the alarm code. Striding across the living room and into the kitchen, her eyes drifted over the framed photographs lining the walls. Married only two years, Claire had managed to fill the house with photos of herself and Gideon. Kit shook her head. Before Claire, she had never seen a photograph anywhere in her brother's house. Not of their parents. Not of her. Gideon wasn't the type to forage through old albums and hang pictures of the past on the wall. A past that they both fought to remember. And forget.

Claire had become his family. His present and future. Every framed photograph proclaimed that. Someday they would have children, and more photos would line the walls. Claire would see to that. She was that sort—the kind of mother figure Kit had missed growing up. The sort that baked cookies and read stories. Her brother would have the family Kit had always dreamed of having. And Kit would have to content herself with reruns of *The Waltons*.

The thought shouldn't have made her feel the way it did. Empty. Hollow inside. Bitter with envy. It was an ugly feeling, and she shoved it back to the deep shadows of her heart.

Lifting the phone off the wall hook, she dialed Cooper's number. She had tried calling him on her cell on the way home but no luck. But given the amount of times he'd called her a pain in the ass, she suspected he didn't always pick up when she called. Maybe if he saw Gideon's number on the caller ID he would pick up. After several rings, the familiar sound of his prerecorded voice filled her ear, and she hung up.

Hand still on the phone, she hesitated, biting her bottom lip and contemplating calling Gideon. At the moment he was at a cabin in the mountains of New Mexico. Safe with Claire. If she told him what had happened tonight he would be headed home before she could talk him out of it. She could handle the situation without him. It had taken her years to convince him that she could handle herself and hunt lycans. Did she really want to play the role of helpless female now?

The hardwood floor creaked beneath her feet as she climbed the stairs. Once in the room Gideon and Claire used as both an office and guest room, she rifled through her duffel bag for clothes. Stripping, she kicked her grimy clothes into the corner with a grimace. She had bought the skirt for her date tonight. Now she doubted she would get the bloodstains out. She had lost more clothes than she cared to recount hunting lycans.

Still uneasy after the events of the night, she took her gun with her into the bathroom. Rafe Santiago had proven himself an expert on matters concerning her. Naturally he would know where Gideon lived. Her skin prickled at the thought of him standing just outside, staring at the house. Was he out there? Watching with those dark eyes? Waiting?

She peered out from the small window above the toilet, her fingers parting the blinds as she looked down on the quiet street, dimly lit from the occasional front porch light. A few random cars were parked along the street. Nothing out of the ordinary. He wouldn't make a move, she decided. Not tonight. Not as long as he needed her brother.

Sighing, she set the gun on the top of the toilet tank and angled her neck in an attempt to ease the tension in her shoulders. Stepping into the shower, she adjusted the valves until a warm spray of water rained down on her body. She worked quickly, soaping her body and shampooing her hair. Turning off the water, she stepped onto the bath rug and rubbed herself dry with a towel.

Snatching her T-shirt off the counter, she pulled it over her head, pausing at her reflection in the mirror. Her light curls looked dark when wet, a tangled mess that clung to her head and neck like ivy crawling a fence. A humorless smile twisted her lips. Her eyes stared widely, almost too large for her face, making her look haunted. Or maybe hunted. And now she was. The hunter turned hunted.

Her eyes looked especially green against her tanned skin. A fluke of genetics, she never needed to tan. As if she would even take the time for such an indulgence. Even at Christmas she looked island-gold. Looking down, she snatched the fresh boxers with dancing penguins off the counter—one of many items Claire had stuffed into her personalized stocking last Christmas—and slipped them on.

Kit and Gideon had never had Christmas stockings before. The whole tradition of a tree, stockings, and turkey with all the trimmings that Claire had foisted on them had been a first in her memory. Her grandmother only ever bought a poinsettia in acknowledgment of the holiday. Christmas morning, Gideon and Kit would sit at the linoleum kitchen table with the poinsettia in the center and open their fifteen-dollar Sears gift cards over a plate of rubbery fried eggs and Spam. The gift cards were for underwear and socks.

Gideon's marriage to Claire had only reinforced all that Kit had missed. All that she still missed. Kit both loved and hated Claire for it.

Dressed, she grabbed her gun off the toilet tank. Her stomach rumbled, reminding her that she had not eaten since her power bar at lunch. She'd left straight from work to make her date with Dan. Another wasted evening—at least date-wise. Not to mention the dent to her checkbook tonight would bring. Friday nights brought the best tips. She rarely took off. Couldn't afford to. Usually she worked the bar until two, and hunted afterward, collapsing in bed at dawn.

She had tried a regular nine-to-five job after college. It wasn't hard to land one; keeping it was another matter. When she trolled the clubs and streets all hours of the night hunting lycans, she was late to work most mornings—and often sporting cuts and bruises that convinced her coworkers she was a victim of domestic abuse.

So what had started out as a part-time gig had soon become full-time. Tending bar was more her scene, anyway. No business suit required. Just a dark, smoke-shrouded club, loud music, and lycans who hunted among the throng of twentysomethings. They never noticed the girl behind the bar; they were too focused on targeting easy prey among the drunken women. But she noticed them—and picked them off later.

So what if she was twenty-six and still living with her grandmother? Sure, her grandmother wasn't the warm and fuzzy type, but aside from Gideon, she was all Kit had.

Entering the kitchen, she flipped on the overhead light. It buzzed and flickered before blazing to full strength. She advanced on the refrigerator, her belly grinding with hunger. Shaking loose her waves from her head and shoulders with a drag of her fingers, she peered inside the well-stocked refrigerator, again courtesy of Claire. Two years ago, Kit would have been lucky to find a stale loaf of bread.

Removing a Lean Cuisine TV dinner from the freezer, she tore into the box and slid the small tray into the microwave. A faint whirring filled the air as the fettuccine alfredo heated.

Her grandmother had never been much on cooking. Her kitchen skills ran to canned tuna on Ritz crackers. Fried eggs and Spam appeared on special occasions. Gideon said their mother had been a good cook. Kit thought she remembered blueberry pancakes, but she couldn't be sure. The memories of her parents had grown dim over the years. Like blurred, faint images glimpsed through water. She tried to remember, to cling to a time when she had stood center stage in someone's life, to recall what that had been like.

Her father, a carpenter, had smelled of wood. Freshly cut cedar and pine. And his hands had been large. One alone could engulf half her head. She remembered that. If little else. Remembered him cupping her face as he kissed her good night. And her mother wore a gold cross around her neck. Kit could see it in her mind, nestled in the hollow of her throat—the skin there had been golden brown, like her own. Warm and smooth, puckered with the faintest gooseflesh. Her face was less clear, only a blurry image in Kit's mind.

The beep of the microwave broke her thoughts. With fork in hand, she removed the tray and peeled back the plastic cover. Stabbing into the pasta, she brought a bite of creamy noodles to her mouth.

Her gaze drifted to the kitchen phone, giving a small start as she noticed the blinking light of the answering machine on the counter. Swallowing her bite, she set down her food and punched Play.

She settled a hip against the counter as Claire's voice emerged.

"Hi, Kit! It's Claire. We just got to the cabin this afternoon. It's so beautiful here. Hope everything is okay there. I forgot to ask you to water the little plant in the upstairs bathroom. Phone reception is bad up here. We're in town for dinner right now, but give us a call. Love you. Bye."

Cooper's voice came next, the deep timbre of his voice oddly sharp in the kitchen air.

"Kit, I just got your message. Nice work tonight. I'll send a cleaning crew out for housekeeping and documentation. Call me as soon as you get this." He paused before adding, "We need to talk." Another pause. His heavy breathing filled the phone line, and she thought she detected an underlying thread of anxiety. "In person." Then the phone clicked dead.

Kit rolled the tines of her fork against her tongue. Did he know EFLA was in town? Frowning, she stood still, her mind spinning as the machine rolled into another message.

Picking up the phone, she dialed Cooper's number first. After several rings, his answering machine picked up. Hanging up, she tried his cell phone. His voicemail came on.

"Coop, it's Kit. Where are you?" She hesitated, about to say more, then instead ended with "Call me back."

She tried Gideon next, ready to warn him about EFLA. He and Claire weren't expected home for another week, but she wanted to make sure they didn't return sooner. At least until she'd hooked up with Cooper. She was sure he could straighten out the mess with EFLA and Rafe Santiago.

Setting the phone back on its hook, she took a few more bites of the pasta. Finding herself too distracted to finish, she tossed the fork in the sink and chucked the small tray into the trash can. She turned off the kitchen light, then the one in the living room.

Upstairs again, she headed for the bathroom. After washing her face and brushing her teeth, she watered the small fern at the edge of the counter, going through the motions of being normal, unaffected—as if her mind wasn't playing over her encounter with Rafe Santiago.

Once in the guest bedroom, she paced the floor for several moments before abruptly stopping and staring unseeing at the tidied desk.

She could handle Rafe Santiago. He couldn't run her out of town. Perhaps in time he would see just how tough she was and reconsider his position on female hunters. *Right.*

With a snort, she flipped off the light and climbed into bed, tucking her gun beneath her pillow. The mechanical clock's numbers turned before her eyes. Ten twenty-eight. Pathetic.

Twenty-six years old and she was in bed alone. Only a gun for company. She shouldn't be going to bed alone. Hell, she didn't *want* to be going to bed alone. She missed men. Missed sex. Hot, heavy, grinding, man-straddling sex. It had been too long.

And yet she had chosen this life. Could not imagine doing anything besides hunting the monsters who had stolen her family from her. Sighing, she stared at the ceiling for several moments, not the least bit tired.

Flipping back the covers, she plucked her gun from beneath

the pillow and strode to the window to peer out one more time. A nagging sense of unease wouldn't let her fall asleep just yet.

Maybe it was the night's adrenaline still thrumming through her veins. But she'd never had this problem before, and there'd been plenty of nights like tonight, when she'd left lycans rotting in an alley. It had to be Rafe Santiago. He had rattled her. He had been, well, *something*.

Her toes flexed against the unyielding hardwood floor as she surveyed the still and silent street, her shoulders tense, her muscles tightening with battle-readiness.

Her gaze narrowed on a dark Hummer that had not been there before. Moths circled the streetlight high above it in an excited flurry.

The streetlights tinged the night blue, outlining the man sitting behind the driver's wheel: a dark, faceless figure.

Her finger curled around the trigger. She dropped one shoulder against the window jam, keeping herself out of view.

No wonder she couldn't sleep. Some SOB was sitting out there watching her house.

"Hmm," she murmured, stroking the barrel of her gun against her thigh as if she had a particular itch. "Let's go introduce ourselves."

# 5

Rafe settled back in his seat, watching the house he knew belonged to Gideon March. For whatever reason, Kit had been staying there for the last two nights. There was no sign of Gideon March or his wife, Claire—a woman who, sources claimed, had been infected by a lycan a little over two years ago. A death warrant to most, but, unbelievable as he found it, Gideon March had helped her in tracking and killing the alpha of her pack and breaking the curse before she shifted and fed, damning her.

The narrow red-brick two-story sat still and silent in the warm night, the leaves of the large oak in the front yard rustling in the breeze. Its roots, thick and gnarled, protruded from the green lawn like bumpy tentacles. The yard was large, like its neighbors, the grass verdant from the muggy Houston climate.

In the far distance, someone had fired up a grill. Charcoal burned on the air, the scent smoky, pungent in Rafe's nose. He inhaled harder, guessing fajitas were on the menu.

One by one the house's lights turned off, first the front living room, then the porch light. Minutes later, the silhouette of a woman appeared in an upstairs window. His heart raced, all his senses kicking into high gear as he studied the slight shadow as it drifted before the window. The blood rushed in his veins and Kit March's face flashed across his mind. The wavy blond hair framing her face had looked soft as a child's, adding to her whimsical, otherworldly appearance. Her elfin features reminded him of the tales of sprites and fairies his mother had whispered him to sleep with years ago.

His brother, Sebastian, almost always fell asleep the moment his head hit the pillow, but Rafe used to lay awake, his mother's soft voice weaving a spell about him, making him believe in romance. In the power of love. That good always defeated evil. Because it was right. Because it *should*. He had believed in such nonsense until the summer of his twelfth year. The summer his mother had been forced to reveal the truth.

The shadow moved from the window, and seconds later the light vanished like a candle snuffed out.

Kit March was not what he'd expected. Her vanilla scent still swirled around him, wrapping him in a seductive fog.

Hell, he had not really thought about her as a person. He had never thought of *any* of them as individuals. Damned inconvenient to start doing so now. They were a job. A mission he dispatched with cold precision. They departed from his life almost as quickly as they entered it. He made certain of that. He had to. But for some reason, he felt in no rush to get rid of Kit March. Something stopped him from closing in on her now—while she slept, at her most vulnerable. She intrigued him, and he wanted to know more about her.

He stared up at the darkened room, the unmoving blinds covering the window. Ten thirty and she was already in bed? Alone.

He thought about the date she had left at the restaurant. Sacrificed in pursuit of a kill. A story he knew well. He had lived it for years. The job came first. Always.

Still, he couldn't imagine her suffering an empty bed. Her small size might make her look delicate and subdued, but a moment in her company had dispelled that notion. She was tightly wound, a fireball of energy, with green eyes that gleamed with light, like a shock of sunshine on dew-dappled grass. Passion hummed through her.

Watching her in action tonight, he'd seen that she could handle herself. And yet she walked a dangerous line. Strong women fell victim to lycans all the time. One slip and she could become a lycan's plaything. A risk he could not take. For her sake—and the world's.

With that thought, he dragged a hand over his jaw, determined to forget how she intrigued him, and committed to remembering his purpose.

Sebastian would never let a pretty face distract him. In many ways, his brother was stronger than he.

Rafe drew a deep breath. He would convince Kit March and her brother to give up this hunting business and lead a quiet life. A safe life away from NODEAL, EFLA, and cities where concentrated populations of lycans thrived. And if she refused . . .

Make no mistake. He would do what he had to do.

A subtle change in the air made him sit straighter in the seat. He scanned the neighborhood, the house, the window of the room where she slept. The skin of his face grew tight and itchy as awareness slid over him with the insidiousness of creeping fog.

He was no longer alone on the street.

☽ ☽ ☽ ● ☾ ☾ ☾

She moved silently over the dark street, walking a brisk, determined line to the parked vehicle, ready to tell whoever lurked there to get the hell off her street.

She kept her gun tucked at her side, close to her bare thigh, all the while scanning the street, making sure none of Gideon's neigh-bors were out and about.

He lived in an older, more established neighborhood in Hous-ton's university section. Most of the residents were elderly. Quiet and retiring, in-bed-by-nine types. Still, it wouldn't do to frighten some blue-haired old lady out walking her dog.

Finger poised over her trigger, she stopped at the driver's-side window and found the seat . . . empty.

The hair on her nape tingled. She pivoted, gun clasped tightly in both hands.

"Looking for me?"

Kit spun around, leveling her gun squarely on Rafe Santiago. "You."

He swiped the gun out of her hand. She reacted, throwing a punch. He caught her fist in his hand the moment before her knuckles made contact with his face.

"You need to work on your approach. I heard you coming like a herd of elephants."

"I wasn't going for discretion," she bit out, struggling to wrench her fist free of his bruising grip. "I came out here to tell you to leave me the hell alone. Take your stakeout somewhere else."

"That's not likely to happen." His fingers tightened around her hand. Hard enough to make her wince.

"No?" She cocked her head to the side and gave up on freeing her hand. Instead, she threw her head forward and crashed it into his face, willing to endure the headache, knowing he would suffer more.

He dropped his hold on her fist.

She jumped back a step and backhanded him across the face. The sharp sound cracked through the air.

His head snapped back, but he did not so much as stagger from the blow.

She waited, balanced on the balls of her feet, watching as he rolled his head around to face her once again, blood trickling from his nose.

She stifled a pang of guilt. Remorse was weakness, and she couldn't afford to be weak.

So he wasn't her standard target. Even mortal, he was still a pain in her ass, and needed to be dealt with.

Smiling, he wiped the blood away with the back of his hand, staring at it for a moment before licking it clean.

Her stomach clenched at the act. So primitive, so male.

"Impressive. What else have you got?"

"Oh, there's more where that came from."

"Let's see it then," he invited, with annoying calm, beckoning her with a mocking wave of his hand.

Irritation zipped through her, feeding her a shot of needed adrenaline.

She came at him, taking a quick jab at his face.

He blocked her fist, smiling that arrogant grin.

Growling, she came at him again. And again.

Each time, he either ducked or blocked her. They moved off the street into a yard. A dog barked somewhere nearby, its frenzied yaps imitating her every strike and punch.

After several more attempts, she paused, panting from both exertion and fury.

Oh, he was good. Her eyes narrowed on him.

He cocked an eyebrow, waiting. *Waiting.*

He was toying with her! Blocking all her blows, but never coming at her or trying to hit her.

"Fight back," she snarled, diving at him.

He ducked and circled her. "I would hate to bruise your face." Laughter gleamed in his dark eyes, which shone down at her in the night.

"Don't hold back! Fight, dammit. Fight! It doesn't matter that I'm a woman."

"No?"

She charged him with an angry bellow, swinging wildly.

He stepped to the side. Before she knew what had happened, he gripped her arm behind her back. Propelling her forward, he slammed her against a tree. Her cheek ground into rough bark.

"Watch your anger," he advised.

"Go to hell!" She kicked behind her, digging her heel into his shin.

He tightened his hold on her arm almost to the point of pain. "Your temper works against you."

"There you go," she spat out, trying to look around at his face. "I knew you had it in you. Knew you could hurt a woman. Nice play at chivalry, though."

He pressed his body against her back, every hard line of him sinking against her softness. His hold on her arm loosened.

"I'll give it you. You are pretty tough." His breath feathered her ear. She shivered, jerking as he brushed a hair off the side of her face. "For a woman," he added.

"For a man," she flung back, heat licking her cheeks, indignation firing through her.

"I suppose," he agreed. "Most men would find you a force to reckon with."

But not *him*? That was his implication. And it burned a bilious trail down her throat. *I'll show you.*

Swallowing her anger, she let herself relax, soften. Thrusting her hips back, she subtly brushed herself against him.

"Most men do," she agreed, dropping her voice in pitch, nearly choking on the provocative words.

His breath caught behind her, the sharp sound rising the tiny hairs on her nape. He released her arm, and she brought it around, splaying her palm against the trunk. She rubbed her ass against his hardness.

She smiled as he pushed himself against her. Then her smile slipped when she felt a certain hardness grind into her ass. Her belly tightened at the feel of him there.

Before things got too far out of hand, she rolled herself around, her back against the tree.

He remained as close as ever, a wall of heat flush against her, staring deeply into her eyes, unsmiling. The hard ridge of him prodded her belly.

"Is this what you do when you're in a tough jam? Tease and give a guy a hard-on?" The centers of his dark eyes glowed brightly.

No. She'd never been in such a bad scrape that she felt the need to use her body. Never before him, anyway.

His gaze slid down. She followed his eyes, not realizing until she felt his hand on her breast that he meant to touch her. He rolled her nipple through her T-shirt, squeezing it until it grew hard and distended.

She gasped at the perfect pain of it. Her belly clenched, and she grew wet. Shifting her legs in attempt to ease the ache between her thighs, she bit her lip to stop from crying out.

"How far would you go, Kit March? Hmm?"

That light at the centers of his eyes intensified as he worked his fingers harder over her nipple. A knot grew in her belly, twisting and tightening. A cry escaped from between her teeth.

He pressed his mouth to her neck, breathing warm air over her flesh. "I, for one, would be very interested to know."

She lifted a hand to cling to his arm. "Please," she gasped, fingers digging into his hard bicep. This was crazy.

"Please what?"

*Rip off my clothes. Put your mouth where your hand is. Take me. Pound into me right here against the neighbor's tree.*

"Stop," she hissed as he turned his attention to her other aching, neglected nipple. His fingers rolled it into a hard, tight bud. "I said stop!"

And then he was gone. His heat. His marvelous hands. *Him.*

She blinked. Gone. Vanished, it seemed.

His hand, his wicked touch on her breasts. As abruptly as it had begun, it was over.

She blinked again. Breath coming fast and hard, she moved away from the tree. Crossing her arms over her chest, she surveyed the neighborhood, craning her neck and looking all around. Nothing. No sign of him.

A humid breeze shook the trees as she stepped out of the neighbor's yard and into the street.

She squeezed her arms tighter over her throbbing breasts, trying to erase his touch. No use. She still tingled and ached, wanted to take her own hands to herself in a simulation of what he had done to her.

His Hummer sat unmoving along the curb, but he was nowhere to be seen. She strained her ears, listening for him, but heard nothing. No sound of running feet.

The night hummed around her, alive. She glanced up at the moon. Almost full. Only a sliver remained. Despite the evening's heat, she shivered. Bending, she scooped up her gun from the street.

How could he have just disappeared?

She eyed a dark line of nearby shrubs for several moments before returning to the house.

⟩ ⟩ ⟩ ● ⟨ ⟨ ⟨

He leaned against a tree, chest lifting in ragged breaths that sawed from his lips as he listened to the light footsteps of Kit March as she moved across the street. He dared not look. Not if he wanted to remain where he was. In his mind he could see her. Her tan legs, her sweet ass, round and firm in her boxers. That was temptation enough.

That's it. Run. Run fast. Run far.

He could still smell her. Clean woman. Her mild scented soap. She had showered, but he still detected on her the faint vanilla from earlier in the evening.

Dragging a hand through his hair, he glanced at the watching moon and cursed. His cock pushed painfully against his jeans, begging for relief. The relief he could have had moments ago. With Kit March.

She hadn't wanted him to stop. At least her body hadn't. He could have persuaded her, could have pushed those boxers down her hips, wrapped her legs around him, and slid inside her heat right there against that tree.

It would have been good. Great.

*Wrong.*

He heard a door open and shut as she entered her house and he heaved a sigh of relief. Hands clenched at his sides, he beat the back of his head against the tree, punishing himself, feeling more alone than he had ever felt before. Bereft. Even worse than when his mother banished him and his brother to the mountains that summer, isolating them from the world. Freaks to be cut off from mankind.

The blood pumped through him, hot and thick. "Shit." This assignment had just gone from tricky to total and utter shit.

He'd stepped over the line. In a big way.

It wouldn't happen again. Kit March was a job. Nothing more. He wouldn't let her get under his skin again.

# 6

Kit woke with a jolt, the remnants of a dream crumbling like dust around her. Chest heaving, she choked on air, a pair of familiar dark eyes flashing across her mind. Dark eyes with unusually bright centers.

Rubbing her chin, she sat up, immediately remembering the night before. Her breasts remembered, too, growing heavy at the memory of his fingers on her, tormenting her in the most wicked ways. Moaning, she fell back on her pillow and pulled the comforter to her neck.

She *so* needed sex. And not with some damn EFLA agent.

Sighing, she stared out the window. The gray dawn air washing the room somehow soothed her. Dawn. She always preferred this time of day. Even when the moon was at its peak, lycans would retreat and head for home at dawn. And so would she. A time of retreat. Rest. It meant she had survived another hunt.

"You look like a little girl when you sleep," a deep voice murmured, cold as glacial wind.

Her hand dove beneath her pillow, and she lurched up in bed

with the gun clasped and ready. For a moment she feared it was him, Rafe Santiago. Again.

That would explain why she was trembling.

There was something about him. Something more threatening to her than his association with EFLA and his not-so-subtle threats to her family. He rattled her. Made her belly tighten and breath come quick and hard.

Her eyes focused through the gloom to the large figure standing before her bed. Pewter-colored eyes glowed down at her.

Not Rafe.

But not someone she wanted to see, either. Even if he wasn't one of the oldest lycans on record, he was one tough-looking son of a bitch. Dressed from head to toe in black, he was the kind of guy who stood out in a crowd. Which was strange, considering he led a fairly discreet existence.

Handsome, she supposed, with a square jaw and hair so black it glowed blue in the light. His lips were well-carved but looked incapable of curving into a smile.

"Darius? What are you doing here?"

In the softening air, his unnerving stare raked over her. "Kit. Charming as always, I see."

Lowering her gun, she snapped, "What do you want? Gideon's not here."

Gideon called him friend, but she did not. Would not. He was a lycan. No different than the monsters she hunted. Like any other lycan. He was damned. Cursed. A predator. Even if he hadn't killed in generations. Even if he locked himself away every full moon to resist the overwhelming need to feed. Remove those walls, and he would kill, feed—on her. On Gideon. Friend or no. She could never forget that. Never trust him. And he knew that. Knew she thought he deserved a bullet in his head.

"I know he's not here," Darius replied in a strange formal accent that hinted at an age lived and lost within the annals of time. He moved closer, with all the grace and stealth of a jungle cat, eyes forever glowing.

She snorted. Of course. Her brother had probably given him an itinerary of their trip.

"Then why are you here?" She pulled the sheets higher, trying to pretend his presence did not affect her, did not make her uneasy. She was accustomed to being around lycans—just not to conversing with them as though they were anything less than blood-thirsty monsters.

A deep breath rattled loose from his chest, a hint of humanity she would never have credited he possessed. Several moments passed before he answered, his deep voice clipped. "Cooper's dead."

His words penetrated slowly through her mind, like a pebble sinking through water. Still, she heard herself ask in a faint voice she did not recognize, "What?"

"Cooper's dead." His lips barely moved as he spoke, and she wondered if he felt anything at all. Or was he every bit the cold bastard she'd always suspected.

"He can't be." She shook her head. "He called here last night—"

"Trust me. He's dead."

"No," she insisted, her hands fisting under the sheets, her chest tightening. "Who told you this? How can you be sure?" The words flew out of her mouth as fast as gunfire. "Cooper wasn't exactly your friend. He only let you live because of Gideon. I doubt you made it to his call-in-case-of-an-emergency-list."

She didn't want to believe him, wanted to deny his words, but she knew through Gideon that Darius had an uncanny way of knowing everything that went on in NODEAL and among the larger lycan packs in the city. He had informants everywhere. If Cooper were dead, he would likely know.

She supposed she shouldn't put it past him to know all the

comings and goings of NODEAL—and EFLA, for that matter. The guy was richer than Donald Trump, living in a fortresslike mausoleum with a full staff to wait on his every whim. Not to mention a state-of-the-art research lab staffed with a pair of Caltech scientists working around the clock to find an antidote to his curse. What a joke. He didn't deserve a chance at redemption. The only thing staying her hand from reaching for her gun was Gideon.

Cooper. Dead.

A terrible pain, swift as wind, swept through her too-tight chest.

She could only shake her head. She should have kept calling last night. She should have driven over to Cooper's house. Done something. Anything.

"A delegation from EFLA has arrived in Houston."

Her mind leapt to Rafe and his ominous dark eyes as he proclaimed himself an EFLA agent. "Yes. I met one of them—"

"You met one? When?" The hard line of his lips barely moved as he spoke.

"Last night."

"And he let you go?"

She frowned, thinking over their tussle out in the street. Staring into Darius's chilly silver eyes, she knotted her hands in the sheet and replied, "Why shouldn't he?"

"For the very reason Cooper is dead," he replied, his accent crisp. "EFLA wants you dead. You and Gideon. I'm guessing Cooper wouldn't go along with it."

"He sounded . . . anxious on the message," she murmured, her lips numb as they moved. She lifted one hand from the sheet and pressed it to her forehead. The skin felt tight and hot as a balloon in the sun, ready to burst.

Had Rafe Santiago been the one to pull the trigger? An angry burning sensation crept up her neck. She should have killed him last night, instead of letting him put his hands all over her. "I don't

understand any of this. Why is it so important to kill us just because we go against—"

"A hit has been placed on you and Gideon. It's all over town.
The packs are allying. You're not safe."

"A hit?" she exclaimed, shaking her head. "That's absurd. Why
are they going through so much trouble for us?"

"EFLA's in charge, Kit. It's what they've been working toward
for over a century. They want to bring NODEAL to heel, rid it of
all rogue agents and policy breakers. Gideon. You."

She pressed both hands to her cheeks. "This can't be happening."

"The top players with NODEAL wanted Cooper gone. They've
never liked the way he handled the Houston division. They knew
he tolerated Gideon and you."

"So they killed him." *Bastards.* She pressed her fingertips to her
suddenly throbbing temples. "None of this makes sense. Even with
everything I've heard about EFLA, I can't believe they would kill
Cooper after all his years of service—that NODEAL would allow
that to happen."

"They believed him untrustworthy. Disloyal."

She recalled Cooper's cryptic message, the urgency in his voice.
She recalled the uneasy feeling in her stomach.

Darius's pewter-colored eyes glowed down at her, his face
a granite mask, impenetrable, incapable of any expression that
might reflect emotion. "It's time to get out of town."

She studied him for a moment, his ink-black hair darker than
the room's deepest shadows. Fury burned in her chest. She did
not want to run. She wanted to make them pay. She owed Cooper
that much. He had saved her life all those years ago. Hers and
Gideon's.

"You'll be next," Darius added, his voice matter-of-fact. Heart-
less bastard. "And Gideon."

"Because we're rogue operators? They'll kill us?" Even for EFLA, known for its extreme measures in the hunting and exterminating of lycans, it seemed drastic. "I don't buy it. There's something more going on here."

His silver eyes drilled into her, steady and piercing. "Maybe," he replied vaguely. "But that doesn't change the fact that there's a hit on your life. Get out of town. And make certain Gideon stays away, too."

Heat burned up her neck and to her face. She surged to her feet and faced him. "You don't think we're smart enough to outmaneuver these bastards? I've seen NODEAL's agents at work before. I'm not impressed. Half of them couldn't find their asses in the dark."

"It's not NODEAL that concerns me."

"EFLA, then?" An image of Rafe Santiago flashed through her mind. True, he possessed an aura of menace, but she knew his weakness now. Her face burned at the memory, and her breasts grew heavy. She. She was his weakness.

The skin near Darius's left eye twitched, the only indication that he was about to tell her something out of the ordinary. "They've released your identities."

The skin at the back of her skull tightened, tingling as though pricked with a thousand needles, drawing forth a dull ache inside her head.

"What?" she whispered, dropping back on to the bed, the well-worn springs squeaking beneath her. She ran a hand through her waves, massaging her scalp with her fingertips. "Released our identities? To whom?"

"You understand my meaning," he replied in that oddly formal fashion that hinted at an age lived and lost. "You're lucky to have survived the night. Lucky I got here first."

She compressed her lips, deciding against telling him that he had not gotten to her first. Rafe had. Twice, the night before.

She nodded slowly. "They've released our identities to the lycan population." She was lucky, indeed. Lucky Rafe had been her only late-night visitor.

"Do you know a better way to guarantee your death?"

"Every lycan in town knows who we are?" Her gaze darted about the room, almost as though she feared the monsters would spring out from the walls.

"If not yet, then soon enough. The packs have a network in place. Of sorts." He smiled grimly. "As competitive as they are among themselves, they'll ally themselves in an effort to destroy you and Gideon. They despise hunters. And a female hunter such as you . . ."

His eerie silver gaze crawled over her. The air seemed to change, grow charged, electric. In that moment, she was reminded of just what he was. Danger. A predator ruled by hunger. Perhaps the most dangerous lycan of all, because he denied himself what he craved. She shivered, her gaze skimming the black strands of hair that reached his shoulders.

"They'll find you an irresistible challenge." His chest lifted on a breath, and for a moment she thought he might approach her. Touch her.

Holding her breath, she tensed, bracing herself.

The moment passed, and he looked to the window, eyes narrowing as though he could see through the blinds. "I imagine they know where you live by now." Moving to the window, he parted the blinds and peered out at the quiet morning. "Every moment you remain here you risk your life."

She rose from the bed and began tossing things into her duffel bag. "I'll go," she ground out, the bitterness filling her mouth, threatening to choke her.

Darius leaned back against the wall, arms crossed over his broad chest. Shoulders of a linebacker. "I'll escort you out."

She snorted and sent him a sharp look. He still talked as if he lived in another century, further reminding her of the gulf between them—of what he was: the very thing she loathed. A bad taste filled her mouth as she studied him. "No, thanks."

He dipped his head and looked down at her with those damnable silver eyes, his voice clipped and reproving, "Kit—"

"No." She flung her last shirt into her bag and fought with the stubborn zipper, careful to keep her gaze away from him, knowing the full power of those lycan eyes, their ability to enthrall, if she let him get the better of her. No lycan had before. She'd be damned if one succeeded now—even if he was an ally of sorts. "I don't need your help."

"No?" His voice was mocking, sharp with skepticism, and she knew what he was thinking. That if it weren't for him, she might very well have gone blithely about her business this morning. And found herself dead.

The zipper finally sang closed. Nostrils flaring, she slung the duffel over her shoulder, ready to move into the bathroom to gather her few things there.

"Thanks for warning me." Even those words stuck in her throat. "Now go. I can handle myself."

One of his dark brows lifted.

She motioned to the door, needing him gone, too flustered when he was around. "I don't need your help."

"You mean you don't want it?"

She shrugged. "Whatever. I don't want it."

After a long moment he pushed his large frame off the wall, the house's old wooden floor creaking beneath his weight. "Very well." At the doorway, he stopped and looked over his shoulder at her. "I only hope your stubbornness won't get you killed. Your brother won't thank me for that."

"I'll survive." It was the principle of the matter. She didn't want to accept *his* help. Regardless of how he lived his life now, he was a monster. He had killed and fed on the innocent. Nothing could change that. Not his friendship with her brother. Not his helping her. He lacked a soul. For good reason.

The heavy tread of his steps receded on the stairs as she hurried into the bathroom to collect her things. Back in her room again, she quickly changed into jeans and a T-shirt. Snatching her cell phone, she stared at it for a long moment, biting her lip until the coppery taste of blood ran over her teeth.

She needed to talk to Gideon, but she couldn't risk it. She was a sitting duck with her phone turned on. NODEAL—and now EFLA—had reach. Most NODEAL agents worked for HPD, with Cooper. It had been the perfect cover . . . and it provided them with access to technologies limited to them otherwise. They could track her phone's GPS in seconds.

They could track her. Just as they could track Gideon via his cell phone—if they hadn't already. Knowing she had to warn him, she quickly typed a text message cautioning him to go to ground and wait for her to join him, confident she could find the cabin where they had vacationed as children.

After sending the message, she turned her phone off and shoved it into her bag. She hoped her brother would get the message soon—before they homed in on his location. He would trust her enough to follow her instructions.

She hit the stairs two at a time, her ears straining amid the silence of the house as she moved into the kitchen and snatched her purse off the counter. Early morning sunlight shot through the large bay window that looked out over the backyard, already warming the kitchen. The day would be a scorcher. Not good. Just what she needed. Lycans were more aggressive in hot weather. They usually avoided it. But forced out into it, they would be in high temper.

A quick stop at her grandmother's for a few necessary items—

namely money—and she would go. Leave town. Temporarily, of course. But she wouldn't stay away forever. Someone would pay for murdering Cooper. For making her run and for robbing her of her freedom, her life.

She had worked damn hard to gain Cooper's acceptance, to persuade him to train her and let her hunt. The only thing she lacked was official authorization from NODEAL and a paycheck. He'd had faith in her. And now he was dead.

*Someone* would pay.

A pair of dark eyes set in a too-handsome face flashed before her mind. She had a pretty good idea who that someone should be.

## 7

Scanning the yard, Kit hurried to her car, her purse and duffel bag slung over her shoulder, bouncing with her steps. A warm vapor rose up to meet her, coating her skin in a sticky sheen of perspiration. She clutched the keys so tightly in one hand that the metal cut into the tender skin of her palm.

Although she spotted no one, her nerves were stretched tight as wire. Imagined or real, the sensation of being watched stayed with her as she tossed her bag and purse into the passenger seat. An instinct not to be ignored. She had honed it over the last few years.

Heat swamped her as she recalled last night, and what had happened when she'd followed her instinct and investigated her sensation of being watched. Shaking her head, she forced herself to forget. To not think about the way he had touched her, the burning sensation that had fired her blood when he put his hands on her.

Ducking her head, she had almost cleared her doorframe when a hard hand clamped on her shoulder. Ready for the bastard, Kit spun around, barely registering a pair of pale blue eyes before she reacted, jamming the heel of her palm into the man's face. Instantly, the grip on her arm vanished. Without stopping for breath, she grabbed her assailant's shoulders with both hands, yanked him closer, and slammed her knee into his gut with the barest grunt.

"Shit!" He dropped to the ground like a load of bricks.

Before she could escape inside her car, someone else yanked her by the wrist and flung her around, slamming her face first into the rear driver's-side door. Pinned, her wrist trapped, she kicked backward at this new attacker, making contact.

A fierce oath gave her a moment's satisfaction. Until a hand grabbed her by the back of the head, tangling in her hair and slamming her head down against the roof of the car with a resounding crack. Pain exploded in her forehead. Her vision blurred, and she clung to the car, struggling not to succumb to the welcoming gray pulling her in, promising relief, escape from the hurt.

Rancid breath fanned her ear. "Don't give me any trouble, March. It'll go easier for you."

Wincing, she twisted her neck around to get a look at this attacker, recognizing him instantly. "Lockhart," she breathed. A few months back, she had killed a few lycans fleeing him. It stung her pride for him to be getting the best of her now.

Lockhart spun her around, exchanging his cruel grip on her hair for a handhold around her neck. He pushed hard against her, pinning her hips and legs between him and the car so that they could not budge.

"You know my name? I'm flattered." He grinned: an unfortunate row of uneven teeth against a heavily acne-scarred face.

"Sure," she replied, breathing deeply against the throbbing ache of her head. "My brother said you were NODEAL's shittiest agent."

His grin slipped. "And I see you're just like that arrogant prick. Must run in the family."

"Waste the bitch." The second guy grunted, clambering to his feet off the driveway. He stared at her balefully from small, deep-set eyes as he leaned forward, one hand braced on his knee, his face red and mottled, a thin trickle of blood seeping from his beaklike nose.

"What's wrong?" she taunted. "Can't take a woman beating the crap out of you?"

"Waste her," the man said again. "That's why we're here."

"Shut up, Davis," Lockhart snapped.

"Yeah, listen to Davis there and do your job," Kit suggested with more bravado than she felt, guessing that their appearance had something to do with EFLA's arrival in town. "You're both EFLA's dogs now, aren't you?" She shrugged. "Maybe they'll give you a nice desk job. All the donuts you can eat."

Lockhart frowned, staring at her intently. Ignoring her jibe, he demanded, "You know about the merger? Who told you?"

"Just tell me this: How did they justify killing Cooper? Did they have a good excuse for whacking him? How can you look yourselves in the mirror? He was your boss. He brought you in and trained you."

Lockhart shrugged. "Cooper had become a liability to the organization. Like you and your brother. He impeded the ultimate goal to rid the world of lycans."

"There's nothing noble about NODEAL anymore." She leveled a glare at both men. "You're just a bunch of murderers now. Assassins. EFLA's dogs."

Lockhart shrugged. "You'd see it that way." Raising his leg, he pulled his gun from his ankle holster. "And what you think doesn't amount to shit."

Kit ceased to breathe as he pressed his gun to the side of her head, the steel cold and unforgiving against the soft skin of her temple.

"Are you such idiots you would shoot her in broad daylight for the entire neighborhood to witness?"

Kit's head whipped around at the droll, rolling voice. Air escaped her in a sigh.

Rafe Santiago stood there, a faintly bored expression on his too-handsome face as he surveyed them.

"Santiago," Lockhart exclaimed, easing the gun off Kit's head. "What are you doing here? We can handle this."

"Can you?" Rafe cocked a dark brow, drawing closer at an ambling pace. "Have you never heard of discretion?" He slid a sharp glance to the gun in Lockhart's hand. "Put that away."

Lockhart hesitated, looking from his gun to Kit, indecision writ in his expression.

She cocked a brow, taunting. "You heard the man."

Lockhart's face reddened and his hand tightened around his weapon.

"Stop provoking him," Rafe growled, looking at her with dark, intense eyes. "If I were in your position, I would say very little."

She thrust out her chin but held silent.

"Now put away the gun," Rafe commanded, his face hardening as he looked back to Lockhart. For all the quiet of his voice, his words came out harsh, an order to be obeyed.

Lockhart complied, putting the weapon back in his holster.

Rafe flicked his hand as if swatting a fly. "Now step away from her."

"You have to watch this one," Davis chimed in, pressing one hand to his nose in an attempt to staunch the blood flow. "She may be small, but she fights almost like a man."

"I fight *better* than a man," Kit goaded. "And I fight better than you." She flicked Lockhart a scornful glance. "Better than both of you."

Rafe's lips gave the barest smirk. "I'm not worried," he assured the agent, eyes locking with Kit's. Something electric passed from his gaze to hers. Heat washed over hers, stinging her cheeks as she recalled their fight last night—and how it had ended. His eyes grew bright, and she knew he remembered, too.

"Sent your goons to do your dirty work?" she challenged, her voice strangely out of breath. She eased away from the car and smoothed her hands down her denim-clad thighs.

He held her gaze, not sparing the two agents a glance. "Hardly. I don't need help when it comes to doing my job. Or handling you."

"No?" She waved her arms wide. "Then why the mass-scale alert?"

"What do you mean?"

She made a disgusted sound. "I know that every agent and lycan in town is gunning for me."

"Do you?" He didn't bother hiding his surprise, cocking his head to the side. "And how is it you're so informed?"

She wasn't about to explain Darius to him. Professing her alliance of sorts with a centuries-old lycan would be a bad idea right now. "Don't you think I was bound to find out?"

"Unless you have an informant, no. Has there been an attempt on your life yet?" His gaze slid from her to the area around them, as if he expected lycans to emerge from the bushes.

"Other than these fools?"

Lockhart puffed out his barrel chest. "Are we going to stand here chitchatting or finish the bitch?" His pale blue eyes were cold as frost.

"Yeah," Davis murmured in agreement, shifting his small eyes along the houses lining the quiet street. "Shouldn't we hurry up with this before any lycans show up? Let's take her inside."

"Yeah, releasing my identity wasn't too clever," Kit continued. "What's wrong? Don't trust yourselves to get the job done, so you recruited the enemy?" She nodded once, clucking her tongue in false sympathy. "Not very well thought out. What if some of you get killed because the lycans you sicced on me show up? I doubt they'll exclude you from their plans if you're here when they show up."

"It wasn't my idea," Rafe said, and from his tone, he didn't seem too pleased that her identity had been released to every lycan in town. His dark eyes gleamed down at her with a menacing light.

"Appears to me your bosses aren't confident you can do your job."

Rafe stepped toward her. "I don't need help from anyone to handle you."

Kit assessed the three men, subtly shifting her weight, muscles tightening, preparing herself to act the moment one of them made a move toward her. She wouldn't go inside the house willingly. That would be tantamount to handing them a knife and offering them her neck. Killing her wouldn't be easy.

Rafe took another step toward her, his full lips a grim line. She tensed, readying for a fight, knowing, with him, just how much of a challenge that would be. But this time, she wouldn't let her body betray her.

Suddenly Rafe stopped with the suddenness of a dead wind. His resolute gaze snapped away from her. A strange stillness came over him. A muscle along his jaw flexed wildly. Ever so slowly, he lifted his head, almost as if he smelled something on the air. From the way his nostrils flared, she imagined the smell wasn't good.

She followed the rapid progress of his dark eyes as they scanned the area around them, looking intently into the trees, the thick hedge of honeysuckle bushes separating her brother's house from that of its neighbor.

Then she heard it. Or rather, felt it.

Silence.

None of the usual sounds filled the air. No birds chirping, insects singing, or dogs barking. Even the faint breeze that had stirred the branches had now ceased altogether. The tiny hairs along her arms stood on end.

"We're too late," Rafe murmured.

"Too late?" Lockhart questioned in a loud voice, discordant in the eerie silence. *Idiot.* "What are you talking about?"

Rafe's eyes swung back to Kit, hard and grim. She knew what he was going to say before she heard the words, and she tensed, readying herself.

"They're here."

# 8

Three sprang out at them from all directions, almost as if borne on air and wind. One lurched over the hood of her car, a faceless blur coming at her, his eyes a bleeding flash of silver.

Before she could blink, Rafe was moving. His fists met the lycan with a loud crack of bone on bone.

The lycan fell back against the car, one arm's length from Kit. Her breath froze in her chest as those eerie silver eyes turned and locked on hers. Recognition lit his face as his icy gaze drilled into her. No doubt he had been given her photograph.

He shot off the car and toward her.

Her gaze darted to her bag, on the passenger seat. Even with the door open, she would never make it to her gun in time.

He never touched her.

Rafe jumped before her, blocking the creature from getting to her.

The hushed zip of a silencer cut the air. She had not even seen Rafe pull out a gun.

Kit peered around Rafe and at the lycan who would have mauled her. A dark hole marred his forehead. A moment passed before blood dribbled out in a thick stream, dark as molasses, running down his forehead and nose. He wobbled in place as the silver infiltrated his system, its poison slowly doing its work. The silvery pewter of his eyes faded to a very mortal hazel before he crumpled limply to the ground, nothing more than a corpse now. All evidence of the soulless fiend he had been was gone.

Her gaze swung back up at the second muted hiss of Rafe's gun. Another lycan fell a few yards before them, clawing his chest as the silver bullet penetrated muscle and flesh.

She looked up, her gaze sweeping the yard. Her heart constricted. *Shit.*

They were everywhere. Easily a dozen of them. Moving too quickly for her to get a precise count. Swarming around them like ants. Even in human form they moved like predators, animals homing in. The air rumbled with the sound of their growls.

One knocked Davis to the ground, mauling the NODEAL agent with his fists in an animal-like frenzy, spittle flying from his lips. Kit knew the poor bastard would be dead in moments.

Lockhart cursed and fumbled for his gun in the holster beneath his pant leg. "Hang on, Davis!"

*Was this it?*

*Would she be killed in Gideon's driveway by a pack of lycans?*

Rafe clamped a hand on her arm and pushed her behind him as he took aim and fired at the oncoming lycans.

It crossed her mind to wonder why he was trying to protect her, but the thought escaped the instant her head was yanked from behind. Pain lanced her neck. She cried out, her back colliding with the car.

Hard fingers dug into the tender skin of her throat, cutting off her airway. Fighting for breath, she scratched and tore wildly at the hand, her eyes straining for a glimpse behind her. A lycan lay sprawled over the roof of her car, his face inches from hers.

She struggled, choking out a scream as he gave another vicious tug on her hair, lifting her off the ground. Before he could haul her onto the car's roof with him and finish her off there, he collapsed abruptly. His face struck the car's metal with a resounding smack.

Free, she turned, and watched as Rafe whirled around and fired on another lycan coming at them. And another.

Kit spun around and dove inside her car. Her blood pumped hard and fast as she stretched across to the passenger seat and fumbled for the gun in her bag, her hand shaking as it never had before. But hell, she had never faced odds like this.

Her fingers closed around the gun's textured grip, the cold steel reassuring in her hand. She tried to slide out of the car, but Rafe blocked her, stopping her from joining the fray.

"Move!" she shouted, her fingers flexing around her gun, ready to unload some silver.

Was he crazy? They needed all the help they could get if they were going to escape from this alive. He could worry about killing her or whatever later. Right now he needed her.

Rafe flung back around to look at her, his face taut, his dark eyes wild and intense as they scoured her. "Go!"

"Look out!" she screamed, her gaze jumping beyond him to the lycan lunging toward him.

Rafe whipped around, fired a round, and dropped the creature before swinging that intent stare back on her. "Go! Get out of here, dammit!"

Bewildered, she stared up at him. "W-what?"

"Get the hell out of here!" He whirled back around to fire another round. "They're not going to quit coming until you're dead. Go!"

"You're letting me go?" she muttered, struggling to understand why he would do that when EFLA had sent the lycans after her.

And crazy as it seemed, she felt cowardly leaving him to face an army of lycans. The other two agents were worthless. She was Rafe's best hope for help.

"Dammit, woman," he swore, swinging back around to glare at her. "Do you have a problem comprehending?" He made a disgusted sound in the back of his throat. "This is the problem with letting females hunt. You can't listen worth a shit!"

Air escaped her mouth in a burning gasp and she forgot about sticking around to help him out. The chump could take care of his own ass.

"Go to hell!" Her hand moved to the door, ready to slam it shut in his face.

His hand shot out to stop the door from closing. She stared at that hand, at the wide palm and long tapering fingers.

Against her will, the wholly inappropriate image of that tan masculine hand on her—on her breast—flashed across her mind. Heat flushed her face, scalding. She blinked rapidly, as if she could chase the image away.

He bent down suddenly. His hand slid around her neck, his warm fingers closing firmly around her nape, burning her flesh.

She stopped breathing altogether, frozen like an animal caught in a predator's sights. The soft zings of Lockhart's gun faded to nothing.

They said nothing. Not a word passed between them as they gazed into each other's eyes.

The air grew charged between them, electric. Sweat trickled between the valley of her breasts, pooling in the fabric of her bra.

"We'll meet again, Kit March. Sooner than you think."

She wet her lips. His brown eyes darkened, following the movement of her tongue.

"You shouldn't make promises you can't keep." She had meant the words to be a self-assured "kiss my ass" farewell, but her voice came out a tremulous whisper.

He grinned, the curve of his mouth wicked and full of sensual menace. Breaking eye contact, he looked over his shoulder and fired two more rounds, dropping lycans like gnats.

Settling those demon dark eyes back on her, he assured her, "Oh, I never break a promise."

She barely pulled back in time before he slammed her door shut. Turning, he resumed shooting, not sparing her another glance.

She stared at his broad back for a moment through the dirty specks on the car window.

Shaking her head, she started the car. Even if he escaped alive, he would never find her. She would see to that.

Looking in her rearview mirror, she nearly backed over several lycans advancing up the driveway, grinning as they dodged out of her way. The car took a quick swerve out onto the street in a dangerous spin.

Slamming on the gas, she sped down the street, glancing in her rearview mirror again, her gaze seeking out the one form battling lycans on her brother's lawn.

Why in the hell would an agent from EFLA bother to help her?

*To get to Gideon.* His assignment was to get rid of them both. He probably wanted to keep her alive only until he had both of them. Of course. She was soft in the head to think he had let her go because he gave a damn about her. He didn't.

Her fingers tightened around the steering wheel, resolve hardening her heart as she banished the hot, seductive pull of Rafe Santiago's gaze from her mind forever.

〉〉〉●《《《

"Good job, Santiago. You let her get away. I thought you were supposed to be the best." The NODEAL agent's lip curled as he struggled to his feet, patting himself down and examining himself with feverish intensity, making certain he had not been scratched or bitten. Even though it wasn't a full moon and the lycans had been in human form, one scratch or bite was all it took to become infected. Finding no marks, he dropped his hands to his sides.

"I am the best. Only, she's tougher than she looks," Rafe replied, looking over each agent with cool assessment, worse for wear, but still alive. Unimpressed, he let them see he deemed them lacking. If this was what NODEAL had to offer, no wonder the organization had been so easily absorbed by EFLA. No wonder the lycan threat in North America was growing at an alarming rate. "Besides. I didn't see you getting the job done. And did you notice how quickly all those lycans disappeared once she left? They were after her, not us. I just saved your asses." He held up a hand. "No thanks necessary."

Rafe turned his attention to the car turning onto the street, studying it closely as it eased to a stop before Gideon March's house. His stomach sank a little as Charles Laurent emerged from the dark sedan.

The two agents beside him immediately straightened in an attempt to look composed before their new boss. Rafe could have told them it was pointless. No one impressed Charles Laurent.

The cold bastard had climbed to the upper ranks of EFLA by stepping on the backs of everyone above him and mercilessly establishing the policies that marked EFLA as nearly as ruthless as the monsters they hunted, policies such as the termination of rogue hunters.

The chief proponent behind the merger, Laurent was not going to allow anyone to stop him from transferring EFLA policy onto NODEAL.

Although they had both been assigned to the Houston division, Rafe and Laurent had different duties: Laurent to do what he did best—dish out policy; and Rafe to focus on his area of expertise—the elimination of *special* targets EFLA deemed in need of killing. Only, Rafe had not killed Cooper. Laurent had done that, on a whim, when he caught Cooper calling the March family to warn them of the hits taken out on their lives. Another casualty of Charles Laurent's ruthless agenda.

"Where is the female?" Laurent stopped before them, assessing each man coolly.

"Bitch got away," Davis grumbled.

Dark anger churned in Rafe's gut at this slur. He flicked his eyes over the agent, his gaze crawling over the beer belly pushing against Davis's untucked shirt, wondering how he managed to track and destroy lycans in his out-of-shape condition. EFLA maintained strict physical requirements for all its hunters. The guy probably couldn't even run a mile.

"She got away?" Laurent echoed. "How is that possible? You're trained agents." His gaze slid over to Rafe. "Santiago. Were you here?" His voice indicated his doubt, his conviction that if Rafe had been there, Kit would not have gotten away. She would be dead.

"I arrived late. Moments before a small army of lycans decided to make an appearance."

Laurent's mouth turned down. "I see."

"I don't think you do. Your decision to inform the lycan population of Kit March's identity was ill-advised."

Laurent's nostrils flared, the only sign of his displeasure at Rafe's challenging him. "Our first priority is to see her dead."

"I know my job. I've never failed before. Don't you trust me?"

"We've never had a target like her before. She's a huntress—among other things. I deemed additional insurance necessary."

"You're aware they may not kill her." Rafe shook his head in disgust.

Laurent shrugged a narrow shoulder. "They may quite possibly have their fun first, true. I'm well aware of the habits that rule ly-cans. But afterward they will kill her. Their hatred for hunters will demand it."

"You're counting on that. But you could be wrong. They could decide to keep her for a while. Torment her."

Lycans often abducted women, keeping them for years as slaves. His mother was proof of that. She hadn't been kept for years, though. Only one afternoon.

If such a fate befell Kit . . . well, then the very thing EFLA most feared would become a reality.

Laurent must have had the same thought. Uncertainty flick-ered in his eyes. Still, he replied with his usual doggedness. "I stand by the decision. Kit March will be dead before the week's out. Mark my words."

Those words sent a small quiver through Rafe.

"So they keep her for a while. Serves the bitch right." Lockhart shrugged. "They won't turn her. Among their kind, that's an honor reserved for a chosen few. Either way, she's out of commission."

*For a while.* His mind reeled at what could happen in that time. His fingers curled, tightening into fists at his sides at the scenario described—a scenario that would lead the lycans to discover Kit's dirty little secret. A secret even she did not know. Yet.

But Laurent knew. He knew all about the Marshan Prophecy. That Kit descended from Christophe Marshan, giving her DNA compatible to all lycans and making her capable of procreation with the creatures. The result would be a hybrid species. A dove-natu, said to be more powerful than a full-breed lycan.

That should have stopped Laurent from siccing the packs on her. Rafe dragged a hand through his hair, stopping himself from plowing his fist into Laurent's face.

Laurent flicked a piece of lint off his blazer. "If you're so wor-ried, then find her first. See that she dies."

"No problem. We're on it," Davis chimed in, wiping at his bloodied nose. "Consider it done."

Rafe laughed harshly. "You two fools couldn't find your asses with both hands."

Davis's face flushed, his jowls quivering in indignation.

"Fuck you," Lockhart snarled. "I'm getting tired of your attitude—"

Laurent waved a slender hand. "Silence." He leveled a cold stare at Rafe. "Just get it done. Both of them. Don't forget the brother."

Rafe clenched his jaw and gave a hard nod.

"You're just sending him? Alone?" Lockhart demanded.

"Santiago is one of our special agents."

*Special.* Laurent had no idea.

Laurent continued. "No one can bring her to ground better." He smiled coldly. "Certainly not you two." Surveying them, he sighed. "The Houston division is a mess. I've got my work cut out for me here. Beginning with assessing all agents and deciding who is expendable and whom we'll keep for retraining."

The two agents started, clearly disturbed to hear that their jobs were on the line.

Rafe nodded in seeming agreement.

"Report to me once it's done." Laurent unbuttoned his blazer, the restless gesture signifying that the conversation had reached its end. Pulling a linen handkerchief from inside his blazer, he mopped the beads of sweat from his brow. "I don't need to remind you how important this assignment is."

Rafe forced a tight smile. No. He didn't need reminding. "Got it." He looked at the other two agents, warning, "You two assholes stay out of my way."

Rafe studied Laurent for a moment, from his blazer down to the cut of his well-tailored slacks and back up to the ruthless line of his lips, wondering if he had blinked an eye over killing Cooper, a man devoted to the same cause EFLA claimed to champion above all else: the extermination of lycans, the preservation of humanity. How could he justify that murder? When had the lines between right and wrong, good and evil, become so blurred?

"It won't take me long," Rafe promised, meaning it.

Laurent sent him a probing, thoughtful look, and Rafe schooled his features into his usual mask of impassivity.

The quicker Rafe finished with Kit March and her brother, the better for everyone, and the sooner he could move on to his next assignment. There were others. Assignments waiting not half as difficult as Kit. Turning, he strode across the lawn.

Perhaps he should quit. Join up with his brother. He missed Sebastian, hadn't seen him in years. Too many years to count. Ironic, considering the times they had nearly killed each other growing up.

Restlessness stirred in his heart. He dragged a hand over his bristly jaw. It was time to move on. To put this job behind him. To play it straight for once. No more pretending to be something he wasn't. Rafe winced. He would always have to do that. To a degree. He had no choice. There was nowhere and no one with whom he could ever be his true self.

The idea of quitting EFLA had never sounded better. The sooner he did, the sooner he could forget a woman he had no business thinking about as anything more than an assignment.

Especially considering he was also a descendant of Christophe Marshan. And the prophecy EFLA feared would come to pass with Kit March had already occurred—with him.

# 9

Kit parked across the street from her grandmother's house, her current residence and the only home she'd ever known. Or rather, the only home she *remembered*.

*Home.* If it could be called that.

Even at the age of eight, she'd felt more like a tenant, a temporary resident, unwanted and unwelcome.

Even now her grandmother made sure of that, collecting rent and Kit's share of the utilities at the first of every month, seeing to it that Kit purchased her own groceries and never ate a scrap of the food she'd bought and prepared.

Kit did not mind pulling her own weight. She only wished her grandmother would see her as something other than an unwanted obligation thrust on her in the golden years of her life. See her as family. See her at all.

Resting her hands on the steering wheel, she scanned the street, looking for anything unusual or out of place. Her grandmother bore the last name of Carlson. Kit doubted she could be traced through her.

Still, coming here felt risky.

Instinct urged her to hit the highway and not stop until she reached New Mexico. Rafe Santiago was not finished with her.

And yet the thought of the weapons and ammo she kept locked in the chest at the foot of her bed stopped her. And then there was the cross. The gold cross her mother had worn around her neck every day of her life. Even though Kit could not bring herself to wear it, it was precious to her. She couldn't leave it behind.

Not to mention the extra cash she kept in her sock drawer. The three hundred odd dollars in last week's tips would come in handy. She knew she could go to her bank. But she also knew that EFLA would be alerted once she made a withdrawal. Considering a lot of agents for NODEAL were cops—like Cooper—she wouldn't make it out of the city before being arrested. They likely already had an APB out on her. She would need to ditch her car at the first opportunity.

After several more moments of surveying the quiet neighborhood, she slipped her gun from her purse and secured it in the waistband of her jeans, out of sight beneath her shirt. Sliding out from behind the wheel, she crossed the street to the one-story ranch-style house, her gaze darting around her, ever alert as she approached the house.

She had thought of moving out, countless times. After high school. After college. Hell, she'd even thought of running away *before* she finished high school—when Gideon had moved out and the loneliness had seemed too much to bear. When her grandmother had ignored her so completely that she began to wonder if she was invisible, if her existence mattered at all. To anyone.

But something kept her from going. Something besides being fifteen years old and having nowhere to go, nowhere to run. Her grandmother was her family. All she had other than Gideon. She couldn't give up on her—on them. Not yet.

Gideon had been there for her as long as she could remember, arms always ready to hold her when she needed someone. But he deserved his own space now. Even at fifteen, she had recognized that. So she had stayed put, taking comfort in sleeping in the same bedroom that her mother had once occupied, staring at the same rose wallpaper that her mother must have stared at. Watching reruns of *The Waltons* and telling herself a family like that wasn't impossible. It could be hers someday.

She'd stayed out of loyalty. Her grandmother was getting on in years. Kit didn't like the thought of leaving her on her own. Nor could she imagine one day putting her in a home, a place where, ironically, she might feel the same loneliness and lack of self that Kit had felt living with her all these years.

But selfish reasons drove her, too. She'd stayed out of hope—and desperation—that one day she would connect with her grandmother.

She hurried up the drive. Using her key, she entered through the back door, letting the screen door slam behind her to alert her grandmother of her arrival. Her grandmother was the jumpy sort, always faintly surprised whenever Kit entered the house—an intruder, even after all these years.

The smell of freshly brewed coffee hit her once she entered the kitchen. The aroma always reminded her of that first night the police brought her and Gideon here.

She had sat at the kitchen table, her feet dangling inches from the linoleum floor as her grandmother prepared coffee for the officers. She had not lifted her gaze from the bloodstained hem of her nightgown, not even as they explained to her grandmother the events of that night—at least *their* version of events.

She remembered watching the police officer's lips move in slow motion as he explained to her grandmother that her parents were dead. Her father butchered, it would seem, by her own mother.

Later, her grandmother put her in the shower, washing Kit with cool efficiency, uttering not a word as she rubbed her daughter's blood from Kit's toes with her chapped hands. With only the steady beat of water filling the air, Kit watched blood swirl down the drain.

Not a word spoken in comfort. Not a word raised in rage or denial over the shocking news that her daughter had murdered her son-in-law—and been shot dead moments before trying to kill her own children.

"Who's there?" her grandmother's voice, rusty from years of smoking, called out.

"Just me." Kit left the smell of freshly brewed coffee and entered the living room, the hardwood floor creaking beneath her shoes.

Her grandmother frowned at her from the couch she occupied with Jack, her boyfriend for the last year and a resident of a nearby retirement community where she spent most of her spare time.

The Food Channel blared loudly from the ridiculously large TV screen her grandmother had splurged on last year because she claimed to have trouble seeing the television set from the couch. As long as Kit could remember, her grandmother preferred the television at decibel-shattering volumes.

Her grandmother looked surprised, faint annoyance lurking in her rheumy gaze. "Kit."

"Good morning." Kit greeted her over Emeril's signature shout-out.

Her grandmother nodded hello, her gray wig so shiny it appeared lacquered. She brought a glass to her bright coral-pink lips and sipped. Even in June, she wore one of her brightly colored cardigans, purchased in bulk from the Dress Barn.

"I thought you were house-sitting for Gideon and Chloe."

"Claire," she corrected, only mildly appeased to see she wasn't the only one subject to her grandmother's disregard. "I needed to get some things."

"Morning, Kit-Kat," Jack chimed in his cheery accent. He rose to press a light kiss to Kit's cheek. When he pulled back, his warm gaze settled on her face with attentiveness. "How are you, little duck?"

She smiled. Jack could always make her smile. "I'm fine, thank you. How are you?"

He flipped a wrist in the air. "Ah, your grandmother keeps me busy. We're going to the cinema this afternoon, a comedy Lois wants to see with that Vince Vaughn in it." He gave a conspiratorial wink. "I think she just wants to ogle the fella and make me feel inferior."

Kit's grandmother slapped him lightly on the hand. "Not true, Jack."

"Inferior? You?" Kit clucked her tongue. "Never."

"Care to join us?" he asked.

Kit's grandmother pressed her lips together so severely they looked as shriveled as prunes.

"No, thank you. I have things to do today." *Like run for my life.*

"Ah." Jack nodded. "Then would you care for a mimosa or a snack?" He held a stained glass goblet up in the air and motioned to an array of tiny quiches on a tray on the coffee table.

With a fond smile at him, she selected a quiche off the tray. She knew her grandmother didn't want her to linger. The older woman conveyed her displeasure as she fished an orange slice out of her glass with one gnarled, arthritic finger. No words needed to be said. Kit knew how to read the signs. Interrupting her date did not meet with approval.

Chewing, she quickly swallowed down the small bite of egg and spinach. "I'll leave you two alone."

Her grandmother nodded, dropping her orange rind on the tray and reaching for one of the little quiches.

Kit hovered in place for a moment, feeling that something should be said. She had no idea when she would return. *If* she ever would. After this morning she had to wonder.

This could be the last moment she ever saw her grandmother. She felt that she should say *something*. Anything. But what? What could she say when there had never been a hint of sentiment between the two of them? No matter how much she'd wished it to be otherwise.

At a loss, she turned and made her way down the hall. To the room she had slept in since the age of eight. The room that had once been her mother's—that still felt as though it belonged to her. To anyone else but Kit.

Her grandmother had led her to that room after her shower that long-ago day. Her hair wet and tangled about her head, she'd settled back on the floral bedspread that felt faintly dusty beneath her. She hadn't bothered to crawl beneath the covers. Simply curled into the smallest ball possible and watched the flickering shadows on the walls, wondering if any of them might turn out to be more than shadow, as real as the monster her mother had turned into. As real as her father's corpse, mauled to death by her mother.

The faded rose wallpaper, wilted and peeling in some places, now looked harmless in the morning light. No shadows anywhere.

She moved to her dresser, taking out clothing and adding it to another bag. Grabbing a backpack from the closet, she unlocked her chest and filled it with additional guns and ammo. Zipping the backpack, she moved to her bedside table.

Her mother's cross hung from the lamp, dangling in the air where she could always see it. Some nights she stared at it until she fell asleep, picturing it around her mother's neck, one of the only clear images left to her, in a past before she ever knew that monsters existed. Outside of fairy tales, anyway.

She closed her fingers around the cool chain and slid it into her pocket. On her bed, a ratty, one-eyed bear sat in the center, cozy between two pillows.

Gideon told her their parents had given it to her their last Christmas together. She couldn't remember, but she lied to Gideon, to herself, pretending that she did, pretending the bear meant something, pretending it held an emotional attachment for her.

Turning, she left the bear on the bed.

Finished packing, she slung her bags over her shoulder and turned to leave the room, jumping at the sight of Jack in the doorway.

"Sorry, duck. Did not mean to frighten you."

"It's all right," she replied a little breathlessly, her heart hammering.

"Thought I'd catch a moment with you while your grandmother freshens up for the movie." His gaze swept over the bags slung over her shoulder. "Already on your way out?"

"Yes."

His gaze lighted on the necklace at her neck. "Ah, you're wearing it. I thought it would suit you."

Her hand flew to the small bronze amulet hanging from the delicate chain at her throat. Her finger absently traced the gold fleur-de-lis pattern at its center. "Yes, I love it." He had surprised her with the necklace a few months back, finding it at one of the many antiques villages he and her grandmother frequented. Too bad he hadn't married her grandmother. Then Kit would have had a grandparent who actually cared about her.

She feigned looking at her watch. "Well, I'm running late."

He stepped aside and motioned her through the door.

She strode down the hall and through the kitchen.

"Kit."

She stopped in the kitchen and turned to face him.

"Is everything okay?"

Her throat thickened for some reason. Because he cared about her? Or because he had grown to know her well enough to know when something was wrong? She blinked fiercely. Too bad he hadn't been around when she was growing up.

"It's nothing," she assured him, walking across the kitchen to press a kiss to his bristly cheek.

He nodded, trying, she knew, to look gruff and unaffected. He waved a hand at her. "Go on your way. I don't want to make you late."

Turning, she hurried outside, the door slamming behind her, the sound ringing in the air with a finality she felt deep in her heart. Her gaze swept her surroundings as she hurried toward her car. Tossing her things inside, she slid behind the wheel.

Pulling from the curb, she noticed a silver Hummer turning the corner and coming up fast behind her. Squinting into the rearview, she recognized the man sitting behind the wheel. Rafe Santiago.

Her foot ground down on the accelerator. He may have let her get away back at her brother's house, but considering whom he worked for—and that they wanted her dead—she wasn't risking another confrontation. And she definitely wasn't letting him follow her to her brother.

Zipping out of the neighborhood, she trusted her knowledge of the area to outrun him. After several more turns, she left the sleepy residential area and turned onto a four-lane highway. Zigzagging out of traffic, she smiled when she noticed him slipping two cars behind. She gunned through a yellow light, chuckling when he got stuck at the red. Before he could catch up, she swerved to the far-right lane and turned. Several more turns put him well behind her.

She continued to swerve through traffic until she reached the freeway she needed to take out of town. Still, it was several more minutes before she relaxed. Before she felt her shoulders ease back down from her ears, the tension ebb as tall buildings gave way to suburbs.

Soon, she would be out of the city. At the next town, she would look for a used-car dealership shady enough to exchange her car without filing the proper paperwork.

Then she would put miles, and one state, between herself and Rafe Santiago.

And forget that she had ever met the man.

# 10

Kit stared at the single-story building through her windshield, feeling herself grimace. She guessed the motel would not require a credit card. That was something. The most important thing. Although whether it would give her lice remained to be seen.

The squat building reminded her of some motel out of a horror movie. The kind that sat along a remote desert highway with hardly any cars in the parking lot. Just your car and that of the truck driver set on murdering you in typical gruesome horror-movie fashion. The main difference—the one that had persuaded her to pull over—was that this motel sat along a busy intersection and several cars occupied the parking lot. Sighing, she grabbed her wallet, left her parked car, and entered the front door, trying to ignore the fact that the desk clerk took her money behind a glass cage and asked whether she wanted to pay by the hour or the night.

Paying her twenty-nine dollars, she stepped back outside. Luckily, she had found an after-hours used-car dealership, and she was now the proud owner of a Taurus sedan. Well, she was the owner for at least another week. That was all the time the salesman had promised her before he would report the vehicle stolen. A small crime, it seemed, for the *gift* of her car. She sank back behind the wheel and drove a few hundred yards, parking the car directly in front of room eleven.

She let herself inside the room. Closing the door behind her, she could not help thinking it had the consistency of cardboard. She gave the simulated wood a pat and grimaced. It wouldn't stand up to lycans. But then, she had always marveled that a steel door and walls of steel effectively contained Darius every moonrise. If any lycans tracked her, nothing except silver would stop them from getting to her anyway.

After driving steadily for the last several hours, she prayed that she was home free. Not for the first time, she wondered if she should even go to Gideon. Should she expose him and Claire to such a risk?

The room smelled of stale smoke and moldy carpet. She dropped her bags on the full-size bed and tossed her brown paper bag of takeout on the small table near the window. Falling gracelessly into one of the chairs, she pulled her gun out and set it within reach, on the table.

Turning her attention to her dinner, she pulled the foil-wrapped burrito from its bag. Despite the appetizing aroma of melted cheese, she could manage only a few bites. Her temples throbbed.

The same questions that had plagued her as she drove still buzzed through her head: How long would she go to ground? Where would she hole up? She couldn't spend a lifetime looking over her shoulder.

Suddenly the dream of marriage and half a dozen kids seemed farther away than ever. As distant as reruns of *The Waltons* she watched over coffee and cereal. Foolish and naïve and completely beyond her reach. Not that the dream had ever loomed close. Gus fixing her up on one date wasn't going to get the job done. Survival suddenly took on larger proportions and made all other wishes foolish and small.

Rewrapping the burrito in its foil, she tossed it in the trash bin and stood, stretching muscles cramped from long hours behind the wheel. How long until Rafe Santiago quit looking for her? Before they all quit?

*We'll meet again, Kit March.*

His eyes had glowed black fire as he said those words. Hard to believe he hadn't meant them.

A warm flush stole over her as she recalled the hard press of his body against hers, the firm feel of his hands on her face as he pulled her closer. Gentle yet strong. She squeezed her eyes tight, banishing the feelings, ordering the heat those memories evoked to dissolve.

Shaking her head, she pressed her fingers to her throbbing temples. Damn if she wasn't confused. He wanted her dead. And her brother. Probably Claire, too. Rafe Santiago's helping her had clearly addled her thinking. He was not her savior. Merely a thug who worked for EFLA and who enjoyed playing with her, like a cat that toys with a mouse before devouring it. And just as deadly. Little better than the lycans she hunted. The only difference was that he was human.

Flipping on the television, she picked up the remote control and scrolled through the limited channels, wishing she could get the Houston news and decipher any NODEAL and EFLA activity. She could usually detect which homicides were lycan hits, especially when some happened to be her doing. Or Gideon's.

Finding nothing, she opted for a *Law and Order* rerun.

Sitting at the end of the sagging mattress, she nudged off her sneakers, laces still tied, and watched Jack McCoy deliver his signature closing argument. If only her life drama could be solved in a one-hour segment.

Getting up, she strolled to the window and peered out through thick canvas curtains, searching for anything or anyone out of the ordinary. The parking lot was lit a hazy red from the motel's perimeter lights. Metallic hoods gleamed ominously in the night. Her sedan sat directly in front of her door, unobtrusive among some of the more vibrant colors of the other vehicles.

Seeing no one among the smattering of vehicles, she let the curtains fall back in place. Stepping into the tiny bathroom, she stripped and took a long shower, letting the warm water beat down on her bowed head and melt the tight muscles of her neck.

She washed her body, one hand slowing at her throat, stopping to caress the necklace Jack had given her, her thoughts softening. At least someone would miss her. Would wonder about her when she never returned home. She would miss him, too. And Gus. The crusty barkeep could always make her laugh.

After several moments, she forced herself to move, scrubbing herself with her loofa and a mild unscented soap she had brought. For once, she decided smelling sweet enough to eat was not such a good idea. With lycans out for her blood, she wasn't looking to attract the creatures.

Not for the first time, she wondered at her insistent need to hunt, to destroy lycans at the expense of everything else in her life: A husband. Kids. Family. Maybe she didn't really want those things. Not as she thought. If she did, she should have been able to set aside her quest for vengeance.

But then, hunting lycans, she supposed, was less work. Finding love, making it work, making it last—that was harder. Maybe impossible.

A few deft twists and she turned off the water and stepped from the shower.

Her wet feet soaked the hand towel she had tossed down to serve as a rug. She rubbed her hair with a larger towel until curls sprang around her face and neck in semi-dry corkscrews. Dragging the towel over her body, she slowed her ministrations as awareness stole over with the insidiousness of a big cat stalking through tall savannah grass.

Utter silence surrounded her. A tomblike quiet that felt heavy, oppressive. The buzz of the television was gone. No voices. No music. Nothing.

Wrapping herself in her damp towel, she pushed open the cracked bathroom door. Its oil-hungry hinges creaked, the sound loud and obscene, pinching her nerves tight.

Darkness yawned before her, thick as smoke. The lights had been on when she entered the bathroom. Of that she was certain. Just as she was certain of one other thing now: she wasn't alone.

## 11

She froze at the threshold, fingers twisting in the towel, knowing that with the bathroom light on, she was perfectly visible. A sitting target for whoever—whatever—watched and waited.

Water from her hair ran down her neck. The uneven rattle of her breath joined with the humming silence. She could not steady it. She squinted, straining her vision to see into the blackness. The showerhead began to drip, each tiny splash on the tub like a rocket explosion in the deafening silence.

Taking a deep breath, she pushed down the fear, the panic that threatened to consume her, and let her training take over.

Her senses sprang into high alert, her hand gripping her towel so tightly her fingers went numb, bloodless.

Her free hand flew to the light switch, dousing the tiny bathroom in blackness, and guaranteeing that anyone watching her, waiting for her, was now as blind as she was.

Assuming he was human, of course.

Rafe's face flashed before her eyes. Dark eyes glinting. Her heart beat harder, faster, the pulse skittering at her neck.

*Let it be him. Let it be him.* As much as she never wanted to see him again, she wanted even less to come face-to-face with a lycan.

Her mind leapt into action, assessing her options, grim as they were. Even if Rafe Santiago had stolen into her room, he wasn't there for idle chitchat.

The gun she had left on the table was now too far to reach without her potentially colliding with her late-night visitor. Later she could kick herself for leaving it there.

Her bag of guns and ammo sat on the bed. One gun tucked beneath the pillow. Not too far. *The pillow.* Her fingers twitched reflexively, readying. Her semiautomatic, with its attached silencer and fourteen-round clip of customized silver-tipped bullets that Gideon had given her upon completing her training two years ago, was just beneath the pillow.

Dragging a silent breath into her lungs, she dropped her towel, tossing modesty to the wind. She did not need the distraction of trying to keep herself covered as she dove for the bed.

She eased one foot out of the bathroom, the carpet dry and flat beneath her damp feet. Another step followed, as silent and slow as the last. She concentrated on *not* running for the gun in a mad, panicked dash. That would only draw attention and get her killed.

Praying that she had just forgotten the act of shutting off the television, that the overhead light had simply burned out, she continued her careful advance toward the bed. Maybe someone wasn't in the room, breathing in the same stale air. Maybe her imagination was working overtime. Maybe, for once, her gut was wrong.

Despite her even breaths, her heart slammed fiercely against her ribs, unconvinced.

Knowing she had to be near the bed, she squatted, her thigh muscles tense and burning, quivering with strain and anxiety.

Her hand brushed the scratchy bedspread, sliding along its surface, searching for the pillow.

Anxious, she set both hands on the bed, bumping into something . . . firm.

Her throat constricting shut, she backed away, hands shaking, hovering over the bed. Her lips trembled on a silent whimper.

A hand shot out and seized her wrist in a brutal grip.

Her whimper spilled free then, startled and terrified as a shock of light flooded the room. She squinted against the harsh intrusion of brightness.

"Hello, there, huntress. We've been looking for you."

Her gaze narrowed on the silver-eyed creature before her.

"No easy task," he added.

She had no time to struggle. He flung her on the bed, the mattress hard beneath her back. Her head bounced, her neck wrenching at the rough treatment.

She blinked past the discomfort and stared up as two lycans crowded her. The one who had flung her down hovered over her on the bed. Shaggy fair hair fell over his forehead and curtained his face, doing nothing, though, to shield the silver eyes crawling over her with a soulless evil she knew too well.

She shrank back into the mattress, agonizingly aware of her nudity, of his relentless hold on her, of just what they would do to her if she didn't figure a way out of this.

From the corner of her eye, she spotted the pillow just to her right.

The lycan's hand fell on her bare leg. She jumped as he squeezed her thigh, his long fingers digging like a cruel claw.

"Do you know what we're going to do with you?" he rasped, his mouth close to hers, the scent of his breath coppery sweet. *Blood-sweet.*

Shivering, she forced her gaze to hold his, to not look away from that cold pewter stare as her right hand crept to the pillow on the rumpled bed.

Determined to keep their attention on her body—not such a challenge since she was nude—she suffered their hungry leers and the savage hand on her thigh as her fingers brushed the pillow.

She let them look their fill, wincing when one reached down to pinch her breast, twisting the tip cruelly between his fingers.

"Sweet," he growled, eyes glittering that eerie silver. He glanced to his brethren. "Perfect timing. We can play with her for two days, then gorge ourselves."

The fair-haired lycan brushed his cohort's hands off her with a growl. "I'm first." He smiled an evil grin.

His hand on her thigh gentled then, his fingers softening on her flesh, feather-light on the skin he had bruised. But the touch was somehow worse, turning her stomach until she feared she might be sick all over the bed. Swallowing down bile, she concentrated on sliding her hand beneath the pillow.

A hand wedged between her thighs, forcing them apart.

*Oh God, please no.*

She forced herself to endure his touch, to resist instinct and not struggle until her gun was firmly in her grip. Without it, she did not stand a chance. Without it, she was dead. Only silver could stop him. Stop any of them.

Holding her legs with both hands, he stretched her open before him, splaying her indecently.

Her throat tightened, trapping the scream that threatened to shatter the air, shatter her sanity as she contemplated his foul touch on her, the depravity he would visit on her in moments if she did not stop him. Her hand fumbled over the rumpled bedspread, straining beneath the pillow, searching for cold steel.

The other lycan crowded behind him, his devil eyes sharing the view, feasting on her.

Shame washed over her, mingling with the fear that swam in

her gut, threatening to spill over in hysteria. She fought for composure, for calm—for a way out of this hell.

"You're small, huntress. Hard to imagine you've put so many of my brethren into the ground," he murmured thickly, his thumbs rotating in ever-widening circles on her flesh.

*And you're about to join them, scum.*

As his hands slid up her thighs, thumbs gliding inward on her legs, inching ever closer to her nest of curls, his nostrils flared wide, inhaling her. "I'd like to keep you alive until moonrise, so that we can enjoy tearing you limb from delectable limb." With a click of his tongue, he shook his head. His fingers dug into her, increasing their pressure. "But I just don't know if I can resist spilling your blood sooner. You smell so damn . . . delicious."

A whimper escaped her lips.

His mouth curved in a cruel smile, clearly enjoying the sound of her pain.

Keeping her movements subtle, she allowed her fingers to meet the cold steel. Carefully, she closed her damp hand around the grip and flipped off the safety. Her palm and fingers tightened around the textured grip, its reassuring weight the final liberation.

*Enough.*

Time to show them they'd messed with the wrong woman.

"After tonight," he continued, "there might not be much left of you."

An angry growl erupted from her then.

She slid the gun from beneath the pillow and swung it in his face.

Silver eyes widened in front of the gun's unwavering barrel.

"Wrong," she bit out, staring down the barrel.

Arm locked straight, she tightened her finger around the trigger and fired.

# 12

*He was too late.*

The sounds of splintering furniture and shattering glass carried through the door, and he knew instantly that they were already here. They had gotten to her first. Evidently with the same information EFLA had fed him regarding Kit's location.

His jaw clenched, teeth grinding together so tightly he tasted the coppery wash of blood in his mouth.

If lycans stood on the other side of the door . . .

Damn Laurent to hell. It wasn't supposed to go down this way. This was the very thing that was *never* supposed to happen.

He knew what lycans could do to a female. He had seen the aftermath, the haunting look that would come into his mother's eyes every now and then. Her soft tears at night when she thought he and his brother were sleeping.

For all he knew, what he hoped to prevent—what EFLA strove to stop—was happening even now. Again.

He begged God that he wasn't too late.

A descendant of Christophe Marshan, Kit could not be violated at the hands of a lycan. He regretted not making that risk clear to her before. He regretted waiting. Regretted not telling her everything. The truth. No matter how she would look at him once he did.

Using his shoulder, he burst through the door, his blood simmering, scalding in his veins at the scene greeting him. He paused at the threshold, fists curling and uncurling at his sides. His bones seemed to expand, to stretch within him at his deep inhalation.

One lycan thrashed wildly about the room, falling heavily to his knees, then on his back, feverishly clawing his shoulder where a bullet had already penetrated. Rafe sniffed, inhaling deeply. A silver bullet. He would be dead in a matter of minutes if he did not dig it out. A real possibility. Some lycans had been known to sever their limbs in an attempt to stop the silver from slowly poisoning them to death.

A second lycan had pinned Kit to the floor. She squirmed beneath him, bare legs thrashing as they wrestled for the gun. He struck her in the face. Her head smacked the floor with a sickening thud, hands falling limply at her sides.

Blood trailed from a nasty gash at the corner of her mouth, the streak of crimson obscene against her skin.

The warm sweet smell of spilled blood floated toward him.

The lycan leaned over her and swiped a finger along her bloodied lip, tasting her and moaning in appreciation.

Typical. The bastard had not even noticed him yet. When it came to their victims, lycans were single-minded in their focus. Especially this close to moonrise, when their hunger was at its zenith.

Something dark and grim—toxic as silver was to these monsters—stirred in Rafe's gut at the sight of Kit's injury, of the lycan tasting her, at the dazed, unfocused look in her lovely green eyes.

Rage flared within him, a dangerous burning in his gut, spreading outward, racing along the path of his bones. The fiery heat burst in his chest, an explosion of force that fed his body.

His skin tingled, smoldered. A familiar scratchy, prickly sensation swept over him. Unwelcome. Yet unable to prevent. He rushed the room, a low growl escaping through his tightly ground teeth.

The bastard atop Kit swung his gaze to look up at Rafe, baring his teeth in a snarl.

A return growl rose up from deep in Rafe's chest. His fingers flexed at his sides.

He felt his bones begin to stretch, pull . . .

The lycan moved off Kit in a low crouch, rolling his shoulders back, readying himself to pounce.

"Rafe," Kit gasped, her head twisting to view him better. The barest moment passed as her green gaze locked on him. Relief flickered there . . . and bewilderment. He knew he must not look quite himself. And yet he knew he had to act. Before *it* took root. Before she made total sense of what she was seeing.

He snatched a lamp off the table and launched it through the air above his head, smashing it into the overhead light. The fixture exploded in a shower of popping and hissing sparks. Broken glass rained down on them as darkness swallowed the room.

Only the dim red haze from the motel's perimeter lights spilled through the open doorway, saving them from total blackness. Rafe's vision adjusted to the dark gloom. The red cast to the room, the crouching lycan, Kit's wide gaze—all lent a surreal quality to the moment. As if they were in an antechamber of hell itself.

But it was dark enough. Enough for what he would do. What instinct demanded of him. What Kit could not witness.

Succumbing to his animal side, a dark rage that he always held in careful check, he surged forward in one lunge.

Blood filled his vision, boiling through him as he met the lycan in a fierce crash of flesh and bone. Their spitting growls filled the room. His hands wrapped around the other's neck, determined to wreak his vengeance.

For himself. For Kit. For lifetimes of past wrongs.

) ) ) ● ( ( (

Kit sat up and squinted into the darkness, wincing as she brushed a hand against her throbbing lip. She inhaled thinly through her nostrils, struggling against the darkness and an aching head to follow the movements of Rafe and the lycan.

*Rafe.*

She had seen his face briefly, registered the anger in his expression, the fierce glittering in his dark eyes. For a moment they did not even look brown, glinting a cool gray, almost silver. Like the bloodthirsty lycans intent on destroying her. Certainly a play of the light. A trick of her imagination. She had, after all, managed only a glimpse before he shattered the light, plunging them into shadows and death.

Why had he done that? Lycans possessed excellent vision. They could see him even in the dark. The lack of light could only incapacitate him.

And yet that single glimpse of him had been enough to reassure her that the only thing he was bent on destroying was her attackers. She didn't know how he had found her, but she felt only relief that he had.

In the fleeting second when the door had burst open and Rafe stood on the threshold like some sort of dark angel—his large shape limned in muted crimson light, quivering, vibrating in the glow— her heart had ceased to beat. Silhouetted at the threshold—the ravaged door hanging only by a single stubborn hinge—it crossed her mind that she faced not a dark angel, but a demon emerging from the mouth of hell.

Then he shot forward in a blur of movement. Impossibly fast. So quick she thought she had imagined it.

She scrambled to her bare knees on the flat, threadbare carpet, peering into the gloom and trying to follow the two shapes locked in a struggle. They appeared almost as one writhing shape. Her hands moved fast, stretching over the carpet in search of her gun, fighting against the dizziness in her head.

A low, gurgling sound reached her ears, followed by a sick, crunching sound—bone on bone. Her hands stopped, hovering over the grimy carpet.

Then the large merged shape broke, fell apart as one body collapsed heavily to the floor, mimicking the drop of her heart.

She went utterly still, staring at the shape still standing. Rafe? Or the lycan?

A harsh silence fell.

Inhaling a deep breath, she fought against the ever-increasing pounding of agony in her head and groped for the bed. Gripping a fistful of the bedspread, she shot a desperate prayer to the night.

Several more moments passed. The silence, thick and suffocating, played with her sanity. She could not stand one more minute of it. She had to know.

"Rafe?" she whispered, her heart beating like a loud drum against her chest as she stared at the figure rising and unfolding to his full height.

The dark shadow moved toward her, his features indistinguishable. The blood glow of light hummed around him, seeming to echo the ringing in her head.

She edged back from the bed. The muscles in her arms straining as she dragged herself away, hands clawing the carpet—and her fingers brushed cold steel. *Her gun.*

With an excited gasp, she fumbled for the weapon, her movements sluggish, slower than she would like, than she needed them to be. *Dammit.* She needed speed and a clear head right now.

A hard hand grabbed her calf, nearly startling her into dropping her weapon.

A quick glance down at the floor revealed glowing, silver eyes moving toward her.

"Shit!"

She had forgotten about the injured lycan, dismissed him, thinking him as good as dead. Even if he was shot only in the shoulder, the silver should have done its work. He shouldn't have been able to crawl across the carpet and hold fast to her leg, to dig his nails savagely into her flesh.

"Just die," she hissed, kicking at his shoulder again and again.

A growl rumbled over the air, lifting the hairs on her arms.

Her throat tightened, killing her breath.

Convinced Rafe had lost, that the shadow rising was the other lycan intent on finishing her off, she adjusted her grip on her gun and fired at the beast clinging to her leg.

With a dying grunt, he released his hold on her and let his head drop with a thud to the floor.

She spun around and fell alongside him from the abrupt motion. Her stomach heaved. Spots danced before her eyes. Fighting against sudden dizziness, she began to squeeze the trigger again just as the shadow lunged forward in a blur.

Gasping, her fingers tightened on her gun, determined not to lose it again.

"I'd really rather you not shoot me."

"Rafe." She breathed, her arm sagging, matching the loosening inside her, the easing within her too-tight chest. The gun dropped from her fingers.

"Kit." In the dark, his hand somehow unerringly landed on her cheek. "Are you all right?"

She nodded, the motion making her all the more dizzy. She swayed on her feet and winced at the show of weakness.

"Kit," he said again, and his voice suddenly sounded so far away, as if he were calling her from a great distance.

His arms caught her as she toppled over, strong bands that felt solid and firm. Warm over her nakedness.

Her lids pulled low, twin weights tugging down over her eyes that she could no longer fight. *Damn.* She loathed weakness, loathed that after working so hard to be the best, to be strong, capable of taking care of herself, she was on the verge of passing out.

"No," she whispered in a weak thread of voice, her hand knotting in his shirt, twisting the fabric as she felt herself slipping away, becoming boneless and limp in his strong arms. Arms that felt good, better than they should. A man whose arms she should flee.

"I'm here, Kit, I'm here," he replied in a voice unusually thick, guttural and low, almost as if his mouth were stuffed with cotton. Still, the sound of it swept through her like an infusion of Claire's Christmas wassail, equally potent, burning a path to her belly.

*I'm here, Kit.*

And she knew he was. Even as she knew that she could not give in, could not let herself surrender.

*I'm here, Kit.*

The words comforted her as they shouldn't. Especially coming from *him.*

Nothing had changed. He was still her enemy. Still someone she needed to escape, but she could not stop herself from sighing against the hard wall of his chest, from inhaling the warm male scent of him. From thanking God he had come.

Her resistance gave out as her fingers uncurled from his shirt.

She succumbed to darkness, dimly accepting that there was no fight left in her—and knowing that when she woke he would be there. With her.

She would fight him then. Later.

$$) \; ) \; ) \; \bullet \; ( \; ( \; ($$

Intense relief swept through him as Kit fell limp in his arms, as soft and malleable as a sleeping child. Cradling her close, he felt her slow, steady breathing ripple through her and pass into him. She lived.

His vision adjusted further to the gloom, assessing the details and nuances of her face, calm and serene in sleep. Her lower lip was puffy, smeared with drying blood. He ran a hand over her head, stopping at the goose egg–size knot buried in her soft curls at the back. Likely a concussion.

A deep sigh rattled loose from his chest. She was unharmed. He inhaled deeply. They had not raped her. The prophecy would not come to pass. At least not in her.

His hands skated over her gentle lines and curves, searching for further injuries, striving to evaluate her with clinical dispassion. The woman was unconscious. Only a bastard would take advantage of such a situation.

Not a stitch of clothing covered her. Not that he needed his eyes to see in his mind what his hands felt. He had already spent more time than he should have visualizing her lithe figure. Naked in his arms. Another first for him. She was a job. One of countless Marshans he had dealt with over the years. Christophe Marshan's offspring had grown into quite the family line. And EFLA wanted them all dead. Those they could trace, anyway.

He had no business looking at her—lusting for her. Nothing had changed. He needed to get rid of Kit March and regain some measure of himself, of the man who never allowed his emotions to get the better of him. Especially when it came to the job. And Kit March, after all, was just a job.

His hands skated over her warm female skin, soft as silk, supple beneath his rough fingers, trying to convince himself that he didn't want her.

Honorable or not, adrenaline sang through him, swimming hot and thick through his veins. He felt slightly drunk, his head heavy, not quite his own. No surprise, in his condition.

The beast in him fought for release, for the freedom to take her. Possess her as instinct demanded. He had to struggle hard to urge him back into his cage, especially following the heady euphoria of his kill. Fighting the untimely erection pushing painfully against the front of his jeans, he kept his fingers stretched at his sides.

Struggling for control, he sucked in a bracing breath. It wasn't the first time he'd surrendered and let himself go. Sometimes he had to. His mother never understood that. She thought the beast should be forever suppressed.

Hunting lycans, how could he not use the full measure of his strength? But it was the first time this hunger, this lust, had followed the aggression. It was the first time he struggled so fiercely to regain himself. The difference, he realized, was that he had been fighting for her. And now he longed to claim her. His instinct begged for it, craved to sink into her soft heat.

Inhaling through his nose, he drew air deep into his lungs as he urged himself to return to normal.

Battling his rush of desire, he readjusted her in his arms and rose to his feet. Moving to the bathroom, he flipped on the light switch and wrapped her in a towel, hoping that the thin barrier might help, and also knowing he could not stroll outside with a naked woman in his arms.

Turning around again, he didn't blink an eye over the carnage of the two bodies, only hesitated at the sight of her belongings strewn over the room. He knew the lycans had tracked her the same way he had. Through a planted GPS.

His EFLA contacts had given him her location. Just as he assumed they had alerted the lycan population. They had not, however, told him where the chip was located. And he hadn't risked asking. It was outside his usual sphere of interest, and he had no wish to raise suspicions by breaking pattern now and asking questions that he had never bothered to ask before. He had a few more years to go before he left EFLA. He needed to make the most of them.

Leaving her things behind, he carried her out into the night, eager to go before any other lycans showed up. Eager to find some place for her to recover, for him to regain control of himself and finish the job he had set out to do.

# 13

Kit woke with a headache from hell. A beer-mixed-with-cheap-wine kind of headache. She opened her eyes, only to shut them again, the brief flash of dim light too much to bear.

Several moments and deep breaths later, she slid her eyes open again, blinking slowly in the murky air. An unfamiliar room washed in muted light stared back at her. She began to turn her head, but stopped, jamming her eyes shut again at the resulting pain in her head. Slowly, she drew air into her lungs and willed the pain to pass.

Memory flooded her. If Rafe hadn't arrived . . .

*Rafe.*

Heart pounding—and not entirely in fear, the fear she should have felt—she opened her eyes again.

Vague images skipped through her mind. Rafe's shadowy figure wrestling with the lycan in the red-tinged motel room. Rafe moving. So fast. Impossibly fast. Too fast.

It was all so fuzzy, as though it had happened in a dream. Surely she had imagined the speed at which he moved.

She brought a hand to her throbbing temple and slid her hands through her hair until she reached an egg-sized knot at the back of her head.

*She had passed out.* How humiliating.

Her cheeks burned at such an uncustomary loss of control. Sure, she'd taken on multiple lycans before—a situation both Cooper and Gideon had advised against countless times in her training. *Isolate your targets. Narrow your risks.*

She could argue that she hadn't picked her targets. They had shown up, intent on killing her—after they'd had their fun.

Still, she expected better of herself. Cooper and her brother had trained her to be better. She knew lycans were hunting her. She should never have dropped her guard. Should have taken her gun with her into the bathroom. Rookie mistake.

Her hands dropped to her stomach, resting over a thick down-stuffed silk duvet cover. The material felt good against her flesh. Smooth and cool.

She frowned, hesitating a moment before lifting the cover and peering down at her shadowed body. *Naked.* She was naked. Of course. She had been naked when the lycans attacked. Naked when Rafe arrived.

Face burning, she dropped the covers back down. When she lifted her head off the pillow, her gaze caught her reflection in a gilt-framed mirror hanging on pin-striped wallpaper across from her. She winced. With her hair a wild mess around her head, she resembled a cartoon of someone who had stuck her finger in an electrical socket. Always the case when she went to bed with wet hair.

Below the mirror sat a crystal vase of cream-colored roses, their sweet aroma filling the room and teasing her nose. Wherever Rafe had brought her, it was a definite step up from the roach motel where he had found her.

She moved her gaze to scan the rest of the room, hoping to spy her bags so she could get dressed and leave before Rafe returned. Nothing had changed. She still needed to reach New Mexico. Needed to get away from Rafe.

Turning her head, she froze.

Beside her, he slept, the contrast of his tan skin and dark hair as shocking as ink against the white pillowcase.

Her chest tightened with a sharp breath. The barest hiss of air escaped her lips. Scant inches separated them. Her breath came easier as she realized that he slept on, oblivious to her.

Tension ebbed from her shoulders as she studied his face, those dark, intense eyes closed in sleep. His impossibly long lashes were dark crescent smudges on the sharp planes of his cheeks. He wore no shirt. His shoulders and upper chest rose sinfully and alluringly above the white sheets pooled at his waist.

Something quivered inside her, swirling downward to tighten in her belly at the sight of all that muscled flesh. She could break a hand on those washboard abs.

Shaking her head, she sat up, turning her back on him.

*Move it, Kit. You can slip out while he's sleeping.*

Carefully, she slid one foot over the edge of the mattress, ready to drop to the floor. At his sudden sigh, she stilled. The sheets rustled. A peek over her shoulder revealed that he had moved. The sheets crawled lower, past the dark line of hair trailing down his navel, where the hair thickened enticingly.

Her throat constricted, cutting off her breath. The sudden quivering in her stomach made her press her thighs together.

Overwhelmed by curiosity—and other emotions she dared not examine too closely—she continued her survey. His chest rose on a deep breath and her palms tingled to touch that flesh. How would he feel? Would his skin feel soft? Hard? Smooth?

Heat exploded in her cheeks, sweeping down her chest in a

blaze. Her nipples tightened as if struck with cold, despite the simmering heat racing through her with the force of a firestorm.

Her face felt prickly and tight at the bold shape of him. So close. Closer than any man had been to her in a long time. Clearly. Why else would she have felt compelled to sneak a look? Especially when she should have been hightailing it out of there?

Biting her lip, she pressed a palm to her cheek, the skin warm against her trembling hand, and forced her gaze away.

She was dizzy, overwhelmed with want from that brief peek. Her hand shook against her face. Feeling every bit the perverted soul, but unable to resist, she looked again.

Her eyes rounded as he grew erect before her gaze.

Gasping, she ignored the answering ache that flared to life between her legs and clutched the sheet tighter to her chest.

Her nape prickled with awareness, her gaze flying to his—colliding with eyes dark as coffee, sinister as shadow, drilling into her with unnerving intensity. He was awake. And aware that she had been watching him, *absorbing* the sight of him.

Her mouth parted, but no sound fell. Scalding heat swept over her face. What could a girl say when caught ogling a man's package? And while he slept, no less?

She pushed herself off her elbow, intent on fleeing. From him. From her humiliation.

He caught her wrist in a brutal grip, stopping her. The touch of his hand burned her there, a manacle of fire, singeing her sensitive flesh.

Their eyes locked and held. She ceased to breathe.

"Good morning," he murmured, looking at her in that consuming way of his, his eyes glinting almost black with something that resembled both amusement and . . . desire? She couldn't be sure. It had been too long.

"You're naked." Even to her own ears she sounded like an appalled schoolteacher.

"Observant."

"But in bed. With me."

"Score again."

"Why?"

"The only rooms available were with a king-size bed." He shrugged one shoulder. "Mary Kay convention."

"And you had to sleep naked?"

He lifted an eyebrow. "Do I strike you as the kind of man who wears pajamas to bed?"

No. He struck her as dangerous. The type of man she had no business sharing a bed with. Even if he wasn't an agent with EFLA. He was the type of man she needed to get far, far away from.

She averted her face and tugged to free her wrist, determined to do just that.

His voice continued its low, sexy rumble, sending a lick of heat twisting through her belly. "Why in such a hurry? By all means, look your fill."

"What?" She blinked stupidly.

"Don't let my waking stop you."

"Are you crazy?"

He continued as if she hadn't spoken. "Touch me, if you like." His dark eyes lightened then, not nearly as dark as they usually appeared, looking strangely gray—like moonlight spilling across an ink-dark sky.

"Touch me," he repeated, his voice a rasp of warm smoke.

*Touch me.*

That voice, his suggestion, rippled over her skin like the teasing brush of a feather.

With a shake of her head, she forced herself back to reality with a reminder of what he was. What she was.

"Easy there, cowboy." She scooted away from him, clinging to the sheets, tugging on her wrist again until he released her.

"I wasn't trying to get anything started. Just assessing the situation."

"Hmm. Disappointing." His top lip curled. "And what is your assessment?"

"Just that neither one of us is wearing any clothes."

"A veritable Sherlock Holmes."

"I just don't usually wake up naked with a—" Heat warmed her face as her voice faded.

His eyes glinted. "No? Interesting."

She had not meant to confess her inexperience.

"A charming woman such as you," he continued. "I would have thought you suffered no shortage of men willing to share your bed."

She glared at him, sure he was mocking her. "I've had more important things to do with my time." A half-truth. She wouldn't have minded sharing her bed with someone. A man worth having. Who wanted her in return.

"More important things," he echoed, his voice faintly accusing. "Like hunting lycans."

Her chin went up. "I could do worse things with my time."

"You have no business risking your neck hunting lycans. There's a reason women shouldn't hunt."

"If you're talking about lycans being able to detect a woman due to her menstrual cycle—"

"For starters—"

She waved a hand. "That never presented a problem for me. I usually set myself up as bait anyway."

"Damn fool," he muttered, dragging a hand through his hair. "There are other reasons you shouldn't—"

"What?" she demanded, leaning forward. "Tell me."

He opened his mouth, lips working.

"You can't," she declared in satisfaction. "You don't have a reason beyond your own sexist beliefs."

With a growl, he flung back the sheets and vaulted from the bed with ease, indifferent to his nakedness. He appeared as comfortable in his own skin as he was in clothes. Perhaps even more. Her gaze trailed down the muscled legs. Even his feet looked good. The toes strong and clean, the nails neat and short.

Standing above her, he bit out, "It's more than that."

Face flaming, she watched, helpless, unable to look away as he strolled to the bathroom. There ought to be a law against men with bodies *that* good.

She tightened her hold on the sheet covering her, acutely reminded of her own nudity. And that he likely knew her body as well as she was coming to know his.

With the door open, she had a perfect view of his taut backside, of the dimples above each cheek at the small of his back. She suffered the sight, mouth alternately drying and watering.

She couldn't even recall the body of the last guy she'd slept with. At least not in any great detail. Oh, she recalled the *guy*. Greg. She remembered him clearly. Remembered that, briefly, she had thought he could be the one. He liked tofu, cycling, and never missed an episode of *Rachael Ray*—for him, the quintessential female.

They had dated nine months. A record. She had contemplated sharing with him the secret of who she was—what she did. Of the evils that stalked the earth, threatening mankind. But something had held her back. A good thing, too. He dumped her for a curvaceous brunette who knew how to flambé quail with Cognac. A five-foot-three-inch blonde with the figure of a twelve-year-old girl wasn't exactly his type. She doubted there would ever be a man to whom she could confess her unusual avocation. How many guys could handle being with a woman who kicked werewolf ass for a living? If they even let themselves believe her.

Looking away from Rafe's backside, she swallowed to bring moisture to her suddenly dry mouth, demanding, "Where are we?"

"Still in Austin," he answered. "I checked us into a more suitable hotel. Rodent-free. Didn't think you'd mind."

Scowling, she sat up and swung her legs over the side of the bed. "I couldn't use my credit card. Good luck trying to find a quality hotel that takes cash these days."

"You might as well have used your credit card." He moved out from the bathroom—still naked. "They found you. *I* found you." He plucked a pair of boxers and jeans from a wingback chair near the window. "You were tracked."

She flashed a bitter smile, not liking the truth, especially when she thought she had done a fairly good job covering her trail.

He snapped the fly shut on his jeans and looked up at her. "You were bugged."

"Bugged?" She felt her eyes widen. "How? When could they have . . ." She shook her head; her voice faded.

He shrugged a broad shoulder. "Don't know. I didn't have the time to rummage through your stuff last night. Just thought it safe to discard your belongings altogether."

Her gaze shot around the room. "You left all my stuff back there!" Her clothes, ammo, hard-earned money.

"Too risky to keep any of it. I didn't want them following us."

Her fingers tightened on the sheet. Escaping this room, him, suddenly posed more difficulty. She pushed to her feet, careful to wrap herself in the sheet. "I don't have any clothes."

A smile tugged at his hard lips. "We'll find you something to wear." His dark gaze slid over her. "I suppose we must."

Her cheeks burned, then she remembered something else.

"My necklace!"

He glanced at her throat. "You're still wearing it."

"No, my mother's necklace. I don't wear it. I just keep it close. I . . . sleep with it next to me."

He stared at her, frowning. "We had to leave your things behind."

"Then we have to go back."

"Kit, there's no going back there." Even though his voice was gentle, his gaze was hard, inflexible.

"Damn you! I have to have it!" Her throat grew thick.

He lifted one shoulder. "Sorry."

"No, you're not." A desperate sort of anger swirled through her. She would never see her mother's cross again. And the blame rested with him. "You couldn't give a shit!"

A muscle in his jaw tensed. Without saying a word, he turned to dig through his bag on the dresser, his back muscles flexing with his movements.

"What about my guns?" she demanded. As a man, he would probably understand that better than the sentimental value of a keepsake. "They're not so easy to replace." Especially her cache of silver bullets. She quivered with indignation. It had taken years and money to acquire those guns and bullets.

"You're with me now." He pulled a black T-shirt from his bag, snapping it once in the air. "You don't need them."

Her fingers grew numb from clutching the sheet. "Why? Because you're my big, bad protector?" She advanced slowly, glaring at the smooth expanse of his back. "Hard to believe, considering you're charged with terminating me." Her gaze fell on the gleaming crystal vase sitting atop the dresser. "Why didn't you just let them finish me off?" she demanded, never forgetting that although he had helped her, he was not an ally. She inched closer to the vase, a sudden plan taking over. "Letting them have me could have saved you the trouble. That's your job, isn't it? What EFLA wants? Me. Dead. Why else did your people release my identity to the lycan population?"

"That wasn't my idea," he replied, slipping his arms into the sleeves of the T-shirt. "There's dying and then there's what they would have done to you. I wouldn't wish that on anyone."

"Oh, you have principles about the manner in which I die?" she sneered, closing her hand around the smooth crystal vase, watching as his dark head popped through his shirt, not really caring about his answer, knowing what she had to do.

She lifted the vase, noting with satisfaction that it felt heavy as lead in her hands.

He began to turn, saying, "I've never said that I want you—"

With a heart that felt surprisingly tight in her chest, she swung, jaw clenched so tightly her teeth ached.

Horror mingled with satisfaction as the vase crashed against his head in a shatter of glittering glass. Rafe dropped heavily to his knees. He remained there, swaying unsteadily, head bent.

She flattened a hand over his shoulder, preparing to push him the rest of the way to the floor, thinking it should be an easy matter to overpower him now. Staring at the dark hair curling against his nape, she muttered crossly, resenting him, resenting herself for doing this to him, even if she had no choice, "You should have listened. I warned you not to underestimate me."

Then she shoved at his firm shoulder, her fingers resisting the urge to caress all the muscled flesh beneath her palm. To her surprise, he didn't budge. In his weakened condition, he should have dropped like a fly.

Frowning, she pushed even harder against the muscle, gasping when hard fingers flew to her wrist with the speed of lightning. His hand flexed around her until she feared her bones might snap, brittle as a branch in his grasp.

Dark eyes shot to hers, alert. Furious.

Alert as they shouldn't have been.

He should have been halfway to unconsciousness on the floor by now.

Lightness gleamed behind the rich brown of his eyes, like

something trapped beneath the surface of a dark ocean, a wild animal swimming wrathfully, searching for a way out.

Dread scraped her spine like the drag of an icy cold fingernail. She tried to tug her arm free, desperate to break free. No luck. His grip grew tighter, bruising. She swallowed a whimper of pain, but held that livid stare, unable to look away.

"Impossible," she whispered, her voice a hoarse croak.

"I've never underestimated you, Kit," his voice rumbled over the air, thick and foreign, coiling like a flame in the pit of her stomach. "It is you who have underestimated me."

# 14

Rafe sucked in a deep breath and waited for the stinging pain in his head to subside. The pain did.

Unfortunately, the deep breath did nothing to cool his fury, a fury that threatened to suck him under, pull him into the darkness that always tempted, begging for free rein.

With a hand on his knee, he pushed himself to his feet, struggling to reel in his temper.

Her green eyes flew from him to the tiny bits of crystal on the carpet, blinking like diamonds. He shook his head, sending more shards raining down.

She lifted her gaze back to him, muttering, "You shouldn't be standing."

"My apologies," he mocked. "Should I have allowed you to kill me?"

Defiance sparked in her bottle-green eyes. "If I'd been trying to kill you, you would be dead."

His gaze crawled over her, prowling, hungry. The way she clutched the sheet molded the thin fabric to her breasts perfectly.

His mouth watered. He remembered rolling his fingers over the turgid little peaks, remembered the mewling cries he had wrung from her. She had been so incredibly responsive. His cock hard, he quickly looked away and dragged in a deep breath before looking back at her.

He heard her breath quicken, and he responded, his body tightening, coiling with an animal readiness. "When you can't even knock me unconscious? Somehow I doubt that."

Color heated her cheeks. "I hit you hard enough." Her voice dropped to a petulant mutter. "Your skull must be steel-plated."

"Something like that." With his hand still on her wrist, he pulled her closer. She stumbled against him. "Let's get a few things straight."

"Such as?" she snapped, struggling against his chest.

"You're not going anywhere without me." He released her wrist to wrap both his arms around her. Her female flesh pressed so close to him. "So get that thought out of your head. No more vases."

"No vases." She gave a sharp nod. "Duly noted. I'll look for something else next time." She cocked her head in mock contemplation. "Maybe a television set."

"There won't be a next time, Kit," he warned, tightening his arms around her. The press of her small breasts against his chest was damned exciting. "You're taking me to your brother." The sooner she did, the sooner all of this could be over. And he could be free of this misery.

The green of her eyes hardened, deepening to polished malachite. "Never."

"Then you're stuck with me."

"Forever?" she mocked. "I don't think so."

"It won't take forever to get what I want out of you." His gaze lowered, assessing the golden slopes of her shoulders, the shadowed dip of cleavage below the bunched sheet. He remembered clearly every curve and angle. The small, perfect breasts with coral-tipped nipples. Those he would never forget. "I generally get what I want from women."

The color in her cheeks deepened. "My, aren't you the charmer. Women must drop at your feet." Her mocking words shook on the air, lacking their usual ring of bravado. For all her toughness, there was a woman at her core, vulnerable and sensitive. This only made his reaction to her more visceral. More dangerous—to both of them.

"But let me assure you I'm not like any woman you've met before," she added. "I won't drop at your feet."

"I can believe that." His hands slid down her back, shifting to the gentle swell of her hips. A reckless move. Foolish. He'd been treading dangerous ground since the moment she woke, attuned to her every move and sound, from the slight shift of her weight on the mattress to the faint rasp of her breath.

He should release her. Should set her from him and drop his hands. Never touch her again.

He'd never touched the others. Never been tempted. And there had been several attractive women over the years. Nice, agreeable ones who never gave him half so much trouble as this one. They had even looked at him with invitation in their eyes. He had no idea what the ramifications would have been if he had mated with a Marshan descendant and a child resulted, but he was not about to risk finding out.

Yet here he was. With his hands all over *her*. With his thoughts wrapped up in *her*.

Of course, he could tell her the truth. But somehow he did not think that would make her more agreeable. If anything, she would fight him all the harder.

His gaze dropped to her mouth. The full bottom lip. Her tongue darted out to moisten it nervously, and something tightened and cramped in his gut.

Her gaze slid from his, moving to his mouth. "Let me go," she whispered.

There were a million reasons why he should have accommodated her, but the sensation of her nipples hardening beneath the thin sheet kept him from obliging her.

"You don't want me to do that."

Eyes wide at his blunt declaration, she shook her head, tossing her unruly curls around her face. The clean scent of her hair drifted to him. He detected no perfume, which only let him smell *her* all the better. Clean woman with a hint of mint.

"Yes, I do." She paused, groping for words, her brow wrinkling. "You want me dead."

She still believed that? Believed he could hurt her?

"You don't think that."

She renewed her struggles, her eyes sparks of green fire in her flushed face. "Let me go."

He hauled her higher against him. Lowering his head, he pressed his mouth near her ear, demanding thickly, "Do I act like someone who wants you dead?"

She stilled. He felt every inch of her quiver.

"That's the way of it then? You're like them. An animal."

He sucked in his breath.

"You want your fun before taking care of business, is that it?"

Her scathing words struck a nerve. He flinched, fingers digging through the sheet and into her back. She winced, and he forced himself to remember his strength and ease his hold before he showed her just how close to the truth she was.

Pulling back, he looked into her eyes, his voice dropping into the charged air. "I'm nothing like them." He had to believe that. He must.

"You're no better! You're just like them," she shot back. "Your methods might vary, but your goals are the same."

*You're just like them.*

His mother's voice came back to haunt him then, the mantra she had drilled into him and Sebastian echoing through his head as if she were standing beside him. *You must never be like them. Never. Never.* The mantra had become his own.

"I am nothing like them. You want me to prove it," he challenged, dark fury rolling through his veins like molten lava, thick and scorching.

Her lip curled. "You can't—"

One of his hands slid up from her back to tangle in her short hair. He gripped the back of her skull, fingers curling into the soft flesh just beneath one tiny shell of an ear. He could feel her life pulse there, dancing madly, leaping against his touch.

He was so close now, his lips a hairsbreadth from hers.

"What are you doing?" The soft words feathered across his lips.

"Showing you that I'm different from them." His fingers shifted, stroking the soft skin behind her ear in a caress.

The words barely left his mouth before he was pressing his lips to hers, covering her warm lips with his own. And discovering true wildness. True, blood-burning animal hunger.

Swallowing her startled cry in his mouth, he deepened the kiss, working to coax a response from her.

She gasped against his open mouth, and he took advantage, delving his tongue inside the warm recesses of her mouth, tasting the wet heat of her. Sweet as wine. And just as intoxicating.

With one taste, he knew it would never be enough. He would never be satisfied until he possessed all of her.

Casting aside the restraint on which he'd prided himself, he growled low in his throat and pulled her closer. But not close enough. Never close enough. His arms lifted her off her feet. Starved, denied too long, he drank from the mouth that had tormented him from the first time he saw it.

Groaning, he let himself go, gave in to the impossible impulses he had felt from the start, since the moment he'd laid eyes on her—a sexy, sweet, vanilla-smelling huntress stalking and battling her prey, her smart mouth lashing out at him, daring him to conquer her in the most primitive of ways.

Mouth still fastened on hers, he gave a single tug on the sheet until it puddled to the floor, leaving her body delicious and bare against him.

He slid his hand from her silken back to her front, dancing his fingers up her quivering belly to cup one breast, kneading the small mound. The soft flesh fit perfectly in his hand. Like he knew it would. Her nipple pebbled against his palm, and she whimpered, kissing him back. Tentatively at first, then more aggressively, sliding her tongue against his as he rolled her nipple between thumb and index finger. He yearned to taste the sweetness of her breasts, to bite and nip at the rigid little peaks until she cried out.

He wedged his knee between her legs, pushing her higher against him. To his delight, she pressed herself down against his thigh.

The core of her burned through his jeans and into the flesh of his thigh, branding him. Releasing her breast, he cupped her face to angle her head better for his hungry tongue, the line of her jaw delicate and smooth in his hands.

She kissed him back more feverishly, matching the thrusts and parries of his tongue, her small hands clutching his shoulders, sharp nails digging through the thin cotton of his T-shirt.

He tangled his fingers through her hair, luxuriating in the silken tresses.

He couldn't stop. Couldn't get enough of her, couldn't prevent his hands from roaming every bare inch.

Down again they slid, skimming the slim line of her spine to cup the deliciously full ass. He groaned and massaged the smooth cheeks, bringing her burning sex against him. Her moistness scalded him through the denim of his jeans. His cock throbbed painfully, aching to be free, to bury itself within her.

But the restraint and discipline that had ruled him through his life obediently reared its head. He withdrew. Slowly, with great pain, he removed his leg from between hers. Then his hands. Then his mouth.

Glassy green eyes gazed up at him, fortunately too dazed to witness any change in his own eyes. And he knew they must be altered—evidence of his desire, proof of what she did to him.

She raised her hand to touch her lips, moist and bruised beneath her fingertips.

"Enough," he managed to get out, the thick, strangled sound of his voice betraying him, threatening to expose him. Then she would see just how much of an animal he in fact was.

He swallowed past the thickness in his throat, struggling to regain control.

He had set out to prove he was not like those beasts, and had only ended up proving to himself that he was perhaps more like them than he wished to be. Never had he come so close to losing himself with a woman. Always before he had been in control.

She shook her head, her fair hair crazy and wild, mussed from his hands. "No," she spat out. Moistening her lips, she grabbed a fistful of his shirt and tugged him close. "Not enough."

He didn't need a second invitation. The last of his willpower vanished. No matter what he was. What she was. His mouth slammed back over hers.

# 15

He was kissing her.

Her eyes drifted shut, lost to the sensation of it, powerless to resist. In that instance, her body's needs outweighed her logic.

Too long. It had been too long since a man had his mouth on hers, his tongue dancing along her own. And his hands. Never had a man roamed his hands so thoroughly, so possessively, over her body.

Now, she decided. This moment, she would take what she could get. Just once. It would be enough. She would make it so.

His warm tongue tangled with hers as his fingers slid into her hair, running through the knots and snarls with a fierceness that rivaled the blood hammering through her veins.

A lick of heat curled low in her belly, tightening and twisting until she grew wet.

His hands slid lower, seizing each cheek, lifting her higher against him.

She moaned into his mouth, winding her arms around his neck, marveling at the insistent ache throbbing between her legs. She'd never felt anything like it. Never had she burned.

Her fingers wove through his hair, reveling in the softness, in the freedom to touch.

Her head fell back, eyes closing. A cry rose in her throat as one of his hands lifted, molding her breast. His rough palm chafed the tender skin. He took her nipple between thumb and forefinger and rolled the pebble-hard peak, gently at first, then increasingly harder, faster, until she thought she would fly from her skin. She arched her spine, closing her eyes as shards of pleasure-pain spiked from her breasts directly to her aching sex.

With a growl, he dragged his mouth down the column of her throat, sucking, nipping at the cords of her neck. His breath fired against her throat. She opened her eyes. His eyes gleamed at her, lights dancing in the centers as though lit from within.

He dropped one hand from her ass.

She slid down him, boneless, the backs of her knees bumping the dresser. Still, their lips clung, drinking, tasting, devouring each other as his hands flew to his jeans.

She brushed his hands away, wrenching the snaps open herself. Shoving the denim down, she sought him, sighing as she closed her hand around the hard length of him, warm and pulsing. She stroked him, her thumb gliding over the tip of him, delighting at his ragged moan. Opening her mouth, she dropped down to taste him. He did not let her sample him long.

With a growl, he seized her wrist. Searing her with the hunger of his gaze, he spanned her waist with both hands and planted her on the dresser, the stinging smack of her bottom on the wood exciting her in a dark, primitive way.

He dropped to his knees, wedging his dark head between her thighs before she could speak or move. His finger ran over her folds, gentle, teasing, playing in her wetness. She shuddered, falling backward, the mirror cold at her back, but she didn't care.

He found her clit, rotating his finger over it in slow, hard circles, every once in a while flicking it with his tongue. She clenched a fistful of his hair, arching herself off the mirror.

Suddenly he ceased his teasing licks. His mouth was there, sucking, drawing the tiny nub into his mouth. She shot straight up, pulling his hair, screaming as an orgasm washed over her. Ripples of pleasure swept over her as she crashed back against the dresser mirror.

But he didn't stop. Didn't quit. He rose between her legs in one motion, his hot mouth seizing a nipple as he sank one finger inside her.

She moaned and lifted her heels up on the dresser, flattening her feet on the smooth wood surface and thrusting her hips forward.

Sucking at one breast, he gripped one trembling knee as he worked a second finger inside her—taking her, reducing her to a babbling, incoherent mess with each press of his hand.

She jerked at the fabric of his shirt, thrusting against his hand, desperate to feel him, to run her hands over the chest she had ogled earlier. She needed her hands on him, skin to skin. "Now. Take me now."

He laughed roughly and stepped back.

She groaned, bereft, naked and wanting where he left her on top of the dresser.

He watched her intently, dark eyes glowing as he discarded his T-shirt and kicked off his jeans.

Panting, she watched him back—his toned, beautiful body effortlessly bending to retrieve a condom from his wallet.

He came back to her then, rolling the condom over his erect penis. Her mouth watered. He fixed his gaze between her legs, jaw locked, a muscle jumping wildly in his cheek.

Reaching out, he teased her sex, stroking her folds.

She whimpered, wiggling on top of the dresser.

"That's it," he murmured, his finger easing back in her with tormenting slowness, eyes hot and hungry, feasting on her. "So lovely and pink. Wet. Weeping for me."

"Please," she begged.

His eyes locked on her. Something passed between them. A shared hunger. A mutual awareness that this was it. The moment had come that began when they first set eyes on each other. No more games, no more pretending the chemistry that burned between them did not exist. No more pretending her body did not crave him more than her next breath. *Sex*, a voice whispered across her mind. *It was just sex.*

His finger slid from her. Her muscles clenched, aching for his return.

It would be good.

He positioned the hard tip of himself at her entrance, teasing, nudging her swollen sex.

Great.

Panting, she braced her palms on the dresser top.

Incredible.

He grabbed a fistful of her hair and tugged her closer, until their foreheads touched.

She grabbed a handful of his hair and crushed her mouth to his in a savage kiss, desperate for him, for what only *he* could give her.

He plunged into her then, buried to the hilt, the hard length of him filling her, stretching her. Completing her.

ᗪ ᗪ ᗪ ● ᑕ ᑕ ᑕ

Rafe forced himself still, body quivering, needing the moment to check himself. Savoring the sensation of her clinging warmth around his member, he reminded himself that she was so much more fragile than he. He swallowed, fighting for restraint, fighting to hold the beast back.

She whimpered, flexing herself around him, the walls of her channel tightening, a perfect silken fist. A growl erupted from deep in his chest.

She worked her hips and he had to move. Pulling back, he buried himself inside her again, this time deeper, harder.

With a deep moan, she parted her legs wider. It was too much. He continued to move, driving into her again and again, watching as her face contorted with the same intense pleasure swelling like a tide though him.

Her moan deepened, and he knew she was close.

"That's it, baby." Dropping his hand, he rolled his thumb over her little nub. With a strangled cry, her trembling legs gave out, heels sliding off the top of the dresser.

He caught her, lifting her shuddering body and wrapping her legs around him.

Their eyes locked, hers glowing brightly as he gripped her by the hips and pounded fiercely into her.

He could not stop, could not take it slow. The beast clawed free and his fingers dug deeply into her flesh, anchoring her for him.

She cried out, throwing back her head, her sweet body tightening, milking him.

He groaned, the sound reverberating from his body and into hers. He readjusted his hold on her. With one hand on her ass and the other gripping her thigh, he moved powerfully, stroking in and out of her. Again and again. His fingers dug into her thigh, pulling her leg higher for a deeper penetration, for a pleasure so intense it bordered on pain.

She writhed against him, shoving him both away and closer, dragging her nails down his back, wild mewling noises spilling from her lips.

"That's it. Let go," he breathed in her ear, taking the velvety lobe between his teeth and biting down, hard. She quivered in his arms.

Every nerve in his body tensed until he felt on the verge of snapping, exploding into pieces. He thrust in and out of her, filling her in a way that was more than physical. More than the endless stretch of days in his life as he knew it.

His thrusts grew harder, faster, stoking the fire within until—at last—he exploded, bursting from within, shattering everything he thought he knew about himself, about her.

She fell limp in his arms, her cheek dropping on his shoulder in trusting sweetness, her warm breath fanning his skin.

He pulsed inside her, the slightest movement in the still and sudden aftermath. He pulled her closer, her lithe body a perfect fit in his arms.

After his mother died, after he and Sebastian discovered her body, butchered by EFLA agents who had tracked her down at long last, he learned to shut down, to block emotion. He mastered the ability to close himself off from others, sealing himself off in a room deep inside himself, where no light penetrated.

Right now, though, he felt as if Kit had burst into that room, bringing with her a warm, reviving light. He had never felt warmer. Or more exposed.

*Shit.*

Carefully, he set her back on the dresser.

She brought her knees together, averting her eyes. She remained just so for several moments as he stepped back, her lovely breasts rising and falling with her deep breaths. Still, she did not move, did not look at him.

A chill chased over his skin, bringing him back to himself. He moved automatically, discarding the condom and dressing himself.

Still she did not look at him. With every second that passed, he could almost see the barriers returning.

"Kit." His hand reached for her cheek. She jerked away before he could touch her.

"Don't." The word fell into the thick air, a sharp explosion of sound.

He dropped his hand.

She lifted her chin, spearing him with cold green eyes. "It was just sex, Santiago. Don't go making anything more out of it."

He felt his lips twist into a cruel smile and could not stop from asking, "Who are you trying to convince? Me or yourself?"

☽ ☽ ☽ ● ☾ ☾ ☾

Kit watched as Rafe moved to the room's single window in a few swift strides. With his back to her, she felt safer, less vulnerable. Out of his sight, she lifted her hand to her mouth, brushing her bruised and tingling lips, willing her hand to still, to stop its feeble shaking.

He pulled the curtains back, and she squinted against the sudden glare of sunlight. Even in the air-conditioned room, she felt the heat of the Texas sun penetrate the glass, almost as hot as his mouth on her body.

"How are you feeling?"

The suddenness of his voice made her flinch. She slid off the dresser and retrieved the sheet at her feet and wrapped it around herself again.

*How are you feeling?*

Breathless. Furious. Confused. Hot and aching from his kisses, from his hands on her, from his complete and thorough use of her body.

But mostly furious. With *him*. With herself for letting a would-be-assassin make love to her.

He turned to face her. "Are you up for travel?"

"Travel?" she echoed dumbly, having trouble wrapping her head around any coherent thought.

"Yes." His dark eyes stared at her with utter coolness, as if nothing had just happened between them.

The mysterious light that had lightened his eyes earlier had vanished. Unremitting darkness stared back at her. Impenetrable. Emotionless. Totally unaffected.

But that was a man for you, she supposed. So able to disconnect from emotion. From the passion that had rocked them only moments before.

"Are you ready to get out of here?"

Swallowing, she fought to gain the same level of composure and indifference he showed. "Definitely." She hefted the sheet a bit higher, clinging to it like armor. "Only, not with you. We'll be going our separate ways."

A hint of light reappeared at the centers of his dark eyes. "Do you really want to fight me on this?" He motioned to the bed. "I can tie you up until you change your mind. Is that what you would prefer?"

Her fists tightened, knotting in the sheet.

"Look," he began with a sigh, holding up one hand in a placating manner. "I promise I'm not out to hurt you. I could already have done that had it been my goal."

"Right," she bit out, ignoring the tiny part of her that was inclined to believe him. "You forget that I know what you are. You already told me it's your job to—"

"You forget," he cut in, his voice razor sharp. "Did I tell you I was going to hurt you? Ever?"

She stared at him intently, thinking over their previous encounters, and mentally answering his question.

No. He had never proclaimed his intent to *kill* her. Not precisely. But the implication had been there. He had not dissuaded her with words to the contrary. Had never once corrected the assumption. *He only helped save your life a few times.*

And why was that?

"Did I?" he pressed.

"No," she murmured reluctantly. Yet wariness still gripped her. She would not have survived these last years had she not learned to sniff out danger before it struck. And everything about Rafe Santiago screamed danger. Perhaps only a different sort than she first expected. Her breasts tingled, nipples pebbling at the memory of being sucked into his mouth.

"Why did I bring you here? Why am I even talking to you if I only want to kill you?" He motioned about the well-appointed room.

"So I'm supposed to believe that you're helping me out of the goodness of your heart?"

He smiled mildly, the curve of his lips devoid of emotion, and shrugged. "You're alive, aren't you?" His dark eyes scoured her like a finely honed blade. "And well satisfied, if the scratch marks on my back mean anything."

Heat swamped her face, but she chose to ignore the jibe. "You work for EFLA—"

"I've never been the most obedient of souls." He jerked his head to the side. "If my mother were alive she would attest to that. The fact that I'm employed by EFLA doesn't mean a hell of a lot to me. I do what I want. When I want." His eyes gleamed darkly, hungry light filling the centers, making her feel hot and prickly again.

"Fine. Let's assume you're going against the orders of your own people." She held his stare. "Why?"

"I don't relish killing innocent humans. That's not what I signed on for."

She nodded slowly. "Then why not let me go?"

He grimaced. "I can't do that." His eyes drilled into her intently, as though willing her to understand. "For reasons I can't divulge."

"What reasons?"

"I can't go into that right now."

She inhaled sharply. "What aren't you telling me? Stop playing games, and tell me what's going on."

Something flickered across his handsome face. Something dark and forbidding. "Trust me. I'm not playing a game. You're simply not ready to hear—"

"Damn you." She pressed a hand against her chest. "Don't patronize me. This is my life you're talking about." Renewed determination filled her, cold resistance sealing her heart. "I can't trust you. Not as long as you're holding out on me. Come clean."

He shook his head. "Sorry, Kit. I can't do that yet. Whether you trust me or not, you need me right now."

*You need me.* A tingle raced down her spine, and her belly tightened.

Despite herself, she looked him up and down, the word *need* rooting itself in her mind, in her blood, working at her resistance. Her body burned, recalling his mouth, his hands, his hardness, the feel of him filling her, the drag of his flesh against her, inside her.

She closed her eyes in one fierce blink, willing the ache at her center—*in her heart*—to subside. God, she was in trouble. She could not stay with him a moment longer. Not when he reduced her to this. Sex one time was excusable. A moment's madness. An itch that needed scratching. Twice, and she had a serious problem.

She had to figure out a way to lose him and continue on to New Mexico alone. Before she did something truly stupid—like sleep with him again.

She opened her eyes to find him watching her. "I don't need your help. I can take care of myself. I can disappear just fine on my own—"

"Like last night?" he quickly inserted, his voice clipped, sharp with challenge. "You looked like you were having quite a bit of trouble when I showed up."

Heat filled her face. "I would have handled the situation."

"Wrong." He advanced, stopping before her. "You'd be dead. Or worse."

Worse. Worse than death. Her stomach tightened, grew queasy. It didn't seem possible, but she knew it was. Knew what could have happened. There were worse things than death.

Sighing, he dragged a hand through his dark hair. "Enough bickering. Are you hungry? I could do with some breakfast. We passed a pancake house not far from here."

"Pancakes?" The idea of eating pancakes with him seemed ridiculous. Far too ordinary. Something two people without an ounce of trust for each other would never do. Even if she was half-starved.

"We have to eat." He scratched at his bristly jaw. "Sounds like a good way to pass the time until I persuade you to take me to your brother."

Did he think he could twist her loyalty so easily? Her lips compressed. He'd learn soon enough.

She glanced down at herself. "Do you plan on having me dine in this? You left my clothes behind, remember?" Her cheeks burned at the reminder that he had seen her naked. And more. So much more. "I need something to wear."

"We can take care of that."

"And a shower."

He waved to the bathroom behind her. "There's a robe on the door. You can wear that until we get you some clothes. I noticed a boutique in the lobby when we checked in." He moved toward the phone. "I'm sure I can call and have them bring up a selection."

"No one said anything when you carried a naked woman into the hotel?"

His well-carved lips turned up at the corners. The sight of them tugged at some place deep in her chest and she averted her gaze again. He really was too handsome. Too . . . everything.

"No. You were wearing one of my T-shirts. I told them you had had a few too many at a party and fell into a pool."

"They believed that?"

"It's all in the attitude. People will believe anything if one is convincing enough."

"So you're an adept liar."

He arched a brow at her, his expression serious. "I haven't lied to you, Kit."

"Right." Turning, she walked into the bathroom, trying not to stumble on the sheet tangled about her legs.

Once inside the spacious bathroom, she crossed the cold tile floor to the marbled vanity. Lifting her gaze to the mirror, she winced.

The woman staring back looked a fright. Purple smudges shadowed her wide eyes, and her blond waves stood out wildly around her head. Even worse than her earlier glimpse in the other mirror. *He had made love to this?*

She turned away from the image of herself. Dropping the sheet, she stepped into the shower. Soon, warm water sprayed down over her body. She let the water relax her sore muscles. Her body loosened, releasing all tension, as her mind worked on a plan.

By the time she stepped out, she had convinced herself that everything would be fine. She would lead Rafe along, biding her time for the right moment to escape. By his own admission, he wasn't telling her everything.

She refused to stay with him, refused to risk Gideon or herself on trusting that he was not out to harm them.

In front of the mirror, she tamed and reshaped her wet locks.

Sliding into the fluffy white bathrobe, she stepped out of the bathroom to find an array of clothes already waiting.

Rafe motioned to the items on the bed. "I guessed your size."

Selecting a pair of black gauchos, a camisole-style tank top, and undergarments, she stepped back into the bathroom and dressed quickly, doing her best to banish the memory of his mouth on hers, the tingling heat, the numbing desire . . .

To forget.

She had her work cut out for her.

# 16

Kit paused, fork poised over her egg-white-and-cheese omelet as she watched Rafe wolf down a tower of chocolate-chip pancakes. Chewing vigorously, he reached for his cup of coffee and took a healthy swig. His eyes met hers over the mug's rim. His throat worked, swallowing.

"Something wrong with your food?"

"No," she murmured, motioning to his plate. "Do you eat like that all the time?"

"I have a good metabolism." He raised a slice of bacon to his lips.

The diner was crowded, voices buzzing around them, waitresses wearing unattractive maroon uniforms zipping busily amid the tables. A heavy odor of grease hung in the air.

He glanced down at her plate and gave a small shake of his dark head. "You don't eat enough."

"I eat plenty." She reached for one of the crisp slices of turkey bacon on her plate. "I just prefer food that doesn't harden my arteries." No sense explaining to him that her stomach was too twisted into knots as she planned her next move for her to eat anything heavy.

Only, with no money, her options once she escaped were limited. Ironically, she had decided that her only hope rested with Darius. No one would be monitoring him or tracing his calls. He was completely off the radar. His death was speculated to have occurred long ago. Certainly no one knew he was in Houston. Otherwise, NODEAL would have captured and killed him years ago.

Once she gave Rafe the slip, she would find a place to lie low and call Darius to come get her. As far as alternatives went, she didn't like it, but she had no other choice.

She watched as Rafe took a bite of bacon and chewed calmly. Four more pieces remained on his plate, alongside several links of sausage.

"You eat like a man destined for bypass surgery."

"I'm fit." One corner of his mouth lifted in a vague smile. A moment passed before he spoke again. "So, was there a special reason your brother and his wife left town?"

Shaking her head, she smiled knowingly. "You won't get me to tell you where they are."

He cut another bite of pancakes out of his stack. "Aren't you worried he'll return to Houston when he doesn't hear from you?"

"They've been warned to stay away. Gideon won't come back."

He looked up at her, holding her gaze. "Even for you?"

She mulled over that. He was right. Her brother wouldn't wait forever. If he didn't hear from her soon after her enigmatic message, he would come looking for her. Just another reason to escape Rafe. And quickly.

"I wouldn't wait," he added, that deep exotic voice of his causing her heart to trip, her blood to race. She suspected she would hear it in her dreams long after she left him. "I would come for you."

A spark raced down her spine at his words. *I would come for you.*

He meant that he would come after his own sister. If he had one. Not *her*. Not Kit. She meant nothing to him, a prize to be served up to EFLA, and she wouldn't mistake his meaning. Still, her hand gripping her fork trembled from his words—and the thrill they gave her.

They resumed eating in silence. Kit glanced out the window to the right of their table, eyeing the crowded parking lot. Apparently the diner was a local favorite. Rafe's Hummer was parked in the far back, in the only spot they could find. It loomed high over the other vehicles. A busy intersection bustled beyond the parking lot. Plenty of traffic. Easy to get lost in. She just had to go about getting lost.

When they finished their meal, Rafe picked the check up off the table and guided her through the narrow aisle between the counter and tables, a proprietary hand on her elbow.

They joined the others standing in line to pay. Four people stood ahead of them—one a young mother with a crying infant on her hip and a whining toddler writhing at her feet.

Kit smoothed a sweating palm against her thigh and lifted her voice over that of the wailing baby. "I need to use the ladies' room."

Rafe turned to level a hard, searching look on her. She fought to hold that stare, to not flicker an eye and give away her thoughts.

Finally, he nodded. "Be quick."

Pulse quickening, she squeezed past the people waiting to be seated and walked down a narrow hallway to the bathrooms. She hurried past the door marked Women, diving into the noisy kitchen.

Dishes clattered. Fryers sizzled and popped. She pushed through the crowded room, past the startled-looking kitchen staff.

A frazzled-looking man wearing a hairnet and a stained apron grabbed her arm. "Hey! You don't work here. What are you doing back here?"

"Where's your back door?" she demanded, heart pounding madly in her ears.

The man stared at her blankly.

With a grunt of frustration, she shrugged off his grasp and pushed on, finding the door on her own.

Bursting through the heavy door, she plunged into the thick heat. The smell of rot from two nearby Dumpsters was thick and suffocating.

Her gaze scanned her surroundings. A Walmart superstore loomed behind the diner, a wide stretch of blue-gray.

She hurried forward, knowing that every moment was precious. She had to find a phone and call Darius. She had to hide. She weaved between parked cars in the diner's back lot, heading for the Walmart.

"Kit!"

She jerked and looked over her shoulder. *Shit.* Had he even paid yet? He had caught up with her sooner than she'd expected.

Rafe's eyes connected with hers across the distance. The fury there was unmistakable.

Turning, she started to run, legs pumping hard, shoes pounding on the hot pavement.

He called her name again. Louder this time. Her shoes pounded the hot asphalt harder.

She darted between the parked cars, shooting through the quasi-road separating the two parking lots, flying in front of a car. It blasted its horn at her.

"Kit!" Rafe raged behind her.

His voice sounded closer now, but she didn't risk a glance over her shoulder, didn't dare look again at the desperate fury on his face. She didn't have to. She felt it. Knew that if he got his hands on her he wouldn't let her slip away again.

This was her only chance.

☽ ☽ ☽ ● ☾ ☾ ☾

Rafe closed in on Kit, wind rushing in his hair. He kept his speed carefully in check, knowing he could overtake her in an instant, but he couldn't risk unleashing himself. It would only raise her suspicion. The last thing he wanted was to see fear and disgust mingle with the distrust in her gaze.

A car whipped past him, tires squealing, the stink of burning rubber filling his nostrils as the vehicle crossed the parking lot at an angle, heading directly for Kit.

"Kit!" he roared as the dark sedan screeched to a halt behind her.

She must have heard something in his voice. Something besides the anger of before.

She turned to look as two men emerged from the car. Lockhart and Davis. The two idiots he'd dealt with outside Gideon's house. They must have been tipped off, as Rafe had been. But he had made certain to leave all her belongings behind. Could she still be wearing the transmitter? What had he overlooked?

She froze. The two men squared off before her, sliding pistols from beneath their jackets.

"Kit. Run!" Rafe shouted, no longer caring if they knew he wasn't on the level.

Dropping all restraint, he sprinted forward in a blur, pulling a gun from the inside of his jacket as he moved. In his peripheral vision, he noted panicked shoppers diving behind cars, screaming and shouting as if in some B-grade movie. He estimated he had five minutes before the local authorities arrived.

"No!" he cried, the shout ripping from deep in his chest as Lockhart aimed his gun and fired at Kit. Everything slowed then. A split second lingered, tearing at Rafe's heart.

Shock crossed Kit's face. Horror. The same horror that seized him.

Her arms flung wide in the air from the impact. Blood bloomed across her bright pink tank top, starting at her stomach and spreading outward. He was instantly assailed with the coppery-sweet scent. Her legs buckled beneath her and she dropped to the asphalt, lying limply, as still as a rag doll tossed to the ground.

A growl ripped from his throat. He sprang, pouncing on Lockhart's back in one leap, sending his gun flying through the air. It clattered several feet away, skidding beneath a car. He wrapped an arm around Lockhart's neck, digging his fingers into soft flesh.

Lockhart screamed, thrashing wildly, waging a useless fight.

"What the hell!" Davis shouted.

"Shoot him! Just shoot him!" Lockhart whirled in a crazed circle, as if he could shake Rafe from his back.

Rafe tightened his arm around the man's throat, knowing he could snap it with little effort. His fury—the *beast*—urged him to do just that. His gaze fell on Kit, on her blood, thick and dark, staining her clothes, spilling out of her. He inhaled, breathing death through his nose.

*No. No!* This was not supposed to happen. It wasn't supposed to go down like this. It never had before. It couldn't now. Not with *her*.

Sirens sounded in the distance.

He didn't have time for this. He needed to get Kit help. But neither could he let these agents carry tales back to EFLA and Laurent. Even if he was at his end with EFLA, the less they knew about him—about the truth—the better.

"Hold still!" Davis shouted, pointing his gun.

Lockhart actually obeyed, finding a position that put Rafe in the direct line of fire.

He heard the click of the bullet leaving the chamber, the slight whizz of the silencer as the bullet burst forth from the barrel, its hum as it crossed through air in a direct path for him.

The moment before the bullet met his back, Rafe wrenched his weight to the side, forcing Lockhart around. The agent took the bullet solidly in the chest. His body jerked against Rafe's.

Shoppers peering over the hoods of cars screamed in terror.

Hopping aside as Lockhart collapsed, Rafe spared only a quick glance at the man, at the vacant eyes staring straight ahead, instantly dead.

He turned his attention on the second agent as the sirens grew to a piercing wail.

"Wait," Davis stammered. "P-please." He waved a hand before him in a defensive gesture and dragged his feet back several steps, even as he lifted his gun again and took aim at Rafe.

Rafe lunged forward before Davis could squeeze off another round. Seizing the man's head in both hands, he ground out, "I warned you to stay away." The words dropped like rocks in the air.

With a hard turn of his hands, he twisted Davis's neck. Instant death. Too sudden for pain to register. Far more humane than the gut shot Kit was suffering on the hot asphalt.

Davis's body dropped like a sack of cement.

Rafe launched himself over the fallen body, dropping to his knees at Kit's side. Hot breath escaped him in an agonized hiss at the sight of the blood flowing thickly from the gaping hole in her tank top, in her stomach, just below her breasts.

He tried to speak, but his words came out garbled, choked and indecipherable.

Her eyes stared straight head, glassy with immeasurable pain. Her lips worked, but no sound escaped.

"Kit," he called her name, running a hand over her brow, wincing at cold, clammy skin.

Those glassy eyes shifted, falling on him with a vague sort of focus.

"Can you see me, Kit? I'm here."

"Rafe," she choked out. The effort sent her into a coughing fit. Blood gurgled at the back of her throat.

Sirens blared, congesting the air.

Cursing, he swept her into his arms just as police cars roared into the parking lot. Cradling her close, he ran, sprinting across the back end of the parking lot, the diner a blur of blue and red.

For perhaps the first time in his life, he suffered no concern for the beast unleashed inside him, the primeval rush that burned through his veins, making him move faster than he had ever moved in his life.

He didn't care if anyone saw him—or the flash of him, a blur before their eyes, more wind than man.

The only thing he cared about was Kit. About making certain she survived. That had been his goal from the start. Even before he knew her. Before he knew how stubborn and infuriating she could be. How strong. How loyal to those she loved. How different from any woman he had ever known. How sweet she tasted.

Now he knew. And he could not imagining living if she died.

He had seen gut shots more times than he cared to recall. He had grown accustomed to the sight. To battlefields swimming in blood and gore. Grown men crying for their mothers. He had swum in death before he ever joined EFLA. So much so that he feared he would never see good in anything again. See *life*.

But he had. He'd come through it all and managed to hold on to a scrap of hope, to retain some compassion and faith in humanity.

But this . . . *Kit*.

This was different.

He would never be the same if he lost her.

# 17

Securing Kit carefully in the passenger seat, Rafe vaulted over the hood of the vehicle. Once behind the steering wheel, he gunned out of the parking lot in a screech of burning tires.

Recalling a hospital he had passed several exits back, he floored the accelerator and zipped onto the highway.

He had no choice. He had to take her there. He would risk exposure before risking her dying on him. The police would interrogate him, as they would Kit, when she regained consciousness. *If* she did . . .

He squeezed his eyes in a tight blink. Not if. *When.*

A sharp, sudden rattle of breath escaped her, more like a shocked gasp, as if she could not breathe and just realized it, as if she were choking on her own blood.

Reaching over, he pressed a hand against her wound. A thick flow of blood congealed over his fingers like warm syrup, swamping him with sick dread.

The erratic rasp of her breathing filled the inside of the vehicle, the sounds growing more desperate. She fought for every breath, the sound rattling on the air.

He pounded the steering wheel with the palm of one hand. "Damn! Why did you run? Why?"

*Because you didn't tell her*, an insidious little voice whispered across his mind. *You couldn't bring yourself to tell her the truth. Because you couldn't stand the thought of her looking at you with loathing.*

"Selfish bastard," he muttered to himself, nostrils flaring against the overwhelming odor of her blood. What did it matter how she looked at him? What mattered was keeping her alive.

Turning off the highway and onto the feeder road, he weaved through traffic and toward the hospital looming ahead. He darted a quick glance at Kit's face. Gunmetal gray. Her head lolled to the side of the headrest, facing him. The sight of those pale, bloodless lips sent a bolt of fear through him.

"Kit," he called, staring into her bottle-green eyes. They looked at him, but didn't see him. Didn't see anything.

He reached over and pressed fingers to the pulse at her neck. Nothing. He pressed harder, determined to find it, to *feel* life in her. She coughed, spraying blood on his arm.

Cursing, he dropped his hand from her neck. Driving with one hand on the wheel, he pressed his palm over the bullet wound.

In that moment, he knew what he had to do. Born of instinct. Wild, brute impulse seized him.

He pulled off the feeder, careening through a shopping center. Maneuvering the vehicle to the back of the sprawling parking lot, where no cars were parked, he jerked to a hard stop on an empty stretch of asphalt.

They weren't going to make it to the hospital in time. The realization settled like a dead weight in the pit of his stomach.

Knowing this, he vaulted from the vehicle. With a vicious

yank, he opened the passenger door, scooped her into his arms, and carried her to the backseat.

Heart hammering like a drum against his chest, he ripped her tank top, severing the fabric in his hands. The bullet wound was a dark, jagged hole in her stomach. Slipping a hand beneath her neck, he lifted her off the seat, bringing her closer. She hung in his arms, a dead weight. Her head lolled limply, eyes at half mast, the green of her gaze peering out dully, the color fading with every breath she struggled to take.

"Kit," he whispered, swiping a palm over the hole in her stomach, attempting to wipe it clean of blood. Impossible. The blood kept coming. As soon as he wiped at the wound, more came, constant as a river.

He splayed a hand against the small of her back, bringing her closer yet. Her flesh beneath his hand felt waxy. *Empty of life.*

An impulse came to him. Sudden and savage. A burning in his veins. Fed by desperation, an urge born of intuition.

Hardly aware of himself, of what he was doing, he brought her closer, his face hovering an inch over hers.

"I'm sorry, Kit," he breathed over her wound, the odor of her death, of the ebbing life, making him sick. "I'm so sorry." And he was.

Sorry if it worked. Sorry if it did not.

Ignoring the voice of logic that warned that this was wrong, he moistened his lips. Only one thing was for certain—being right, safe, normal . . . *human*—would not keep her alive.

And she had to live. There really was no choice. Not for him. Not for her. He was determined to keep her alive. Even if she never forgave him for it. Even if unleashing his power pushed at the boundaries of right and wrong, good and evil. All his mother had warned against. He didn't care.

For once in his life, he would risk everything. For Kit.

Later, he would examine when and how she had become so

important to him that he could do such a thing, that he could ignore the advice his mother had given him and Sebastian time and
time again over the long years.

No longer thinking, he moved his blood-soaked hand to her
neck, covering the beat of her pulse, monitoring her life as it ebbed,
a slow thread that barely jumped against her skin. He slid his hand
from her neck, leaving a trail of blood on her golden flesh until he
reached her stomach. Blood swam everywhere there. He felt dizzy
from the cloying scent. Clots formed around the bullet hole, but
still blood flowed, a river that could not be staunched until death
took its final claim.

Slowly, so slowly, he could hear the thudding beat of his own
heart in the close confines of the vehicle, he lowered his head,
bringing his mouth down, down . . .

His nostrils flared, the sweet tang of her blood a heady, intoxicating thing. Empowering. Frightening.

"Kit." The hush of her name fell from his lips, soft as a feather
stroke. "Forgive me."

No question about it. The next time she looked at him—*if* she
looked at him again—it would be with the loathing he had hoped
to avoid seeing in her lovely eyes. But that he could live with. Her
death he could not.

His head swooped down, lips covering the bullet hole.

He gripped her with both hands, fingers burying in the soft
flare of her waist, the blood making his hold slippery.

The serrated edges of her torn skin teased his mouth, and a part
of him hesitated, horrified . . . excited.

He pressed his lips more firmly against the wound. With several deep, catlike strokes of his tongue, he surrendered himself.

He'd always been careful about crossing the line, of putting
himself in a position where his demons might get the best of him
and drag him into a hell from which he might never return.

With a tiny mewl of sound, she moved beneath him, thrusting herself closer, pushing herself into his mouth as though she would crawl inside him. A dangerous mix of hunger and desire spiraled through him.

One hand rose to delve in his hair, tugging him closer, seeking survival with an instinct that matched the primal force thundering through his blood, demanding he claim her.

With a groan, he opened his mouth wider, tasting her ravaged flesh, drawing out death, taking it deep inside himself, knowing it would have little power there.

A dark need ripped through him, intoxicating, staggering. Trembling against her, he forced his hands to gentle, his mouth to soften. Rafe gave, pouring all that he was into her—and hoping it would be enough.

"God," he sighed, letting His name—his mother's god—fall in the air between them, heavy and solemn. A benediction of sorts. A plea.

He had never been certain whether God heard his prayers, despite his mother's insistence that he and Sebastian never give up on God, that God was there for them, that their existence mattered—no matter what they were.

All hard to accept when God had not been there for her, never heard her pleas. Both as a girl, and later as an old woman.

Still, he found himself praying, staring hard at Kit and praying as he had never prayed in his life.

*God, let this be enough.*

# 18

Pulling back, Rafe swiped at his mouth with the back of his hand, shoving back down the wild beastly lust burning through his veins. He dragged his gaze to her face, scanning her rock-still features, listening to the harsh sound of his breath fill the closed space.

A streak of blood marred the fragile curve of her chin, a shocking red against her tanned flesh. He ran a thumb over the stain, but it held fast. His gaze fell, surveying the damage.

The bullet hole decreased in size, growing tighter, shrinking, sealing itself before his very eyes.

Regeneration had begun. Her newly altered DNA was working quickly, just as he had hoped.

Her breathing evened, became less labored. He pressed a hand to her neck, satisfied to see that her pulse was growing stronger against the test of his fingers, no longer the light, skipping thread of moments ago.

"That's it." He breathed, the invisible band about his chest loosening. "Good girl," he murmured, pushing a springy blond curl off her sweat-damp forehead as he examined her.

Positioning her on her side, he tucked her legs so the car door could close. He slid out from the backseat and shut the back door. Once in the driver's seat, he gripped the leather steering wheel and dragged air into his lungs, containing himself, burying the beast back within, deliberately avoiding glancing at himself in the rearview mirror. Knowing what he would see.

The sight of his bloody hands was enough. Kit's blood. So much covered him. And her. So much that she shouldn't be alive.

It was not the first time someone's blood stained his hands. But it certainly was the first time the sight ever gave him pause.

He wore Kit's blood. *Mortal* blood. Not that of the lycans he felt justified in killing. He shivered, and glanced back at her stretched out on the seat. Mortal no more. Only precisely what she was—*like him?*—he had yet to learn.

It was the first time the blood of a Marshan colored his hands— if one did not count his mother.

He drove for a while, heading north, glancing over his shoulder and keeping an eye on her in the rearview mirror as he left Austin city limits. He needed to find someplace private, remote, without prying eyes. A place where they could hole up while she recovered.

He scanned the billboards lining the interstate until his gaze caught a sign for La Cantera, a lakeside resort twenty miles away boasting private, secluded cabins.

He veered off the interstate at the advertised exit and followed another sign, taking the road that led to the resort.

After forty-five minutes, he arrived in the small town. He passed a feed store with a dirt parking lot full of pickup trucks, a single grocery store, a restaurant boasting the world's largest chicken-fried steak, and a mechanic's with more boats than cars parked in its multiple garages.

He continued following signs, turning off the main drag and toward the lake and driving over a bumpy one-lane road until reaching a small wooden and red-stuccoed lodge. A quick glance back at Kit assured him she was still asleep.

He hopped out from behind the wheel. With a wary glance around him, he climbed in the back with Kit. Watching the rise and fall of her chest, he quickly changed out of his bloody clothes.

Dressed in clean clothes, he stepped out of the vehicle and sprinted inside the building. The bell over the door tinkled his arrival. Within ten minutes he had the keys and directions to a cabin the clerk vowed to be their best.

Back behind the wheel, he maneuvered the Hummer along a narrow path crowded with thick cedar and oak. Snatches of a glass-blue lake occasionally peeked through the tree line on his left. His heart rate spiked at a sudden moan from Kit. He knew Initiation could be difficult, the transition traumatic.

He accelerated, eager to reach the cabin.

"Kit," he called, almost as though he expected her to answer him. He knew she couldn't, yet still he talked, hoping some part of her could hear him. "You're going to be okay. It will feel like you're dying . . ." his voice faded and he blinked once. *Idiot.* Probably not what she wanted to hear. Even if she could hear him.

The trees finally broke to reveal the lake. Sunlight glinted off its surface, bringing diamonds to life along its gentle wind-tossed swells. A few boats dotted its expanse. In the far distance, skiers chased one.

He rolled up before cabin sixteen, glad to see the considerable distance separating the single-story wood-and-rock house from its neighboring cabins dotting the lakeshore.

With a quick scan to assure himself no one was about, he swept Kit into his arms and carried her inside. Settling her on the bed, he pulled the shades shut on the cabin's large front window, robbing them of the lakefront view. Submerged in privacy, they were enveloped in cool darkness, and still he perspired. From the shock of all that had happened, he guessed. All he had done. All that would yet happen as a consequence of this day's work.

Sighing, he hurried to the air-conditioning unit against the far wall. Although cool, he knew it needed to be cooler. Knew that the fever would soon grip her. He adjusted the dial. The unit rumbled, and icy air gushed from its vents.

He lowered himself onto the single king-size bed beside Kit, the mattress releasing a slight squeak at the additional weight. Except for the wretched state of her clothes, shredded and soaked in blood, she looked like a child asleep. A little girl with her curls tousled about her head, her elfen features relaxed in slumber.

Some of the color had returned to her face. He pressed the back of his hand to her cheek, wincing at the fiery sensation of her skin. The fever had already begun.

Crouching over her, he stripped her of her ruined clothing. After several trips to the bathroom, he managed to clean most of the blood from her with several wet hand towels and washcloths, pretending not to notice the delicate curves of her body. She didn't make a sound as he worked, didn't move a muscle. No matter that the memory of her body had been playing through his mind since they made love. Had it only been this morning? He shook his head. It seemed a lifetime had passed since he discovered her naked at that roach motel.

*A lifetime.* And for him, a lifetime was truly long.

One hundred and twelve years, to be exact.

# 19

Rafe awoke with a start, coming wide awake in an instant, senses alive, muscles strung taut as wires as his eyes adjusted to the darkness with ease.

It had always been that way for him. Sleep never came easily . . . or deeply. It was the same for his brother. Years of running, fleeing from town to town, staying one step ahead of their enemies.

Such an existence had taught them never to sleep too soundly. Never to grow too comfortable. Never to feel safe.

And to never trust. Only each other. Only their mother. No one else.

Letting people in, growing close to others, only invited pain. Pain could drive anyone mad. And madness was a luxury he could not afford. He needed to remain in control at all times. He'd promised his mother that, promised never to descend into the darkness, never to corrupt his soul.

And yet staring down at Kit, he let pain flow in, seep into that room, past the locked door, and he felt that control slip. Felt the dark beast stir in his heart, a dangerous rumble that threatened the safe life he had built for himself all these years.

Tearing his gaze from her, he reached over and turned on the bedside lamp. He scanned the room, keeping one arm around her, curled close to his side. Her body generated heat like an electric blanket. Still, he spooned his larger body against hers, needing to feel her, craving her as he had no right to. Needing to feel her heat, her breath, her *live* body.

She was all right. She was going to be all right.

It soon became apparent what had woken him. Sleeping alongside her, he was attuned to her every whimper, her every move, right down to the ever-increasing spike in her body temperature.

He felt her brow with the back of his hand. Dangerously hot. Flaming to the touch, hotter than any human body should be. *Or could be and survive.*

But then that was it. The heart of the matter. The very thing that could drive her from him forever. Make her despise him as she despised lycans.

She was no longer human. Initiation had begun.

He'd never gone this far before. Never known if he could. Hell, he still didn't know what the outcome would be—whether she would survive past Initiation. She could still die.

Memories flooded him. He recalled what it had been like. The violence of it. The excruciating agony. Like dying, he imagined.

He lowered his hand to Kit's neck. Her pulse thrummed against her neck in a rapid-fire tempo. Moist curls clung to her damp throat. Like moss on a rock. He swiped them away, wincing at her sharp little cry, well imagining the demons chasing her in her dreams.

"You're going to be fine," he murmured. He stared at her starkly. "You'll hate me, but you'll be fine. I promise. I'll see you through this, Kit." *See that the beast, the darkness, never overtakes you.*

Even as he thought this, he wondered how he could ever make such a promise. Kit alone would decide her fate.

Moving off the bed, he settled himself in a deep armchair. He covered himself with a throw and sank into the chair's depths. Propping his feet on the edge of the bed, he watched her. Waiting. Knowing it would be days before she woke.

At that moment, his cell phone vibrated in his pocket. He dug the phone out and read the sender's information, instinctively knowing before he looked who it would be.

With a grimace, he flipped the phone open. "Hello, Sebastian."

"What's happened?" His brother wasted no time getting to the point.

Rafe sighed. He shouldn't feel surprised. As brothers, as twins, they were close. "Your timing couldn't be better, little brother."

"You'll never let me live down those five minutes, huh, *big* brother?"

"With you, I need every advantage."

Sebastian chuckled in his ear. "I've missed you, brother. When are you going to give up this stupid game you're playing with EFLA? You could make a hell of a lot more difference with me than working for those bastards."

As long as he remembered, Sebastian only ever referred to EFLA as bastards. A sentiment Rafe did not disagree with, but unlike his brother, he was able to control his animosity in order to meet his goals. Goals that weren't very different from Sebastian's. They just followed different paths in reaching them. Whereas Rafe had infiltrated EFLA's ranks, Sebastian preferred to go it alone, hunting lycans independently. And that is where their objectives differed. Sebastian was content simply to hunt and destroy lycans. Rafe wanted to do that and more.

"Yeah, I've missed you, too. It's been too long."

"Seven years."

Seven years already? He didn't monitor time too closely. Not when years rolled by like days, frequent and unnoted.

His gaze fell on Kit tossing restlessly on the bed. That was what had led him to this moment. To her. He had wanted to help her. Others like her. Others like his mother.

From where he sat, he could see the fine sheen of sweat coating her skin. He rose, tossing the throw aside and walking to the bathroom. He just hadn't anticipated helping her quite like this.

"Rafe? You there still?"

Returning to Kit with a wet washcloth in his hand, he replied, "I'm here." He pressed the cloth to her warm forehead, and murmured, voice laced with derision, "Oh, I think I might be making a difference. More than I ever planned."

For better or worse.

A heavy pause stretched before his brother spoke again, repeating his first question. "What are you talking about? What's happened?"

"Nothing," he hedged, reluctant to confess the truth, knowing how Sebastian would react. The same way Rafe would have reacted had his brother been the one to attempt turning someone.

Sebastian's voice scratched roughly on the air. "You forget whom you're talking to. Something has happened. Something big. I can feel it."

He couldn't pretend nothing had happened with their damned bond hanging thickly between them, humming across continents, linking him with his brother whether he willed it or not.

"Where are you?" Sebastian demanded, beginning to sound genuinely worried.

"Texas," Rafe answered, glad for one simple, uncomplicated question.

"What in hell are you doing there?"

"I go where I am told."

Sebastian snorted in his ear. "Right. What's EFLA doing in Texas?"

"I'm part of EFLA's assimilation efforts in North America."

"You mean they've done it? They've really expanded the operation. Great. Just what we need. More of those fuckers dealing out their brand of justice."

Rafe did not need to hear the sarcasm in his brother's voice to know how Sebastian felt about EFLA. The organization had killed their mother. Butchered her long after she had carried out the much-feared prophecy.

"Sorry, brother. I find it hard to believe you're making a difference by helping EFLA expand itself."

"No?" he queried, watching as Kit tossed onto her back with a moan, the sound low and terrible, raising goose bumps on his arms.

"What was that?"

Kit's face contorted in her sleep, her delicate features twisted with the dark agony that he recalled from his own Initiation.

"I've done it." His words fell softly, almost inaudible.

Heavy silence met his hushed proclamation. Then: "What?"

"That thing we've always talked about. Always wondered about." His hand tightened around his cell. "Remember, Sebastian?"

Their mother had made it a point to educate them on lycans. Desperate for them to understand the powers and limitations of the soulless creatures. But they had been left with questions concerning themselves.

He watched the rapid rise and fall of Kit's chest. Her breathing fell harshly in the room as she fought her fever, fought the demons in her head.

"Rafe? Are you there?"

He gave his head a small nod. "Yes. I'm here."

"Shit." A gust of breath followed Sebastian's expletive. "It really worked? Who? How?"

"She was another assignment."

"And you *turned* her?" Sebastian broke in, his voice accusing. "You never turned any of the others. How did it happen? You didn't attack her, did you?"

"Hell, no!" he cried, hot indignation sweeping through him. "What do you think I am? A fucking animal? EFLA tracked her. She was shot. I didn't have a choice."

"Yes, you did. You could have let her die rather than take such a risk." Sebastian's voice lowered, grew grave. "We talked about this. We never knew if we could even turn someone—"

"Well, we can."

"And we decided never to try. You know what it was like for us. There's no guarantee who we turned wouldn't become dangerous."

"Kit won't be like them." It was all he could say, all he could offer as an explanation. Nothing else could be said. He couldn't have let her die without trying. Simple as that.

"Ah." Sebastian sighed, the sound heavy with understanding.

"What do you mean, *ah*?"

"Come on, Rafe. You forget who you're talking to. I know what you're saying even when you're not saying it."

Rafe grimaced, flinching outright when Sebastian added, "So are you prepared to spend eternity with this woman?"

"Who said anything about eternity?"

"You turned her. She's yours."

*She's yours.* The words gave him a thrill he shouldn't have felt. His eyes drifted to Kit's lips, barely registering his brother's voice as he continued talking.

"You don't turn someone and leave her to fend for herself. She's your responsibility now."

"I'll see that she's properly initiated."

Sebastian chuckled, the sound deep, smug and knowing. He

could almost see his brother giving him that leering wink he gave when a particularly attractive woman walked past. "I'll bet."

"Get your mind out of the gutter, little brother."

"You mean you haven't thought about doing her every which way? Come, be honest."

"That's not why I did it," he replied even as he knew his answer acknowledged his brother's assertion that he had thought about sleeping with her. Hell, he had.

Hell, why deny it? Sebastian would know he was lying. That was their gift, and their curse.

Kit had fascinated him from the start. And he wanted her. He couldn't say whether he would have done what he had if he hadn't wanted her so damned much.

At that moment, she arched off the bed, crying out and clawing her cheeks as if she wanted to tear the skin from her body.

"Shit. I have to go."

"Sounds like you have your hands full," Sebastian said in his ear. "Go for now, but I expect you to keep me in the loop. Call me. I don't like any of this, Rafe. As a matter of fact, why don't I—"

"I'm fine," he bit out. "We'll both be fine. Stay where you are. I don't need a babysitter. I'll call you in a few days."

"Call me tomor—"

Rafe shut his phone, letting it fall to the floor with a thud as he dropped down on the bed beside Kit and gathered her in his arms.

Her cries tore at his heart. He tugged her hands down from her face, wincing at the long, bleeding scratches she had given herself.

Pulling her into his arms, he held her tightly as she thrashed, determined that she not hurt herself, determined that she survive this. Determined that this not be the end of her.

The end of them.

# 20

Kit fought against sleep. It was like fighting free from a great thick fog. Her mind shook free of the mist, eyes slowly opening. She stared straight ahead, gaze fixed on wood rafters as she tried to make sense of where she was—and what had happened.

Lockhart's face floated before her, and it all came back with blinding clarity.

Her hand flew to her stomach, meeting nothing save the cool cotton of a T-shirt. Grabbing the neckline, she peered down her shirt. Shadowed flesh met her gaze, breasts bare and trembling. No wound. No blood. Not a scratch.

Her gaze flew up at the sound of a door opening. Rafe stood at the threshold, fast-fading sunlight haloing his tall form, arms full of brown paper bags. A tantalizing aroma carried to her nose.

Squinting and shading her eyes with a hand, she whispered in a parched croak, "What happened?"

"You were . . . hurt."

She nodded, everything flooding over her in a rush. The explosion of pain in her chest. Her burning flesh. Hot, unforgiving asphalt colliding with her back. And Rafe. His face looming over her, etched in panic—concern she could not credit. Hardly the reaction of a man determined to kill her.

"I was shot."

He said nothing, simply stared at her.

"I'm alive," she murmured, hands drifting down to her stomach again, feeling herself through her T-shirt. Not wounded. Alive. *Incredible. Impossible.*

"How?" she demanded, beginning to grow worried at his silence, at his unflinching stare, at the way she imagined she could hear his very heart beating a steady rhythm against his muscled chest. Crazy. "Did you take me to the hospital?"

Averting his gaze, Rafe moved from the door, kicking it closed with his foot. The savory aroma from the brown paper bags reached her, distracting her.

He shook his head, answering slowly, "No. Not the hospital."

Her brow wrinkled in confusion. She eased herself up on her elbows. "How . . ." She shook her head. "I was shot, right?" She remembered the pain. The burning agony in her stomach. The white-hot fear, the sudden, absolute knowledge that death was at hand. She couldn't have imagined that.

"Would you care to eat while we talk?" He set the bags down on a table near the window.

She eyed him carefully. Dressed in black from head to toe, dark hair disheveled, he looked like something out of *Mission: Impossible.*

"I thought you might wake soon," he went on to say, "so I got some food. Glad I wasn't gone long." He smiled mildly. A vague sort of smile that revealed nothing. "You woke sooner than I expected."

She dropped her gaze to the bags in his arms. Surprisingly, she was hungry. Hungrier—she couldn't help thinking—than someone recovering from a gunshot should be. But then she bore no wound. Nothing made sense. Shouldn't she feel weak? Sore? Achy? . . . *Something*?

Beginning to think she had lost her mind, she tossed back the covers. "I could eat," she allowed. Standing, she felt another need assert itself. Turning, she moved into the bathroom, sensing his eyes on her bare legs as she moved.

After emptying her bladder, she stared at herself in the mirror as she washed her hands, wondering what was different about her reflection. She looked the same—yet not.

She pressed her palm over her chest, felt the steady beat of her heart for a moment. Strong and persistent, it thudded against her hand. She slid her hand down, splaying her fingers over the thin cotton T-shirt, still marveling at the absence of a wound. Had she dreamt it all?

"You okay in there?" Rafe's voice carried through the door. The deep rumble of it made the hairs on her arm stand on end. A tickle fluttered inside her belly.

Stepping from the bathroom, she observed him as he set the bags of food on the table. Tugging on her T-shirt, trying to make it extend past mid-thigh, she approached the table. "What happened to my clothes?"

He motioned to a leather chair. A small stack of clothes sat there. A neatly folded gray top and blue jeans. Before she could ask him about her clothes from earlier, he asked, "You like barbecue? They seem to have a lot of that around here."

He nodded to the bags. A part of her longed to refuse the food, to demand answers first, but her belly rumbled in protest as he began to unload several items wrapped in white butcher's paper. The tempting smell of smoked meat intensified her torment. Her stomach cramped in hunger.

"It's Texas. We do barbecue," she replied, lowering herself into a chair and shrugging lightly, as if the prospect of food mattered little to her. When he unwrapped a sandwich laden with thick slices of juicy barbecued brisket she had to restrain herself from snatching it up.

"Go ahead," he encouraged. "You need the protein."

Lifting the heavy sandwich to her lips, she wondered at this strange remark. "And why is that?" she asked before taking a bite.

He lowered himself into a chair across from her, an unwrapped sandwich before him. His demon-dark eyes fixed on her, steady and intent. "The calories are . . . important."

"What are you talking about?" she asked around a mouthful, her fingers pressed to her lips to cover the fact that she was talking as she chewed.

Instead of answering, he opened a container of creamy potato salad and handed her a fork. Accepting the container, she dug into the chunky potato-and-egg mixture.

"Here." He pulled out a couple of liters of sports drink from another bag. "Hydrate yourself."

"Yeah," she murmured. "This could hydrate a small village."

"Come on," he directed.

She lifted the heavy jug and sipped. At the first small swallow of liquid, it struck her how parched she was. As he watched, she drank deeply, heedless of the liquid dribbling out of the sides of her mouth.

His gaze followed the trail down her neck, his dark eyes lightening, the centers glowing almost white as his look traveled over her flesh. Fire licked her cheeks.

Clearing her throat, she fought down the rising heat in her face and murmured, "I thought we were going to talk about what happened today. In the parking lot. That bastard Lockhart shot me." Her hand dropped to her stomach. "Or not," she muttered. She shook her head and snorted lightly. "Guess not. That guy couldn't shoot the broad side of a barn. Did I fall and hit my head or something?"

How else could she have imagined being shot? Imagined the hot asphalt at her back. Rafe leaning over her. The sweep of death's cold hand over her cheek?

"Or something," he muttered so low she barely heard him.

"What?"

"Not today," Rafe murmured, his voice still low. "You weren't shot today."

She leaned forward in her chair, shaking her head, confused at why he'd emphasized *today*.

"But I was shot?"

Rafe dragged a hand through his hair. The locks fell back in place as if he had not touched his hair at all. "Look, Kit, this is complicated." He stretched his neck, rotating it in small circles.

Lifting her sandwich, she took a bite. Swallowing, she wiped barbecue sauce from the corner of her lip and studied him. "Since I met you, everything has gotten complicated. That's nothing new." Setting her sandwich down, she gave him her sternest stare. The kind her grandmother used to give her and Gideon if they dared act like the children they were and intrude on her life. If they dared to be anything more than invisible. "Lay it on me."

With a heavy sigh, he began, "Nothing happened *today*. You've done nothing but sleep . . . today." He motioned to the rumpled bed as if that were evidence enough.

"What are you talking about?" The way he'd stressed *today* made her nervous.

He shifted in his chair. "You slept the day away. And yesterday. And the day before that. Today is Wednesday."

"Bullshit." She shook her head and released a nervous little laugh. "That's impossible." A knot grew in her chest at his stoic expression. "I would have woken up. It's impossible to sleep that long."

"Yes," he agreed. "Normally it would be."

"What do you mean *normally*? What are you saying, Rafe?"

"You're not normal anymore." The lightness from his dark gaze had long since fled. Obdurate black gazed at her. Eyes so dark, her reflection could be seen in them. Bleak, desperate.

Tossing down her napkin, she leaned back in her chair, narrowing her gaze on his impassive face, on the hard, unyielding lines that her palm itched to slap. "What are you telling me?"

"All right." He crossed his arms over his broad chest, his face hardening as if he were about to perform an unpleasant task. "The reason EFLA wants you dead isn't because you're a rogue hunter."

She leaned forward, ready at last for the truth, knowing all along he had been holding out on her. At last, she would have her answers.

"It isn't?" Her stomach clenched and stirred with an unsettling flutter. Suddenly she wasn't so sure she wanted the truth.

"It was easier to let you believe that." He released a heavy sigh. "In the grand scheme of things, EFLA couldn't give a damn about sending out their special agents to assassinate a couple of rogue hunters. They've got bigger prey to hunt."

She had always thought the same thing. Thought it rather silly for them to care so much about her and Gideon. To demand their deaths when they were hunting like enemies. *Bigger prey to hunt.* But that meant they saw her as the bigger prey? A shiver chased down her spine. Why?

"But they *do* want me dead. And Gideon."

"Yes." The words dropped as heavily as a stone from his lips.

"Why?"

"You're a descendant of the Marshan line. A *female* descendant. As far as EFLA is concerned, you're a dangerous commodity." His gaze narrowed sharply on her. "Doubly so because you place yourself in the sphere of lycans."

She shook her head. "Is that supposed to mean something to me?"

She had never heard the name before—not that she knew anything about her family's genealogy. Her grandmother certainly wasn't interested in the subject. If either of her parents had been, they had not lived long enough to share the knowledge with her.

"It will. It does."

Shrugging one shoulder, she asked, "So what if I descend from this Marsan line."

"*Marshan*," he corrected her.

"Again, what's any of this supposed to mean to me?"

"You have never heard of the Marshan Prophecy?"

"No."

"Cooper knew. He knew your family was descended from the Marshan line. It's why he saved you and your brother all those years ago. And it's the reason he's dead now."

Her throat tightened at his words. "He died protecting me?"

Rafe nodded.

She released a shuddery breath. A part of her had always resented Cooper—his closeness with Gideon had, at times, made her feel inferior, alone, a secondary consideration to both of them. But he was the reason Kit and Gideon were alive today. He had been there, arriving moments before their mother turned to kill them both. And now he was gone. Dead. Murdered.

And if Rafe were to be believed, he was gone because of her. Because of some prophecy about which she knew nothing.

"Why?" she demanded. "What's so wrong with descending from this family?"

"You're descended from Étienne Marshan, born approximately A.D. thirty. You're descended from him—*before* he became the world's first lycan. You're descended from his child, Christophe Marshan. A single child who escaped, who was not infected with his father's curse."

Kit stared, unable to speak, struggling to wrap her head around what he was saying.

Rafe leaned forward in his chair. "Do you hear what I'm saying, Kit?"

She nodded dumbly.

"You share DNA with every lycan in existence." His voice scraped the air, grating her frayed nerves. "A female of the Marshan line can successfully procreate with a lycan to create a new species of lycan. A hybrid, neither fully human nor fully lycan—a *dovenatu*. Loosely translated to mean double birth."

"Bullshit." The word exploded from her mouth at missile speed. "You want me to believe that I'm a potential"—she groped for the right word—"*carrier* for some prophetic species?" A damned brood mare for the bloodthirsty monsters she had made it her mission to hunt? She closed her eyes and shook her head, suddenly unable to look at his handsome face. To look into his eyes, to see the truth there.

He went on as if she had not spoken, penetrating the wall she struggled to erect between him and his horrible words. "A dovenatu can assume the strengths of both humans and lycans." Softly, he added, "Unfortunately, the dovenatu can also assume all the weaknesses, too. The flaws."

*Flaws.* The flaws of lycans were many. Horrific and numerous.

Opening her eyes, she asked sharply, "Meaning?"

"A dovenatu can be evil."

"Can be?

"They possess free will. Like any human. It's possible that a dovenatu could be a scourge on mankind. And for that possibility, EFLA is determined that the prophecy never come to pass."

The image of her mother as she had last seen her—the only way she remembered her: a monster who killed her husband, who tried to kill Kit and Gideon—flared through her mind. He was telling her she could give birth to one of those creatures? The very thing she hunted? *Never.*

He nodded. "But a dovenatu can be good, too. Free will, remember? They don't have to be like lycans."

*Good?* Nothing remotely similar to a lycan could ever be good. As far as she was concerned, a dovenatu would be as bad as a lycan. And she would never bring one of them into the world. No matter what he said. She would never let herself produce such a child. Not if she had to tear it from her womb herself.

A flash of heat seared her cheeks, scalding. Her pulse grew to a hammering beat at her neck, blood pounding loud as a drum in her ears. A sense of forbidding swept over her. She shook her head fiercely at his explanation. "I've never heard any of this before. You expect me to believe—"

"Kit, I know what I'm talking about," he broke in, his voice hard, inflexible. His dark eyes scanned her face as swiftly and intently as a hawk.

She held his stare, her mouth drying. A sick premonition swept over her. The tiny hairs at her nape stood on end.

"How? How do you know?"

His eyes drilled into her, the darkness sinking into her very soul, grabbing her heart in a tight vise. "I know," he repeated. "I know because I'm the very thing EFLA is so afraid you will bring into this world. I'm a dovenatu."

# 21

N o!" She shoved back from her chair, sending it toppling to the floor behind her.

Heat washed over her, blistering fire over her skin. Only her heart felt cold. Deadly cold. She'd slept with him, for God's sake! Her stomach churned. He had deceived her in a way she could never have fathomed.

Shaking her head, she said again, her voice a harsh whisper, "No."

In that instant, she didn't know what she was denying. The existence of some prophetic hybrid species? Or that he was one of them.

Deciding not to take a chance, she stepped around her chair, her movements clumsy, almost drunken. "Get away from me."

"It's true, Kit. Trust me. I know." Rafe rose, following her, stalking her like a cat, his movements lithe, predatory. Hadn't she noticed before the way he handled himself? More animal than human? *Because he was.*

He was this *thing* he claimed to be—a dovenatu. A monster.

"Stay away from me." She held out a hand as if to ward him off even as heat continued to wash over her.

His features hardened, marblelike and beautiful in their fierceness.

"Kit." Her name fell softly from his lips, but there was an unmistakable edge to his voice, a ruthless glint to his eyes. As though he were feigning mildness in order to coax a wild animal near. She grimaced at the comparison.

Her mind worked feverishly, searching for logic. Strange, considering she had long known the world to be far from sane. Nothing was black and white. Gray colored everything. The sight of her mother—a beast one moment and a corpse the next—had taught her that.

And he was telling her he was *one of them*. A man she had slept with? A man who had brought her body such incredible pleasure? *No.*

Shaking her head savagely, she spun around, ready to flee him and the horrid reality he was shoving at her.

He caught her. A hard hand dropped on her shoulder and spun her around. She balled her hands into fists and pounded on his chest.

One arm snaked around her waist and slammed her close, trapping her fists between them.

"Stop it," he growled.

She looked up into his face, gasping at the change in his dark eyes. She had not imagined it those times before: His eyes did not change to silver, but they did change. The darkness ebbing, the centers glowing like a candle's pale flame.

That wasn't the only change.

The lines along his face blurred for a split second, shifting, sharpening, hardening into an almost feline-like aspect. Not ugly. Not the monstrous appearance of a lycan during moonrise, just not human. Not mortal.

"Oh, God." Her breath came fast and hard, serrated rasps on the air. She leaned back as far as she could in his arms.

"Easy," he instructed, and she recognized his voice from that night in the motel. Thick and strangled. He had shifted then to this . . . this *thing* when he fought those lycans.

*Easy? Easy?* A slow tremble eddied through her. She struggled to stave off her fast-rising panic.

He inhaled slowly, closing his eyes for a moment, and his face changed again, returned to its usual handsome mask. Familiar. Human.

Relief skittered through her, and her breath fell less harshly. Gradually, his arms loosened around her.

"I'll let you go, if you promise not to run." He stared at her expectantly.

After a moment, she nodded, desperate to be free of his over-powering nearness.

He dropped her arms, and she stumbled back a step, rubbing her arms where he had gripped them.

She moistened her lips, eyeing him warily. "If you're a dove-natu, how can you work for EFLA?"

"Because they don't know," he explained, still advancing. "Ironic, isn't it? They pay me to terminate descendants of the Marshan line. Because they fear the prophecy of the dovenatu. A prophecy that already exists. In me."

"I don't get it. Why would you hunt your own kind? Well, essentially the Marshans are your own kind, right?" She moved backward as she spoke, trying to increase the space between them.

"In a way." He followed her step for step. "Yes."

Her back hit the door. She could go no farther. "So, why would you hunt Marshans?"

"I don't. I infiltrated EFLA to help descendants of the Mar-shan line from being butchered. I track Marshans with the assis-tance of EFLA in-house archivists. Then I explain to the targets what they are. Help them assume new identities and relocate."

He sighed. "I stage their deaths, leave no trail, then tell EFLA the job is done."

Cocking his head to the side, he paused, dark eyes probing, gleaming in silent challenge as he lifted a tendril of hair off her cheek, rubbing it between his fingertips.

She stilled, like prey caught in a lion's grasp.

"I'm not a monster," he whispered.

But he was. She had just seen that with her own eyes. And it wasn't even a full moon. If she had slept the last two nights, as he claimed, moonrise had come and gone.

She had no concept of dovenatus' limits . . . if they possessed any. But he had just proven he could shift at whim, that he was not bound by the moon. She had seen the change in his eyes. His face.

The only advantage hunters ever held over lycans was the fact that they shifted at moonrise. And only then. The rest of the month, their powers, while strong, were subdued. But he could shift at will. She could not wrap her mind around such power, the potential threat . . .

"I'm not a monster," he repeated. "So you can stop looking at me like that." He leaned in, his breath hotly fanning her cheek. He inhaled near her neck, like an animal savoring her scent. Goose bumps feathered her flesh, and her adrenaline kicked into high gear.

"How am I looking at you?" she asked.

"With fear."

Resolve shot up her spine. Her fists knotted at her sides and she pulled her head back until it bumped the door. "I'm not afraid."

And yet his dark eyes drew her in. She felt herself slipping, drowning in his dark gaze. She struggled against the mesmerizing effect, reminding herself what he was. Brethren to the beasts she hunted. Evil. Soulless. Only, staring at him, it was hard to remember that. Hard to believe.

She gave her head a hard shake. This must be how Gideon felt about Darius. Why he felt compelled to foster a relationship with the age-old lycan. Maybe she should not have judged Gideon too harshly, after all.

His lips twitched. "So proud," he muttered. "I've been with EFLA for twelve years now." All hint of a smile had disappeared from his mouth. "And I've never met a Marshan like you before."

"How so?"

His chest rose on a deep breath, nearly brushing the front of her T-shirt, and she couldn't help wondering if he had kissed any of the others. Had there been some beautiful woman so grateful for his protection that she fell into his bed? Her gaze scanned his hard-edged face. Not that most women would need an excuse to fall into bed with him. She should know.

"No one ever gave me so much trouble. They're always a little reluctant to believe what I'm telling them. They don't even know lycans exist, remember? But once I've convinced them of the matter, they're eager to cooperate, eager to help themselves." He stroked her cheek with his thumb. Her pulse spiked at his touch. She swallowed, struggling to shield her reaction.

*Eager?* "I'll bet."

He continued as if she had not spoken, his thumb tracing a small circle on her cheek that left her breathless. "To do whatever it takes to help themselves." This he uttered with a fair amount of accusation.

"Maybe things would have been different if you had been honest with me from the start," she returned, indignation eddying through her in bitter waves.

"Doubtful. The reason I didn't tell you from the beginning is because I knew you would react this way. With all your biases in place. So damned distrustful . . ."

She pressed a hand to her chest. "I have a reason to distrust lycans—"

"I'm not a lycan," he quickly countered. Something in his voice stopped her from arguing further. A menacing edge.

With the door at her back, the hard wall of his chest at her front, and his face so close to hers, she felt vulnerable, exposed.

Damnable heat smoldered through her, and she wondered if she suffered a fever, if she was, in fact, sick.

"You already know about lycans. You're a hunter." He angled his head, staring at her so intently, so . . . strangely. "I never knew a woman like you could exist."

Something in the way he said that, in the way he looked at her, sent a flutter through her belly. Warm and languid, she pressed her thighs together where she stood and willed herself not to feel. To keep a cool head and *think*.

She squirmed against the door, resisting touching any part of him. Inexplicably, she itched to tear off her large shirt, as if it added to her discomfort, chafing her overly sensitive skin. She squeezed her eyes shut in a long, tight blink, forcing herself to inhale a steadying breath. A mistake. The scent of him overwhelmed her. All male. Intoxicating.

"Kit."

Slowly, she opened her eyes. He stared at her darkly, eyes fathomless, ageless. Ageless?

Then something he said penetrated. "Twelve years? You've been with EFLA for twelve years now?"

"Yes. I'll have to stage my death soon. Can't have them wondering why I never get any older."

"How old are you?"

He hesitated a moment before answering. "One hundred and twelve."

*One hundred and twelve years old.*

She closed her eyes again. Nothing he had said before made her realize what he was more than that single statement.

"Your mother was of the Marshan line, then? Like me?" she asked.

"Yes."

"What did she do when—"

"When she gave birth to me and my brother?"

"You have a brother?"

"We're twins."

Two dovenatus? Two darkly handsome lost souls? She moistened her lips, asking again, "What did she do?"

"What do you mean?" he asked, dark eyes narrowing dangerously.

"Well, did she know it was a lycan who'd assaulted her? Did she know what you and your brother were?"

"When we came of age, it was clear we weren't like other boys. She knew then."

"And . . ."

"And what?" he bit out, a muscle along his jaw jumping wildly. "She didn't poison our soup or throw us out with the garbage, if that's what you want to know. She loved us."

"She must have been a strong woman," she murmured, not meeting his gaze, unwilling to test his temper with her true thoughts. *She loved her cursed sons. So much that she set them free on the world. Damned selfish fool.*

Every lycan Kit had ever encountered flashed through her mind. Their grotesque appearance, their thirst for blood, their indiscriminating tastes. No one was safe. Man, woman, or child. Kit could not imagine allowing such a creature to exist. Blood relation or not.

Clearly she had not experienced a mother's devotion. Memories of her own mother were too vague, but Kit could never do as Rafe's mother had and overlook her children's monstrousness. A shiver raced through her. She wouldn't—not that she ever intended to be put to the test.

So she was a Marshan. That didn't mean she was doomed. Didn't mean she was like Rafe.

She took several gulps of breath, telling herself that it wasn't the end of her world. Being a descendant of the Marshan line didn't mean she was a lycan.

So she shared compatible DNA. So what? She just had to be sure she never let herself become impregnated by a lycan. She wasn't like Rafe's mother, some girl from a dead era who hadn't a clue about defending herself. She didn't even need to quit hunting. She could handle the situation. She had made it to twenty-six without bringing about the prophecy, and she exposed herself to lycans all the time.

Chin lifting, she vowed in an ugly sneer, "I won't be a vessel for some lycan. Don't worry about me. I can handle myself without giving birth to—"

"What?" The muscles along his jaw knotted. "Without giving birth to what?"

*Him.* She thought it, but dared not speak it. The dangerous glint of light was back in his eyes again. For the barest second the contours of his face blurred, and she feared he would transform before her.

And she hated that fear. Hated the way her breath hitched, hated the way he made her feel like a lost girl again, weak and small, witnessing her mother transform into a nightmarish creature.

"Me, you mean," he growled. "You think I'm a monster, Kit. Just say it."

She swallowed against the awful thickness in his throat. "All lycans are. Whatever your differences, you're not human. You lack control, a conscience. You're like them—"

"I'm not. If I were like them, you'd be dead." His stare burned through her. "Worse than dead."

She shivered. He spoke the truth.

She shook her head, unable to accept that he could be trusted. Not if he possessed even a scrap of lycan blood. The proclivity to kill was there. One bad day, and he could succumb to it.

"I'll allow there would clearly be differences in a hybrid species," she said. "Perhaps you're not as blood-driven, but—"

"Let's just agree you don't know anything about me." The words sprang from his lips. A look came over his face then. So harsh and severe, a frisson of alarm skittered down her spine. "Not a damn thing. And you don't know anything about yourself, for that matter."

Her brow tightened. "What do you mean?"

"Here's a reality check for you, Kit." His hand moved suddenly to grip her face, long fingers sliding around to cup the nape of her neck. His thumb pressed into the soft flesh of her cheek. "You like me a hell of a lot more than you're willing to admit." His gaze roved over her face, lingering on her mouth. "You even want me again, no matter what you think I am."

She tried to shake her head in denial, but he held her face in place, fingers tightening at her neck.

"And . . ." His dark gaze, the flame dancing in the center, lifted to her eyes. "You're not simply a Marshan anymore."

She blinked. As far as she was concerned there was nothing simple about being a Marshan.

"You're so much more," he whispered.

*More?*

"You're me."

*"What?"*

"Like me," he amended. "A dovenatu. I turned you. After you were shot. It was the only way I could save you." The pressure of his hand on her face increased as his eyes drilled into hers.

"No. You only said I was a Marshan, a potential carrier . . ."

she accused. *Pleaded.* "How can I be a dovenatu? How could you turn me?"

"You remember what happened in that parking lot. You *know*. You were shot. Dying." His lips compressed into a grim line. "I saved you the only way I could. I don't regret it."

"No?" She winced at the sharpness of her voice. "Well, I do!" He had turned her into the very thing she most hated in the world. The thing she had watched, helplessly, her mother become. Bile rose high in her throat. "You know about my parents. And you turned me. Just like some fiend out there infected my mother. You should have let me die."

Emotion flickered in his eyes, then vanished, his gaze returning to steadfast, obscure blackness. "I couldn't."

She surged against him, wrenching her face free from his hand. "Don't touch me!"

The warmth that had been simmering through her burst free in a rupture of hot fury, burning her veins. Her heart hammered at a frantic tempo, the air rushing out of her mouth in spurts. Dipping her head, she moaned low in her throat, still trying to shove him off her.

He grasped her by the shoulders, trying to pull her up, to face him.

A scratchy, tingling sensation that bordered on pain overwhelmed her body. Powerless to resist, she threw back her head and arched her spine, moaning louder. Clutching her cheeks, she felt her bones altering, ever so slightly stretching, pulling . . .

She struggled to hold on to herself, to what she knew, but it grew increasingly harder as her body twisted inside itself.

"Kit, no!" Rafe shouted, wrapping both arms around her and hauling her against him. "Calm yourself."

She couldn't. Couldn't control her raging emotions.

The face of every lycan she had killed, the sight of her father's mutilated body, slain by her mother, flashed through her mind in a searing blaze. He had done this to her. Turned her into one of them. A red haze of fury filled her vision.

The sound of his voice came to her from a great distance, as if he called to her from the bottom of a well.

"Kit! Kit! No! Relax. Don't shift!"

# 22

He had no choice.

The only way Rafe could hope to restrain her, to keep her from hurting herself or him, was to let himself go, to surrender to that which he always kept in careful check. The beast he controlled with a firm hand and released from its cage only rarely, when absolutely necessary. As a last resort.

So, with Kit struggling like a wild animal in his arms, nearly breaking free of him with her newfound strength, he shifted.

Kit froze at the sight of him, screaming.

Her own face mirrored his, distorting before his very eyes. The sharpened features, the white-gold light dancing at the centers of her pale green eyes. Although she didn't know it. Relief washed through him that she could not see herself.

"Kit," he growled, the thick sound of his voice telling him what he already knew. He was in full form. His voice purred from deep within his chest. "Take a deep breath. Calm down, and you'll shift back to normal."

She shook her head, her hair tossing wildly about her head. She surged against him again, sending them both crashing to the floor. "Kit, stop it!" Grabbing a fistful of her hair, he forced her to still, holding her gaze as they strained against each other, chest to chest.

He remembered the pain of his first shift, his confusion, his bewilderment at the changes overcoming him. The absolute terror. But his mother had been there, talking him through it, her voice a lifeline, a soothing balm. He would be the same for Kit—if she let him.

He loosened his grip on her head, threading his fingers through her silken mop. Gently, he lowered his face, pressing his forehead against her sweat-dampened skin, making a shushing sound. She continued to struggle against him, and he swung a leg over her, stilling her against the carpet.

"Easy. Easy there," he murmured as though coaxing a wild animal, wincing when she pulled her head back and brought it crashing into his.

Spots filled his vision. Swallowing a curse at the pain, he massaged the back of her head, holding her in place, and ground out, "Let me help you."

She made a whimpering sound and gradually ceased her struggles. His hand descended to her back, his palm rubbing a circle over the thin cotton T-shirt. He could feel each and every tiny bump of her spine beneath his hand—the sensation erotic, tantalizing. The tension ebbed from her. Her body relaxed in his arms, turning from the angry, smoldering heat of moments before to a different kind of heat. Like the warm welcome of a flickering fire on a cold night, she lured him.

"Good," he breathed, his lips almost brushing her mouth as he spoke.

The sweetness of her breath escaped her lips and he sipped at it, drinking it inside him. She trembled in his arms. Unable to stop himself, he feathered a kiss over her quivering lips. She jerked as though stung. Hunger twisted inside him, and he followed her mouth, claiming her lips, pulling her flush against him.

She sighed, parting her lips wider for his questing tongue. Animal hunger erupted in him at the sound, at the sugary taste of her—the very hunger he'd spent a lifetime holding carefully in check. He may have not lived life as a monk, but he was careful never to get carried away with a woman. Never until recently. Until Kit.

*And Kit wasn't mortal anymore . . .*

A dangerous thought in itself. If he allowed himself to think along those lines, she would be on her back and he would be parting her thighs before he could stop himself.

With a groan, he broke the kiss and pulled back to look at her, relieved to see she was Kit again. Well, almost. The wild anger may have fled, but in its place something else simmered. Her green eyes glowed brightly; her mouth was parted, lips glistening invitingly.

He slid his leg off her and put more space between them. She didn't want this. Not anymore. And he couldn't stomach her hating him anymore than she already did. He wouldn't take advantage of her. Not when she wasn't fully herself. Hell, but then she never would be. Not entirely. Not like before.

His hands flexed at his sides, but he willed himself to remain normal. *Human.* Tension thrummed through his muscles. Instinct swamped him, demanding he take her, make her his. She was part of him now. The same. A dovenatu.

She thought him a monster. He knew it. Had seen it in her eyes, heard it in her voice. Damned if that didn't wound him. Damned if the dark side of him didn't want to spread her legs beneath him and hear her cry out for him—a monster—as he took her fast and hard.

Desire coursed his blood . . . and anger: anger at himself for being drawn to her when he had no right.

"Rafe," she sighed, her wide eyes fixed on him.

The sound of his name on her lips sent a lick of heat twisting through his gut. He couldn't resist. Not her. Not when he remembered how good it had been between them the last time.

She scooted near, closing the space between them, fed, he knew, by the hunger he had awakened in her. He knew what she wanted. The beast in her had been roused and demanded satisfaction. She didn't have the strength or experience yet to deny herself this.

Neither did he.

Rolling her onto her back, he hovered over her. He stared down at her, her hair a puddle of sun-kissed gold around her face. His mouth went dry. Dark need burned a fierce path to his belly. Only the thin barrier of her T-shirt hid her nudity. Only that thin shield barred him from total access to the body that had haunted his dreams for nights.

A soft sound escaped her lips. Her green eyes appeared a bit unfocused, dazed. Calling himself a bastard that he would do this to her, fresh after her Initiation, he grabbed the hem of her T-shirt and pulled it up over her head in one quick motion.

His breath escaped in a hiss as he devoured the sight of her small, pert breasts, the dusky nipples, the gentle slope of her belly. It was too much. The sight finished him, made him tremble like a new foal.

He greedily drank in the sight of her, bringing one hand to her breast. She followed his gaze.

A growl sounded from deep within his chest, and something hot and animal erupted low in his gut. His gaze ran the full length of her body, roaming over the sleek lines and gentle curves.

He laced his fingers with hers and pinned her hands above her head, watching the rise and fall of her breasts.

She rotated her hips and opened her legs, cradling him between her thighs. Such a primal invitation enflamed his desire to have her, to give up the fight and fall—to descend into the very depths of the abyss he had spent a lifetime fighting.

There was no fighting it, no strength left in him to resist.

"I won't be gentle." He couldn't be.

Releasing her hands, he grasped the smooth and supple outside swell of one hip. His breath hitched, catching in his throat as he slid his hand around, cupping the taut fullness of one cheek.

Her gasp reached his ears, different than any sound he'd ever heard, ripped from some place deep in her throat where animal pleasure hid. "Good."

His fingers flexed, digging into the roundness of her ass, forcing her closer, rubbing her wet heat against him. He pressed his full length against her, moaning at her softness, her silken limbs, her warm body.

Her wide eyes locked with his, the green of them glowing like precious gemstones in the firelight.

Dipping his head, he scoured her neck with his teeth. She groaned, and he bit down, reveling in the savage shudder that tore through her and reverberated through him.

Closing his eyes, he trailed the backs of his finger along the sleek flesh of her back, over each tiny bump of her spine. He wanted to skim his mouth over each and every one.

His hands continued their exploration, roaming every inch of her. The delicate shape of each rib. The soft curve of her belly that quivered under his fingertips. His hands grazed the underside of each breast, testing their slight weight. He brushed open palms over her hard nipples. Her breathing grew harsh, arousing him nearly as much as the silky feel of her.

Past stopping, he closed a hand over each breast, gripping the firm, petite mounds, squeezing, kneading, rolling the distended peaks.

The beat of her heart vibrated against the palm of his hand in sync with his own, and he lowered his head to kiss where her heart beat, worshipping the life forever bound to his own. The life that he had come so close to losing.

She would have no gentleness. She tugged on his hair. Her desperate keening filled the air, sharp and animal-like, knifing through him, making him burn, banishing the sane, mortal side of him that whispered for him to stop, to love her with slow, easy thoroughness.

Her hands grabbed his forearms, her nails cutting his flesh in a pain that bordered on pleasure.

"Rafe," she whimpered, begging, pleading.

A strangled laugh rose up in his throat. He was powerless to resist. Releasing her breasts, he delved one hand between her thighs, brushing feather-soft curls damp with need. He tested her readiness, stroking the folds of her sex, already slick for him.

Her fingers dug like talons into his arms, and she leaned forward, resting her damp forehead against his chest as he worked his fingers feverishly along those folds, back and forth, back and forth, each time brushing closer and closer to that tiny nub. Finally, he landed there, rubbing his fingers over the pearl in fast, little circles. Her body tensed, and she released a loud, shuddering cry.

He drank in her rapturous expression, branding that look in his mind, knowing he would never forget it. Then, as the waves of her climax were still rushing over her, he parted her legs and put his mouth to that exquisite pleasure point and sucked, tasting her desire.

Arching her back, she came up off the carpet, releasing a cry. His eyes devoured the breasts quivering above him, shuddering golden orbs, as another climax tore through her.

She collapsed back on the carpet, her body panting and humming from her release. He never took his eyes off her as he stood to tear off his clothes, his movements eager and clumsy as a boy.

Her eyes lifted to his, the clouded green searching, questioning.

He shook his head, one boot hitting the floor, then the next. His pants followed, then his shirt.

Naked, he stood over her. Her eyes flitted over him, surveyed the broad width of his chest, nostrils flaring wide at the evidence of his lust, smelling his hunger, just as he smelled hers. A heady steam on the air.

He held her gaze, waiting for her to object, wondering if he could stop himself if she did, praying that he did not have to find out.

He was past reasoning, past caring about all the reasons they couldn't do this.

He would have her again. Like this. He'd finally descended into the abyss, to the darkness his mother had always warned against.

Kit was right about him. *You lack control, a conscience.*

But not even that could stop him now or make him regret what he was about to do.

# 23

She should stop him, this . . . *herself.*

But when Kit looked into his eyes and saw the fire in his feverish gaze, the desperate need flickering in the glowing centers, she knew what he felt. Because she felt it, too. Not just her own desire. But *his.* On top of what she felt, she could feel his emotions, his hunger—as true as her own, as though physically linked, as though his turning her had in fact bound them.

Bound? Right.

She was not bound to this guy. She was not bound to anyone. And yet . . .

His arms, taut bands of steel, trembled with restraint. She marveled that he—more animal than man—could restrain himself at all. The greatest shock of all was that *she* did not want him to.

She drank in the sight of him: the shadows pooling in the sharp angles and hollows of his face, the play of his sculpted muscles, the dark wave of hair falling over his brow. Her gaze fell lower, eyeing his manhood springing from between his legs, daunting in its size. The hard length pulsed before her very eyes, summoning her touch.

Her stomach clenched in response. The place between her thighs throbbed in memory of him, and her breathing grew labored. Eager for him to be inside her, to continue the incredible torment that his mouth had begun on her aching body, her eyes shot back up to his.

"Oh, yes," he muttered, as if he had the ability to read her thoughts. And perhaps he did. "Touch me."

His rough voice, combined with the desperate intensity of his gaze, would have her do anything he asked.

Rising to her knees, she reached up and touched the center of his chest with one finger. Pressing her lips tightly in determination to take this slow, she trailed that finger down, over the hard stomach, the washboard abs, her nail slightly scraping the firm skin. His breathing grew harsh.

Her finger dropped lower, arriving at his jutting manhood. She was close enough to take him in her mouth. Smiling wickedly, she touched the head of him, growing more aroused when a tiny bead of moisture rose to lick her fingertip.

He groaned and buried a hand in her hair.

Emboldened, she closed her hand around his throbbing length and gently squeezed, aroused at the soft texture of him—silk on steel in her palm. Her tongue darted out to taste him. Slowly, she licked him. Again and again, until she couldn't resist closing her lips around him.

"Stop." He pulled her up. His jaw clenched, the muscles knotting, demonstrating his hard-fought control. "I can't wait."

Her smile deepened, thrilled to see her power over him, to know how badly he wanted her, that he was holding himself back.

Ready for his control to snap, she arched her spine and rubbed her bare breasts against his chest.

Twin lights flared at the center of his dark eyes. His hands clamped down on her hips and he guided her back to the bed. She spread her thighs, sucking in a breath as he positioned himself over her.

His breath caught in a hiss as he pushed himself in, one inch at a time. Her muscles stretched, burning in pleasure-pain at the fullness of him inside her.

His gaze, dark and fathomless as a moonless night, mesmerized her, lodging deep in her soul as, with one final push, he was fully inside her.

Whimpering his name, she dug her fingers into his tense forearms, urging him on, desperate for more of the wild, twisting heat swimming through her.

Moaning, she angled her hips to take him in even deeper.

A choked cry escaped him. Muttering her name in a garbled voice, his breath fanning hotly against her throat, he slowly began to move.

With the throbbing burn of him deeply inside her, Kit shook her head from side to side on the bed, desperate for him to move harder, to slide in and out as fast and furious as the animal need surging through her.

"Kit," he gasped, warning, "We need to go slow. It may be too much, too . . ."

"No," she growled in a voice she did not recognize as her own.

Letting go of his arms, she skated her palms down his back, skimming the smooth skin until she clutched his firm buttocks with both hands, forcing him to thrust himself deeply inside her. Hard. Savage as the burning in her blood demanded.

Their cries mingled, filling the air. Shock waves rippled over her, convincing her that she would never again be anything except a part of him.

His body pressed heavily upon her, comforting and thrilling in its weight. She had to move, to take. Writhing beneath him, she rotated her hips, tightening her inner muscles and clenching him, her body begging for more, for an end to the incredible fire that he had stoked within her.

Groaning, he moved, withdrawing himself nearly out of her before thrusting back inside in a deep slam of flesh.

Ripples of white-hot pleasure washed over her as he repeated the action, pumping in and out of her. The feel of his hardness hammering into her, the strong fingers digging into her hips, anchoring her for his assault, drove her over the edge.

Her head rose off the bed, a scream building from deep in her throat, hovering on her lips. His frenzied stroking carried her higher, created an explosion of desire that finally wrung a wild, air-shattering shout from her lips.

He pumped several more times, the violent sounds of their bodies coming together thrilling her in the deepest, primal way. With a deep growl, he plunged into her, stilling as he poured into her.

A tightness gripped her chest as she studied his face. In the fierce grip of desire, the sharp lines and angles blurred, reminding her at once that he was no mortal. Rather, a dangerous animal. That what they had just done was not making love, but the coupling of two beasts. Wild and unrestrained. So wrong. Wrong in too many ways.

Mortifying heat washed over her. Because in that moment she knew he was right: she was like him.

The heavy fall of his dark hair obscured his eyes, yet she longed to see them, to see if the eerie bright light still glowed at the centers. A solid reminder of why she could not feel close to him. Why she could not let the best sex of her life affect her. He'd lied to her. He'd turned her even when he knew she would hate it. And now he intended to make her his captive. How could she ever trust him?

Suddenly he looked up, tossing the hair back from his forehead, and she found herself pinned beneath his searing, cursed gaze. Flickering light filled his pupils. Did her eyes look the same?

Sick at heart, she dipped her gaze. Squeezing out from beneath him, she sat up, hugging her knees to her chest, resisting a sudden sense of desolation.

"Kit."

She turned at the hushed sound of her name.

Sprawled naked, bold and unashamed beside her, he reached for her arm, and she saw that some of the light had ebbed from his eyes. But not all.

She pulled back before he could touch her, an awkward flush creeping up her neck. Absurd, considering what had transpired between them.

"Don't," he commanded. "Don't do this to yourself."

"Do what?"

"Don't punish yourself for this. For us."

She laughed, the sound cruel and bitter, poison to her heart, but she could not stop herself. She needed to stop this. Forget it. Forget all that had happened. Forget him. A *liar*. "There is no *us*."

Careful to keep her eyes on his face and not the appealing length of his body, she stood and snatched her T-shirt off the floor and pulled it over her head. "This is just a manifestation of . . ." Her brow tightened, struggling for the words final and cruel enough to build a wall between them. "Of my being like you. An animal of instinct. It didn't mean anything."

"That's bullshit. We did this before I ever turned you."

Standing, she glared down at him. "Don't pretend this was something beautiful and romantic. Even before you turned me into a lycan, I've never been a Hallmark kind of girl. The truth is you lied to me from the start. And now you think you can keep me captive?"

He was on his feet in a flash, his face blurring into all that she hated again, all that she feared.

He grabbed her arm and hauled her close. "Cheapen it all you like, but there's something between us. Something real. Even before you turned, it was there."

She shook her head violently, resisting the childish urge to fling her hands over her ears. She ripped her arm free and stumbled away. Chest heaving, she held his stare, relieved to see his face resume itself.

"Kit—"

Lifting a hand, she shook a finger in warning. "Don't touch me again."

Turning, she fled into the bathroom, slamming the door so hard it shook the air, and covered the sound of his voice.

Trembling, she yanked off her shirt and stepped into the shower. Twisting the faucet, she let ice-cold water rain down on her, crying out when it hit her feverish skin. She welcomed the sting, embraced the pain of it, let it cool the burn of emotions flooding her. After a few moments, her teeth began to clatter, but she felt herself again. She only wished the memory of what she had done could be wiped out as easily.

She remained beneath the pounding water for several minutes more, washing her hair and scrubbing her body until her skin glowed red, chafed. Only the sensation of him on her flesh lingered; his hands, his mouth. Damn. Shutting off the water, she stepped from the shower, pulled a fluffy towel from the towel bar, and rubbed her goose-puckered skin dry.

No sound carried from the room beyond, but she knew he was still there. Felt him there, on the other side.

She stared at her reflection for several moments. Her eyes appeared normal. But would they always? Had they remained their usual green when she was going at it like an animal with Rafe?

Dropping her head, she sucked in a deep breath, dreading facing him. Seeing him made her see herself as she was now: a half-breed lycan.

Wearing the shirt again, she opened the door and stepped carefully from the bathroom. The lights were off. Rafe's large shape reclined on the bed, beneath the covers. She grimaced. Just like a man. Asleep and dead to the world following sex.

With the stealth of a cat, she crept past the bed, moving toward the chair containing her clothes. Her hand fell on the shirt when his voice spoke. "You don't think it's going to be that easy."

Stopping, she turned to stare at his dark shape.

"You'll have to do better than that to get rid of me. You need me now. Whether you want to admit it or not."

"You think I'm that hard up? Arrogant—"

"It has nothing to do with sex. Who's going to train you?"

Train her? Was he kidding? She wasn't going to stay like this long enough to require any training. There had to be a way out of this mess. Her brother had saved Claire. And Darius believed he could find a way to reverse his curse. Surely there was a way to reverse what Rafe had done to her.

His sigh filled the air, the sound weary. "Get into bed, Kit. It's late. We can talk about this tomorrow."

Biting her lip, she looked at the door.

As if he could read her thoughts, he added, "You can try to escape tomorrow. For now, get some rest. You're going to need it."

Grabbing the throw off the back of the chair, she pulled it over her as she settled into the soft leather, swinging her legs over the arm.

He lifted his head from the pillow. His eyes gleamed at her from across the room. "That can't be comfortable."

"I'm not sharing a bed with you." *No way do I trust myself enough to do that.*

His head fell back down on the pillow without a word. Her

heart sank a little. What had she expected? That he would at least protest?

She squirmed in the chair, attempting to get comfortable. Fortunately, her body was too exhausted to really care where she slept. With her cheek resting against the too-firm back of the chair, she dozed off.

She didn't know how much time passed before two hard arms slid beneath her and lifted her from the chair.

"What are you doing?" she demanded, her voice sleep-heavy as he settled her in the center of the big bed, lacking the forcefulness she would have liked.

"Putting you to bed. Go to sleep." His voice sounded beside her ear, fluttering strands of her hair against her cheek.

Like this? With him? Impossible. She gasped as he curled his big body next to hers, pulling her to him as if he had every right, as if she belonged at his side. As if he were a man she could trust.

"Sleep," she echoed, her every nerve stretched tight, achingly alive. Sleep. Elusive as smoke circling overhead. As the new moon outside their window. Invisible, but there just the same. Dark moon, she mused. It was there even when you couldn't see it. Like Rafe.

His affliction wasn't nearly as visible or apparent as a full-breed lycan, but he was afflicted nonetheless. She hadn't seen it at first, but now she did. Now she knew. The beast was there. Inside Rafe. *A dark moon.*

His hand splayed over her hip, large and possessive, a veritable paw anchoring her to him.

She wet her lips, searching for her voice. "Tomorrow," she began, relieved that her voice did not quake as her insides did. "I'm going." Damned if she wasn't. She was no man's prisoner.

"You can try," he said against her neck, his voice mild, unbothered, the moist fan of his breath making her belly flutter.

"I will . . ." Her voice tore, twisting into a sharp gasp as his teeth bit down on her earlobe. Desire, hot and savage, spiked through her, melting her bones and burning her blood as she fought to finish her sentence. "I thought we were going to sleep."

"We will," he breathed in a voice warm as the sun, thick with need. He raised his head to look at her. His hair fell forward. Light and shadow flickered over his features, casting his face into sharp lines and hollows.

Her hand wobbled on the air before pushing the hair back from his face. His eyes gleamed down at her, those twin lights returning to the dark fathomless pools, pulling her in, swallowing her whole. She moistened her lips, needing to speak, to say what burned on her mind, even as *he* burned through her blood and body. "You know you're everything I despise."

He tensed and took his time responding. For a moment, she thought he would not answer at all. "I know. But I can change your mind. I can earn your trust."

"And if you don't? You'll hold me captive for how long? Forever?"

Shadow fell over his face, but he didn't answer.

A secret part of her wished he could change her mind. That she could just accept all he had done to her. Forgive. Accept him. Accept herself as she now was.

Turning his head, he pressed a moist kiss into her palm. "I'll prove to you that you can still be everything you ever wanted . . . and more." His eyes met hers over her palm.

His hand traced the line of her collarbone, the brush of his fingertips chasing away her thoughts. That hand lowered, trailing a fiery path between her breasts.

"Trust me," his low voice reassured her, a caress in itself. A slow lick of heat curled in her belly at his words, a serpent's coaxing plea.

She arched beneath his hand, thrusting her breast into his ready palm. Her hand circled his neck, dragging his mouth down to hers. She didn't have to trust him for this.

# 24

Kit woke slowly, her body leaden, muscles warm and liquid, sated. Opening her eyes, she found herself staring directly into Rafe's dark gaze. He was dressed, standing over her.

Instantly, she remembered last night, seeing those eyes as she had in the darkness, flames flickering in the dark depths at the height of his rage. And passion.

"Good morning." His voice rumbled through her, swirling in a vortex of heat in her belly, threatening to pull her under as it had last night. Fire scorched her face.

She could only respond with a fierce nod. She was the very thing she loathed. The very thing that had stolen her parents, robbed her of the life she was meant to have, a life that might have given her a sense of wholeness, completion, filling the void that ached dully inside her now.

"I was just about to step out."

"Out?" she replied, still feeling rather lethargic, groggy. "Why? Where?"

"I was going to get supplies to last us while we're here."

He made it sound as though they were staying a while. She shook her head. That couldn't happen.

"No. I can't stay here. I'm leaving. Remember?"

His eyes glinted with challenge. "And I said you're not. Remember?"

Scooting up in the bed, she moved to tighten the sheet about her . . . and found one of her hands trapped, pinned to the bed frame. She tried to pull free. The steel cuffs simply rattled. Useless. "What the hell is *this*?"

Rafe looked down at her, his face impassive as stone.

She jerked at her wrist. "You bastard. You can't keep me chained to this bed. Is this what you meant about gaining my trust?"

His lean chest rippled in a dance of sinew and muscle beneath his black shirt. "You have much to learn before I set you loose on the world. Staying put is a good idea right now. You have a lot to understand—"

"Why? So I can stay here and be your fuck buddy some more?"

"I didn't hear any complaints last night."

"Like I had a choice."

His jaw tensed. "I didn't force you."

"No? You turned me into you. An animal. A creature driven by her instinct."

Something bright and dangerous flickered in his gaze. "You wanted me before all this. Need I remind you?"

"I know you find it hard to believe, but I don't want you, or anything *from* you now! Including lessons on being a lycan." Perhaps, for a moment, she had softened toward him last night. Considered dropping her guard, letting him in. But he dared handcuff her like some sort of hostage? As if *she* couldn't be trusted? He was the one who had lied to her from the start!

"You can't bury your head in the sand and pretend—"

"I'm not. I'm perfectly in tune with reality, and I'll figure all this out. On my own. Without you." She glared at him. "Last night was a mistake I won't repeat again."

In a move so fast she hardly saw it coming, he grabbed her, lifting her off the bed as far as the handcuffs would allow, flexing his hands over her shoulders. "You need me."

Her heart leapt at his words, betraying her. Just as her body betrayed her last night. Her gaze clung to him, careful to keep her eyes from straying south, from rousing her hunger and succumbing to the madness of the night before all over again. "No."

*Need.* She had always wanted someone, needed someone. An aching hollowness had always been with her. More pronounced now that Gideon had found someone, and needed her less than ever. But Rafe was *not* what she had in mind. Nor was this heart-leaping thrill for him. He was not safe. Not the man she had been looking for. *Not human at all.*

But then, neither was she.

She squirmed free and fell back down on the bed, having nowhere else to go. "You want me to trust you?" she ground out, tugging on her wrist. The handcuffs held fast to the brass bed frame. "Let me go."

A long moment passed before he asked, "If I did, where would you go? To your brother?"

She couldn't go to Gideon. She *wouldn't* go to him. Not as she was. Not until she figured a way to reverse what Rafe had done to her. There had to be a way. Her brother had saved Claire. Done the impossible. The very thing she had told him couldn't be done. He had proved her wrong. And she would prove Rafe wrong, too.

"Home," she finally answered.

"You cannot return home. You won't survive."

"I'm tougher than I look. And thanks to you, I'm now harder to kill."

"Harder. But not impossible." He splayed his hands wide before him. "Kit, you have much to learn. Let me teach you—"

"You've done enough. Thanks."

His jaw knotted. He spun around and snatched his jacket from the table, adjusting his holster around his middle with rough, angry movements. "You can't change this. You need to accept. Adapt."

As she stared at the unforgiving lines of his face, the dark eyes that drew her in, her resolve hardened. She refused to believe him. Refused to believe that she was stuck this way.

One face appeared in her mind. *Darius.* Even if he did not know she and Gideon were of the Marshan line, he must know about the prophecy. She may not have trusted him before, but what choice did she have now? Perhaps his antidote research might help her.

She glared at him. "You can't keep me chained to this bed forever."

"Not forever. Just until you see reason."

"You mean until I see things your way," she snapped.

He scowled. "No one ever gave me as much trouble as you. Any of the others would be safely secured in their new life by now, and I would be on my way. You're one uncooperative pain in my ass."

"You can still be on your way." She jiggled her hand. "Unlock these and go on."

"For now I'm going to keep you alive. Even if you're too stubborn to realize that's what I'm doing." He pulled the door open.

"Bastard," she hissed. He'd lied to her. Taken everything from her. Her choice, her life. Now he dared take her freedom?

"Letting you go would be tantamount to killing you. Not to mention others. You can't handle—"

"Save it," she bit out, fighting the swelling heat of her anger. All her life she had heard men tell her she couldn't *handle it.* Her brother. Cooper. NODEAL. "How long do you plan keeping me prisoner?"

He lifted one broad shoulder in a shrug. "I don't know."

"Not good enough. How. Long."

"Until I'm satisfied. I can't set you free right now, not knowing . . ." His voice faded.

"Not knowing whether I'll give in and become a bloodthirsty killer." Her voice dripped acrimony. "Yet you claim we're so different—not like lycans."

His mouth pressed into a grim line. "My brother and I never slipped. We mastered the beast within us. In time, with my help, you will, too."

"*Slipped?*" He made it sound so mild. One *slip* and she became a slave to the hunger. Soulless. Like Darius. Never free. "How is this right? First, you turn me, now you imprison me. What's next?"

He looked her steadily in the eyes. "Acceptance. I hope."

"Hope." The word rang hollowly, dead inside her. "Well, you know what I hope? I hope that when I close my eyes, you'll disappear. That I'll open my eyes and discover this is a bad dream."

A muscle ticked along his jaw, but he said nothing. Just stared at her with such damnable calm. As if ice water flowed through his veins. Rage thrummed through her, hotter than fire, almost too much to bear. Damn him, this is what he meant, why he claimed he had to keep her with him. Raw emotion threatened to consume her, rule her—and he knew it.

Breathing in through her nostrils, she drew air deeply into her lungs. She would show him she possessed control. She didn't need him. She would escape. Put her newfound powers to good use and break free.

She would get the better of him, go to Darius, and everything would work out. *Darius.* The thought of him made her mouth twist. Ironically, she had more in common with a full-breed lycan than with Rafe. Like her, Darius wanted to change his fate.

And yet the truth was there, staring her in the face. Even if she ran from Rafe, she could not run from *it*, from herself.

She was a dovenatu. Like him.

# 25

She hated him. And he couldn't blame her.

He had lied to her. *Turned* her. Then taken advantage of her newfound susceptibility and slept with her. Again.

He walked the length of the cabin's wooden porch, his feet thudding over the planking. The sun sank below the trees, beams spilling through branches to gild the lake in yellow, gold, and red. A boat's engine purred in the distance.

The smell of food cooking wafted to his nose from the neighboring cabins. He inhaled deeply the mingling aromas: Steak. Fish. Some kind of dessert. Pecan pie.

He was acutely aware of her movements in the cabin behind him, the muted hum of the television. The rise and fall of her every breath. As with his brother, he felt bound to her. Linked in a way that was metaphysical.

He had freed her upon returning to the cabin with groceries. After unloading enough food to last the week into the small refrigerator, he stood in the kitchenette for an awkward moment, suffering her glare, before striding outside, eager to escape the accusation in those green eyes.

She schemed for a way to escape him. He would have to be on guard. She was now a greater match for him.

He simply couldn't let her go. She was a threat to anyone who crossed her path. He couldn't set her loose on mankind until he was certain she could control herself.

*Liar.* A small voice whipped across his mind. *You don't want to let her go. You want her for yourself. You wanted her from the start and now you have her. It doesn't matter one damn bit if she wants you back.*

"No," he muttered to himself. He wasn't that big a bastard. That selfish. He hadn't put her in the path of those agents. He hadn't shot her. He had just tried to save her when they did.

He prowled the porch, stopping when another scent struck him, sending the hairs on the back of his neck into stiff salute.

It was always this way. He felt them before he saw them.

Quick as a flash, he sprang from the porch and vaulted himself atop the cabin. Crouching low, he waited, watching, barely breathing, still as stone in the fading twilight. He brushed the sun-warmed roof in lazy swinging strokes, so at odds with the tension coursing through him, the spine-tight readiness coiling through him. He waited. Watched. Half-tuned to Kit below him in the cabin, he turned his head slowly, surveying the cabins in the distance, the surrounding woods, the wind-rippled waters of the lake beyond.

He sat atop his perch, undetected, focused on cooling his body's heat level, making himself undetectable, blending into the approaching night.

Somehow they had tracked them. Again. Too coincidental. He had rid Kit of her belongings. Were they tracking her through him? How? Had his cover been blown? Was Laurent on to him?

Pushing the concerns away for later reflection, he narrowed his gaze on the ground below.

They approached from all sides. Four of them. Two moved in fast and hard, coming directly for the front of the cabin. Anger threatened to swamp him at the thought of the bastards getting their hands on Kit.

Squatting on his heels, he rotated, observing the remaining two moving in behind the cabin, winding through the trees like stalking beasts. They could wait. He would save them for last—after he dispensed with the two barreling for the front of the cabin.

He dropped down directly before the first lycan advancing up the porch steps, landing lightly on the balls of his feet. He slid the serrated knife from inside his jacket. In a crosswise swipe, he cut the lycan's throat, simultaneously pulling his revolver out with his free hand.

Silver eyes dilated wide in shock and pain. The lycan's words gurgled free. Choking on blood, he clutched feverishly at the gushing opening in his throat. The wound, lethal to mortal man, would not kill the bastard. In minutes, it would stop bleeding and seal itself, his DNA doing its job and regenerating. It only hurt like hell. And slowed him down.

The second lycan charged up the wooden steps, releasing a bellow of rage as he flew past his comrade. Rafe tightened his finger and squeezed off a round. The shot zipped through the air with a muted hiss. A dark hole appeared squarely in the lycan's forehead, followed by a thick trickle of crimson. The creature dropped, eyes staring vacantly ahead, the silver instantly fading, reverting to a very mortal, lifeless shade of blue.

The lycan with the cut throat staggered down the porch, trying to flee until he recovered from his temporary wound. Rafe aimed at his back and fired, watching grimly as the lycan dropped to the dirt.

The door behind him flung open. Kit stood there, wide eyes taking in the scene, mouth parted with unspoken words. Her gaze flew to Rafe. She gasped. "Your face!"

"Inside," he barked.

He didn't need a mirror to see what she saw: the beginning of him shifting.

He spun back around, senses sharpening, burning along his nerve endings. Branches snapped and leaves crumbled beneath the feet of the two remaining lycans, soft, undetectable to the human ear but as loud as a car horn to his.

"Stay in the cabin," he growled over his shoulder.

"What—"

"Now!"

He broke into a run and circled the cabin, disappearing into the trees. He paused, nostrils flaring, sensing an approaching lycan, feeling the race of the other's heart, the fall of his uneven breathing on the humid air.

With a single jump, Rafe swung himself up into a tree the moment before the lycan became visible, moving stealthily through the press of cedar.

He waited until his prey was directly below him before dropping, blood pounding through him like the beating of drums. Landing directly behind the creature, he grabbed a fistful of greasy hair and pulled back the lycan's head, firing the gun into his temple.

The body fell lifelessly at his feet. Rafe stepped over it and moved on, taking a position behind an oak large enough to conceal him. He listened, detecting the movements of the coming lycan.

This one moved cautiously, each step measured.

Rafe flexed his hand around his gun's grip, waiting. Sweat trailed down his spine. He held his breath.

Suddenly the steps halted. Too suddenly. He'd been detected.

Stepping out into the open, he found nothing but wind and trees before him. He rotated on the balls of his feet, gun at the ready, scanning the area, seeing nothing.

Scalp tight and tingling, he continued to turn in a full circle—until he came face to face with a smug-looking bastard with flashing silver eyes.

Before he could fire, the guy was on him. The gun flew from his hand. They crashed to the ground. Burning curses flew as they rolled in a violent collision of arms and legs. Bone crunched bone. Fingers clawed, scratched. Teeth snapped, bit with animal fury.

A growl rose from deep in his throat, and the beast within him sprang free. He felt his skin tighten, his bones stretch. His strength increased, power swelling in a liquid-hot surge.

Rafe jammed his feet to the lycan's chest and shoved him off, sending him flying several feet. He landed in a cloud of dirt.

In a flash, Rafe was on his feet again, gun back in his hand. He aimed.

"What the hell are you?" the creature demanded in a harsh snarl, chest rising and falling with heavy breath.

Gasping, with a hot rush of adrenaline, he bit out, the sound of his voice thick and distorted, "If you think really hard, I'll bet you can figure it."

Shock flickered across the lycan's face the instant before Rafe squeezed the trigger and the silver bullet rushed across air to penetrate his chest.

Sliding his gun back in its holster, he headed back to the cabin, leaving the body behind, ready to reassure Kit.

In the distance, an engine gunned to life, stopping him in his tracks.

*Son of a bitch.*

Fury rippled over him. While he was getting his ass kicked, Kit was bailing on him.

The beast burned hotter, hungrier, furious.

He didn't care that she had told him she would try to escape. He knew only anger. And betrayal. And possessiveness.

A fire-hot determination to keep her with him—and punish her for daring to leave him—crashed over him.

# 26

He made it to the cabin in seconds, the rage churning through his gut intensifying as he saw brake lights glowing in the sultry dusk air.

Springing forward, he landed beside the driver's door as she was backing from beneath the tin-roofed carport. Kit jumped and cried out at his sudden appearance, slamming on the brake. He tried the door handle.

"Unlock the door or I'll break the window and pull you out."

She hesitated only a moment before putting the vehicle into park and shutting off the engine. With a wary glance at his face, she unlocked the door.

He yanked it open and hauled her out. Without a word, he dragged her toward the cabin, stepping over bodies as if they were no more than litter in his way. And that's all they could have been. All his attention, all his fury, was caught up in Kit.

He slammed the cabin door behind them and flung her on the bed.

She immediately rose up on her elbows, her eyes skimming

over him, the barest hint of light flickering in their green depths. "You're covered in blood."

He didn't spare himself a glance. "Leaving?" His voice escaped in a growl as he came down on the bed.

Her throat worked as she inched back. "You shouldn't be surprised."

He cocked his head. "No." But he could still be angry. "I shouldn't." He straddled her, settling his knees on each side of her hips. Her head fell back on the bed to glare at him.

Her nostrils flared. "You reek of blood."

"That's what happens when you kill a pack of lycans hunting *you*—who want to kill you."

He shrugged free of his jacket, flinging it violently to the floor. Grasping the hem of his shirt, he pulled it over his head and let it join the jacket.

She quivered beneath him, eyeing the breadth of his chest. "I never asked you to protect me."

"You never asked for any of this, did you? But you have it. This is your lot. NODEAL, EFLA. The Marshan Prophecy." He leaned over her, bracing his arms on either side of her head, coming closer with each word he uttered. "Life as a dovenatu. *Me.*"

With that final word, his lips swooped down and claimed hers. His hands tangled in her hair, holding her still for the assault of his mouth. He swallowed her gasp, delving his tongue into the sweet heat of her mouth, tasting her desire, her anger . . . her fear. A fear that she tried suppress with her prickly exterior, her tough-girl façade.

That fear cooled his anger as nothing else could, made his hands soften their tight grip in her hair. As if his mother were whispering in his ear, urging him to control the beast, to shove it back into the dark, his lips gentled, nipping gently, coaxing forth a response.

She arched beneath him, purring like a stroked cat. Her female scent undid him, the faint powdery odor of her soap—and something else, something that was innately Kit.

He shed her clothing—and his—his hands moving in a rapid blur.

She rose up to meet his first thrust, fingers digging into his back, scoring his flesh in savage swipes. His head flung back as he moved, taking her hard and fierce, claiming her with a driving need. He had never taken a woman with such ferocity before—a mortal woman. But with Kit there was no holding back.

His hands covered her breasts, squeezing, kneading, rolling the distended tips.

A sharp keening rose from her throat and he drove into her harder. The sound of her desire, the feel of her soft heat tightening like a fist around him, milking him for all he was worth, pushed him over the edge.

Releasing a cry, he shuddered, spilling himself inside her. Sated, he collapsed over her, his hands still holding her, luxuriating in the soft texture of her flesh.

Only a moment passed before she slipped out from under him. Donning her shirt, she sat on the edge of the bed, fingers gripping the mattress, knuckles whitening.

"Are you no more than an animal?" she whispered. "You knew I didn't want to do this with you. Not again. I told you that."

Bitter cold washed through him at her scathing words—followed by the savage burn of the beast clawing through him.

All his life he fought to make a difference, to make his mother proud, to prove to her that he could overcome the darkness. That he lived only in the light.

And Kit refused to see that. Refused to recognize that there could be something between them beyond animal passion. That he—she—was more than an animal, more than a beast. He rose from the bed in one fluid motion. Picking up his discarded jacket, he pulled his revolver free.

Facing her, he grabbed her wrist and forced her to her feet, slapping the weapon into her hand.

"You think me an animal?" he demanded, his voice thickening, a warning. The beast lurked close. But he didn't care. Let her see it. She did anyway. Whenever she looked at him, it was all she saw. All she would ever see. "You think I'm the same as them? A mindless killer?"

She looked from the gun to him with unsure eyes. Her mouth parted, the tip of her tongue darting out to wet her lips. Despite himself, his gut tightened, responding to the sight.

Shoving the unwanted feelings down, he tossed out "Then do what you do best." He nodded decisively at the gun in her hand. "End this. Put me out of my misery. And yours. If you think I'm a soulless killer, then that's what you should do, right?" At her stunned silence, he barked, "Right?"

She held the gun limply in her hand, staring at it as if she had never seen one before, as if she did not know its function.

"Do it!"

She jumped.

Impatient, he grabbed her hand and forced her to point the gun at his chest, its barrel cold and hard against his heart. "Shoot me. I'm a monster, right? A soulless demon. You've said as much." He flexed his fingers over hers, bringing the barrel against his chest. When she tried to tug her hand away, he jabbed the gun against his flesh, digging the barrel in. "C'mon," he barked. "Make me pay, Kit. Maybe that will reverse your curse. Have you thought of that yet? Let's find out, eh?"

She blinked, and he realized she had not considered this possibility. "Maybe that's what it takes." He shrugged as if it were a small matter and not the end of his life they were discussing.

"Maybe. Kill the source of your curse and you'll be free. That's how it works with full-breed lycans, doesn't it?"

Suddenly pale, she nodded, mouth parted with words that would not come.

"Find out, then," he snarled, jerking her hand, tired of her denouncing him and hurling insults. The time had come for her to decide where they stood. He knew she wouldn't shoot him. He just needed her to realize it, too. Hopefully with that realization, others would come, too—such as her not really considering him on the same level as a full-breed lycan.

"Shoot me," he invited. "If I'm such a bad guy, shoot me, Kit."

A small, strangled sound escaped her mouth. Her fingers stretched wide, lifting off the gun. Still he held her hand, forcing her to hold the gun.

"No?" He shook his head. "Strange. I thought you were trained to kill monsters."

He turned his back on her. With rough, angry movements he dressed, noticing that she followed suit, moving slowly, head bowed, silent as death. He tossed her his keys.

She caught them with a fumble. Her forehead drew tight in confusion. "What are these for?"

"You want to leave?" he asked. "Go."

She would never accept his help. Accept him. He could try to teach her his ways, but she would fight him at every step—and hate him in the process. He saw that now. Saw that he had to release her.

"You're letting me go?" she whispered.

He crossed his arms over his chest. "That's what you want, isn't it? Your freedom." He waved to the door. "Go."

She moved toward the door, her steps a slow shuffle. "You're letting me go?" she repeated.

He nodded, resisting the urge to place himself between her and the door. He had to do this. For her.

Some of her spunk returned then. Lip curling over her teeth, she asked, "What? Is this some kind of trick?"

"No trick." He waved at the door again, the gesture mild, at odds with the emotions churning darkly through him. "Go on."

She opened the door wide, letting the early night inside the room. Chirping crickets sang out as she looked over her shoulder at him, a question still in her liquid-green eyes. Her lips worked, clearly searching for words. "Good-bye, then, Rafe."

"Good-bye." He nodded stiffly, the words thick as rocks filling his mouth and throat—and just about as unsavory. "Take care of yourself, Kit. Because I won't be there to look out for you."

Color spotted her cheeks. "I don't need you covering me." Her chin lifted higher. "I don't need you at all."

Then she was gone.

Without shutting the door, she hurried down the porch steps, skirting the dead lycans and vanishing into the deepening night.

He listened, following her movements, the light fall of her feet on the ground as she walked, forcing himself to stand still, to not go after her. His hands clenched into fists, fingernails digging into his palms.

A door slammed shut. The Hummer's engine purred to life. Rock and gravel crunched beneath rolling tires, the rumble of the engine fading as she drove away.

Into certain danger. And out of his life.

# 27

K it. This is unexpected. I thought you'd be in New Mexico by now. Shopping for turquoise or horseback riding or . . . something," Darius murmured with deceptive laziness. Only the sharp glitter of his pewter gaze sliding over her told a different story.

Something dark and menacing lurked in his eyes as he surveyed her from head to toe with languid slowness, crossing strong arms over his broad chest. Deceptive indeed. *Languid* was a word that could not be applied to him. He reminded her of a coiled snake hidden in tall grass. A secret killer.

With her newly honed senses, she could almost *smell* how dangerous he was, how capable of destruction. The hair at her nape prickled. She was abruptly reminded that he was alleged to have killed Étienne Marshan. True or not, it would take a lycan of extraordinary power to kill the world's first lycan.

Sliding her hand in her pocket, she caressed her mother's necklace, gaining strength from the feel of it. Perhaps unwise, but she had returned to the motel Rafe had taken her from the night the lycans attacked and retrieved the cross before heading to Houston. She had to. Feeling it close gave her courage now.

She had also called Gideon and assured him she would meet him in New Mexico at the end of the week. Once there, she would explain everything to him. Once she spoke with Darius to see if there were some way out of the mess her life had become. In person. Not over the phone.

Kit stopped in the center of the vast sunken living room and glanced around at the expensive furniture and art framing the walls. She didn't need to know anything about art to know they were all priceless works. And old. No doubt as old as the lycan himself, who lived in Houston's high-end River Oaks. Darius had probably known the artists.

Her thoughts drifted to Rafe. Was he accustomed to such finery? The gulf separating them yawned ever farther, convincing her she had done the right thing by leaving. Even if he had turned her into a creature like him, she was nothing like him. On any level. She never would be.

She'd never been to Darius's home before. Wouldn't have dreamed of accompanying Gideon or Claire on their visits to evaluate the progress of his research. But she knew where he lived, had made it a point to find out. If he ever fell off the wagon, she wanted to know where to find him.

Again Darius's rich, formal tones rumbled over the air, reminding her that she had not answered him. "Kit?"

She tore her gaze from an elaborate tapestry hanging on the wall.

He did not look as she had remembered him. Oh, he still seemed dangerous, still had the appearance of a caged predator. But his chilly pewter gaze did not illicit the usual feelings of hatred in her. For the first time, she felt pity for him, a tormented soul with no say in his damnation.

She dragged a deep breath into her lungs and looked away from his harshly handsome face, accepting the sudden glaring truth. She had changed. In more ways than one. Why else would she be here? Seeking help? From the one person whose help she had stubbornly refused in the past. Even when Gideon had always insisted that Darius could teach her more about lycans, teach her to be a better hunter.

"What's happened?" He frowned, those eerie eyes narrowing on her. "I thought you were leaving town? What are you doing here?" His nostrils flared ever so slightly, and he took a step closer. She heard him inhale, drawing in her scent. His eyes seemed to glow brighter. Her stomach quivered, her response primal, unwanted as he took yet another step closer, an encroaching wall of heat, overwhelming her with his nearness. "What's happened to *you*?"

She shivered and pulled back her shoulders, alarmed that he would immediately be able to sense that she had changed, that she was different. The fault must lie with her. With her inability to camouflage herself. She winced. No doubt one of the many things Rafe had insisted she needed to learn.

She picked up a bronzed figurine of an armored knight from a side table. She turned it over in her palm. It looked very old, the details blunted from age. "What do you mean?"

"Something's different. *You're* different."

She set the figurine down and looked directly into his silvery gaze, lifting her chin. "Tell me about the Marshan Prophecy? About dovenatus?"

For a moment, the hard mask of his face cracked. Surprise flickered across the hard lines of his face, a muscle feathering in his square jaw an instant before the mask fell back into place again. "How did you hear of that? Who told you?"

She crossed her arms and cocked a brow, waiting for him to put his finger on what precisely was *different* about her.

It did not take him long.

He slowly looked her up and down. "You?" he demanded. His silver eyes drilled into her. "How can that be?"

"Apparently I descend from the Marshan line. I'm one of the *lucky* females EFLA is determined to eliminate."

He nodded slowly. "I see. You're a descendant of Étienne Marshan." He searched her face, and she wondered if he saw a resemblance to the lycan he had allegedly killed.

She shrugged. "Or rather, Christophe Marshan."

He nodded. "Now it makes sense why they want you dead so very badly."

She felt her features twist with bitterness. "Apparently the prophecy that has everyone gunning for me has already come to pass. Hybrids have been alive and roaming around for over a century." She laughed mirthlessly and dropped onto a buttery brown leather couch. "I'm a dovenatu. But by no means the first one."

"Dovenatus already exist?"

"Yes. Two brothers. Twins. Their mother was attacked by a lycan over a century ago in a small village in Spain."

"These brothers. You've met them?" Darius sat across from her on the ottoman, his large shoulders tensing beneath the black linen of his shirt. "You know where they are?"

She thought of the last time she had seen Rafe, his face hard, his dark eyes remote. As much as she swore to detest him for all he had done to her, the image would stay with her until the day she died—along with his taste, the feel of his lips on hers, the memory of them together, the sensation of his hard body over her, in her . . .

She brushed her fingers against her mouth as if she felt him there.

Shaking her head, she dropped her hand from her lips. "I've met only one of them, the one that turned me. His name is Rafe Santiago. The brother is in Europe somewhere."

Darius rubbed the hard line of his jaw. "Do you realize what this could mean?" He motioned behind him. "He may possess the answers I need. A blood sample from him—and you—and we may be able to create a genetic history."

"A blood sample," she muttered. Darius didn't want to help her. He only wanted to use her. *Screw him.*

He leaned forward on the ottoman eagerly. "Where is he?"

She opened her mouth to snap at him that there were no answers, no solutions to his quest to reverse the curse and regain his soul, but then she stopped herself. Wasn't she hoping to do the same? Return to herself? Reverse what Rafe had done to her?

His silvery gaze fastened on her. "You must meet with Dr. Howard."

"Who?"

"The geneticist I've hired to conduct research." At her mulling silence, he continued, "This Rafe Santiago has given you a great gift, Kit."

"A gift?" Her spine shot ramrod straight. He'd lied to her, held her captive, then freed her as if he couldn't stomach the sight of her. "To be like you? Cursed?"

His expression grew grim, the skin stretching tight along the hard lines of his face. "Still pig-headed, I see. Unwilling to change, to learn."

She breathed thinly through her nose. His words stung. It was the same song. She'd heard it on more than one occasion from Cooper. From Gideon and Claire, when she had refused to give Darius a chance.

*From Rafe.*

"You're hardly cursed," he continued. "You still keep your soul . . . and live in the light. Not darkness."

Something in his voice, in the hard mask of his face, shook her. For a moment, she glimpsed the darkness he spoke of, the darkness that dragged him down every second of every day, weighing every breath he took. How many souls had he killed over the centuries? Did each one haunt him still?

Not liking the realizations she was reaching, or the way she was beginning to feel sorry for him, she turned and started to walk from the room, calling over her shoulder, "Forget I came here."

Before she knew it, Darius stood before her, having whipped past her in a blur her eyes could hardly register.

His eyes glittered as hard as ice. "It's time you hear a few hard truths."

"From you?" she demanded, snorting. Hot, familiar rage swept over her, heating first her face and neck, then spreading down through the rest of her. "How about I tell you a few hard truths instead?"

His face revealed nothing. Such calm irked her. He was the monster. Why should he appear so unaffected when her emotions raged out of control?

"You're a murderer, Darius. No matter how long it has been since you've killed." She gestured wildly, knowing his research lab lurked somewhere in his spotless mansion. "All your research, all the Caltech scientists you buy can't save you. No antidote will ever give you back your soul." Her chest heaved by the time she'd finished speaking.

He still did not move, did not speak. A damned pillar of stone.

Her heart hammered wildly in her chest. Blood rushed in her ears as loudly as cars speeding on an interstate. She forced her chin up and held his hard stare.

"Why are you here, Kit?" he asked at last. "Why did you come?"

"I don't know." Her voice came out a choked whisper. "I thought you could help me."

"Hybrids are an entirely different species, even if some genetic traits tend to be the same. You're not ruled by the moon or a need to feed. You can shift at will. Why not accept that you are a dove-natu and—"

She shook her head even as she thought of the last time she'd shifted. The sensation of her body stretching, twisting, tearing in pain. The terror of losing control. Losing herself.

She hadn't willed it. She had simply been too furious to stop it. Rafe had talked her through it, the warm whisper of his voice leading her past the red haze of her rage until she felt herself returning to normal, but she had left him. Her stomach churned, knotting tightly, and suddenly she feared she would be sick.

"Is it really so bad?" Darius's voice slid over her quietly, seductive as the drag of silk. "Why not embrace what you are?"

"What's good about it?" she retorted, heat swarming her face. She pounded a hand against her chest. "I'm not *me*! Not human."

Darius's mouth twisted cruelly. "What did being human ever get you, Kit?"

She flinched as he stepped nearer, cringing as he inhaled near her cheek. His dark scent swirled around her. "I can smell him on you, this dovenatu. His scent is all over you. You belong to him now. What are you doing here?"

She gasped, her feminist hackles quivering with indignation.

"He belongs to you, too," he added, as though reading her mind.

She stared at Darius, his words shocking and thrilling her in some buried, primal way.

He stepped back, jaw locked and resolute. "I'm sorry, but I can't help you."

"You're not sorry."

"If I were you, I would find Rafe Santiago again. You need him right now." He cocked his dark head, blue-black strands of hair brushing his massive shoulders. "But then, you know that already."

*Need him.* His words burned her up, fueled her anger. They were the same words Rafe had used.

"Well, you're not me," she snapped, loathing that she recognized a truth in all he had said.

Stepping around him, she stormed from the living room, stalking over the limestone foyer and out the front door, wondering if leaving Rafe, walking away from him, might have been the biggest mistake of her life.

# 28

Kit sat behind the Hummer's wheel, the leather vibrating against her palms as she drove. The lights of oncoming traffic blurred before her. She swiped a hand at her burning eyes, refusing to let tears fall. *Damn.*

There must be some explanation for the sob that scalded the back of her throat. A side effect from her unwelcome transformation? Could Rafe's turning her have truly bonded her to him? Something had to explain the loss she felt inside, the dull ache in her chest. *Something.* Anything except that she actually cared for him.

The likelihood of that very thing shook her.

*She missed Rafe.* Propping her elbow on the armrest of the driver's-side door, she shook her head. It made no sense. She missed the very thing she fought. A man who lied to her and chained her to a bed. The only one, she now realized—she now accepted—who could help her. She trusted him. Another word rose in her mind, a nagging whisper.

Her mind shied from the word, but it was there, a shadow in the far corners of her mind.

Whipping across two lanes, she exited the freeway. Heading into the familiar. The loud, boisterous din where she always managed to drown out the world and forget the void in her own life.

Right now, forgetting seemed a good idea. It didn't even faze her where she was headed, or that EFLA or lycans might also be there. In her mood, she relished the idea of a good fight.

Two hours later, and too many shots of Crown to count, she realized she wasn't the least bit drunk. Not even buzzed. Apparently another consequence of her new dovenatu status. That and her ultra-sensitive nose. The hot stink of too many bodies overwhelmed her.

Gus poured her another shot from behind the bar. "What's eating you, babe?"

Kit shook her head and slammed another shot. "Nothing."

"Only two reasons a woman goes drinking alone," Gus volunteered over the heavy thrum of voices.

She nearly snarled when someone bumped into her, sloshing the amber liquid in her glass onto her fingers. Repositioning herself atop her stool, she downed the drink and slid her glass across the bar's sticky surface, muttering, "Lay it on me."

"Well." Gus shrugged a well-muscled shoulder. "A: because she's alone. No woman ever wants to be alone." He held up a broad palm as if he thought she was going to object. "I don't care what feminists say."

Kit's brow winged up at that. Despite Gus's chauvinistic attitude, the middle-aged biker had always been good to her— covering for her when she was late, picking up shifts when she couldn't make it in, even loaning her money a time or two when she came up short at month's end.

"Or B," Gus continued, "because she's got a man, only he's a no-good loser she'd be better off without." Gus shook his bald head. "Which is it, babe? You seeing someone?" He snorted. "Not Dan, I know. Last time I ever set you up." Gus poured another shot. With a quick glance around to make sure the owner wasn't looking, he slammed it back. With a smacking sigh, he added, "Milly stopped baking me those magic cookie bars of hers because you stood up her precious son." He patted the belly pushing against his Harley T-shirt. "Lost five pounds already."

*Dan.* Kit had almost forgotten about him. No surprise, considering the man who had filled her life—her world—of late. She hopped off the stool, suddenly accepting that Gus's particular brand of philosophy wasn't making her feel any better. "Thanks, but I'm outta here."

"Hey, you okay to drive?"

Kit smiled grimly, not the least affected from the half-dozen or so shots. Unfortunately. She wouldn't mind the dulling influence of alcohol right now. "Sure."

Gus eyed her dubiously. Kit stared back.

With a slow nod, he asked, "When you coming back to work?"

"I don't know." Her appearance tonight would no doubt make the rounds. If she didn't call in for a shift soon, the manager would fire her. But Kit couldn't summon a shred of worry. Her job was the least of her concerns now. Gideon was expecting her in New Mexico. And considering she didn't know how to find Rafe . . . if, in fact, that is what she wished to do, she had no clue where he'd made off to.

"Night," she called, diving through the Friday night crush, squeezing her way to the back door, the quickest exit. Kid Rock reverberated all around her, rattling her bones.

With a grateful sigh, she broke free, the scarred steel door thudding shut behind her, stifling the din. Inhaling the night's warm, smoke-free air, she burrowed her hands into her jeans pockets and rounded the building, walking through the parking lot toward Rafe's Hummer, the black hood gleaming beneath the clear, moonlit night.

The rush of cars on the nearby highway hummed like a drone of bees in the distance. Other sounds penetrated. The faint buzz of an airplane in the distance. A passing car, the bass throbbing on the air.

Gradually, more noises rose, eclipsing the others. Even if they were not as loud.

Skin tingling, she stopped and listened, identifying the sounds. The scuffling of feet on loose gravel. The sharp cries of someone in distress. Her hand balled into a fist in her pocket.

She resumed walking, her pace increasing. She followed the faint sounds, passing her own car. Feet crunching over asphalt, she exited the parking lot, skipping across the street.

Her skin tightened, stinging with keen, primal awareness as a woman's voice reached her.

*Stop! God, stop—no, no, no, no.*

Sliding her hand from her pocket, she broke into a run. Arms pumping at her sides, she crossed a railroad track, hauling ass through a vacant lot with weeds as high as her knees.

Her senses sharpened, guiding her. No thought entered her mind. Instinct—pure, darkly primitive—drove her.

The sounds became more distinct. The woman's wrenching cries for mercy echoed through her head, joined by rough, snarling laughter.

Something strange tickled the inside of her nose. The faint odor burned, stung like a foul chemical.

*Fear.* Thin and stinging. A definite smell.

Saliva pooled in her mouth. Her nostrils twitched, flared, catching another scent. Familiar. Heavy as sweat, as smoke drifting on air. *Lycans.*

She vaulted a chain-link fence, dropping lightly to the pavement in a crouching position, fingers brushing the ground. She was close now.

Pausing, she straightened, smelling the air before proceeding, her feet light, skimming the ground as she ran into an area consisting of warehouses and run-down commercial office space. Buildings whipped past in a blur, their windows watchful, blackened eye sockets. Hot wind singed her cheeks. Scattered perimeter lights cast the drab buildings a hellish red—fitting, considering the demons who prowled close at hand, torturing the night's chosen victim.

Her senses guided her, an invisible hand leading to the unfortunate soul. She found the creatures between two buildings. The victim was pinned down on broken asphalt, surrounded by ramshackle crates that smelled of mildew and rot.

Kit counted five. More than she had ever faced alone. She slid her gun free just as they lifted their heads, catching her scent on the breezeless night.

Two of them removed themselves from their tight circle, lips peeling back in cruel smiles. She braced her legs apart, muscles coiling in readiness.

The other three lowered their heads and continued their assault on the female who thrashed beneath them as uselessly as a bug.

"Come to join the party?" one asked Kit, silver eyes roaming her from head to foot as he approached in a loose-legged amble.

She lifted her chin. "Bring it," she bit out, the low, guttural sound of her voice strange to her ears.

They sprang in unison, flying through the air.

She held her gun in her hand and was firing before she even realized she had pulled the weapon.

One lycan dropped. The scent of his blood, acrid as cordite, singed her nose.

She fired at the second beast.

He fell, clawing his chest, blood pouring freely from the wound.

The coppery taste of fresh blood floated on the air, curling around her like tendrils of poison gas. She compressed her lips, trying to seal herself off from the noxious taste.

"She's the hunter! The one!"

Two more flung themselves off their victim, charging Kit, eyes silver flames in the dim alley, testimony to their animal fury. Only one remained over the woman, slave to his savage lust as he worked her over.

They moved in on Kit quickly, using all their considerable strength and speed. Still, it took no time for her to aim and squeeze off two more rounds.

They were falling through the air, the last one not yet hitting the ground, and she was moving, pouncing on the remaining one and wrapping her arms around his neck in a ruthless grasp.

Blood rushed her veins, the pump of adrenaline making her heart pound harder. A dull roar filled her ears. The lycan thrashed, trying to throw her off him. Still, she held on, nails digging, tearing into his flesh. He howled an ungodly shriek.

The lycan's victim opened her mouth wide on a scream. Gazing at Kit, she stumbled to her feet, holding the tattered fragments of her dress over herself. And Kit knew. Knew what she saw. Knew what terrified her.

She was in full form. She likely looked as Rafe had with his face transformed into sharp lines and angles. Almost feline in appearance. Not human. But not lycan, a voice whispered. Better. Stronger.

Power surged through her like an electrical current. She knew she could rip this lycan apart. But that would be plain savagery—a dark side to herself she did not ever want to unleash.

She released him, and he dropped like a sack of grain, moaning and clutching the bloody scratches scoring his neck.

Like a rabid dog, he needed killing. Not the butchery of a savage attack. And only silver could do that.

The woman whimpered and huddled against the wall of the

building. Her face was badly beaten, one eye swollen shut, her nose crushed, blood seeping from her nostrils and sliding down into her mouth. "Don't hurt me," she choked, staggering to her feet. Sidling close to the wall of the building, she stumbled over crates and garbage, fleeing.

Kit didn't stop her, had no wish to frighten her more.

Returning her attention to the lycan, she picked up her gun.

With one hand pressed to the swiftly regenerating flesh at his neck and the other hand clawing the ground, trying to crawl away, he spat out, "What are you?"

She lifted her arm, a great feeling of peace sweeping over her. The tide of animal fury ebbed, subsided. She felt herself returning, the beast receding to its cave within her. "*Not you,*" she said, firing, forever stilling the lycan.

Elation swelled inside her. She had killed five lycans without breaking a sweat. Five beasts she would not even have detected if not for her newly turned self.

Human life had been saved. Because Kit had been there, been able to help in a way she never could before. Because she was a dovenatu.

Because of Rafe.

Suddenly she felt herself smile. A great lightness rolled through her, chasing away the cloying darkness that she had permitted to shadow her heart. Myriad emotions washed over her. Relief, gratitude . . . shame.

A tremble snaked through her as she recalled all the horrible things she had said to Rafe before leaving him. She fought to swallow the sudden bitterness coating her mouth.

Her eyes shut in a pained blink. Slowly, she shook her head from side to side. Her knees suddenly felt weak, too weak for her to stand. She dropped to a boneless pile, the smack of her knees a loud crack on the asphalt.

"Rafe," she whispered to the night, knowing in that moment that the nagging ache in her chest was for him. It had nothing to do with her physical transformation and everything to do with *him*.

She rested her forehead in her palm. *Idiot.* She had said and done everything in her power to push him away. *Are you no more than an animal?*

Why should he have wanted her around anymore? No wonder he had tossed her his keys and told her to hit the road. She'd been stubborn, at times cruel. She dragged a hand over her face, wishing she could take it all back, wishing she could see him again.

"Kit."

Her head snapped up. A large, dark shadow stood at the mouth of the alley, still as stone, frozen, and yet there was something in his stance. Her nostrils flared as his scent came to her. She would have known him anywhere. In the darkest of nights, in the most packed crowds, her nose would find him, her heart would know him.

"Rafe!" She exploded off the ground and launched herself across the distance separating them. He still didn't move, not even when she flung herself against him, wrapping her arms around his lean waist. "Rafe, what are you doing here?"

"You didn't think you'd seen the last of me, did you? You know me better than that."

She pulled back to stare into his dark eyes. Their dark depths stared down at her intently, the lights banked at the centers. "You've been with me all along? All this time?"

He moved then, one hand brushing her cheek. "I couldn't let you leave without knowing you'd be safe."

She dropped her face back to the warm wall of his chest, inhaling the scent that had become as familiar as her own.

He had never left her. Her chest tightened. She'd been such an ass, and he had never left her.

His voice rumbled in her ear. "I had to be sure you could handle yourself." He drew a shuddering breath. "Now I am."

She lifted her head, suddenly uneasy. "Rafe?"

"More important, now you can be sure you can handle yourself. Never doubt that, Kit."

"Rafe, what are you saying?"

His hand fell lightly against the back of her head. "You're strong. Stronger than me. I was born to this, and it took years for me to gain full control over myself." His fingers flexed over her hair, and his breath turned to a soft hiss. "You'll never lose control."

She nodded, knowing she could continue hunting, could make a real difference now. Could save lives that she never could before. "I know I won't, but why does this sound like good-bye?"

With a sigh, he set her from him, his hand sliding from her head. His dark eyes scanned her face intently, as if memorizing it, branding it in his head. An uneasy feeling began to root in her gut, intensifying as he said, "Because it is. You don't need me. I told myself you did in order to try to keep you for myself. I won't be that selfish. Good-bye, Kit."

Coldness washed through her. She shivered in the humid night. "Rafe, *no*."

"I watched you." His lips curved in a humorless smile. "I saw you." He nodded. "You were good. Very good. You can handle yourself."

She snatched his arm. "I—" What would she say? That she didn't want to do this alone. That she was sick to death of being alone. That she could not face the stretch of time, the generations yawning before her like that. Alone. Without him.

She decided on the truth. "I need you." The words spilled from her mouth in a burning rush.

He shook his head. Slowly. Regretfully. "No, Kit."

She dug her fingers into his arms, determined to convince him. "Yes."

Standing on tiptoe, she pressed her mouth to his in a crushing, desperate kiss. She splayed herself against him, rubbing her breasts to his chest. Touching, tasting . . . loving.

"Please, Rafe." Her voice broke on his name.

With a groan, he finally surrendered, delving his hands through her hair. Blood pounded in her veins, urgent and hard as he slipped his tongue inside her mouth. She whimpered, struggling to get closer, suspecting she would never be close enough.

This, she realized with a jolt, was what it felt like to love a man. To feel a deep connection with another soul. The very thing she had spent her life craving.

She wasn't about to let it slip from her fingers.

# 29

With a groan, he wrenched Kit from him, holding her back, with his hands braced hard on her shoulders.

"No," he panted, the word a hard bite on the air.

"Yes," she gasped, straining to return to his arms. It took considerable effort to keep her at arm's length. "You were right, Rafe. We do belong together. You turned me. We're both dovenatu—"

"No," he ground out, dropping his hands from her shoulders as if the feel of her burned him. "That's no reason."

He turned from her and began to walk away, his pace quick and fierce, heading back down the alley. She followed him. "You've been through a lot, Kit. You only *think* you have to settle for me. Because we're alike. Because it's easy. Because aside from my brother, a continent away, we're the only two dovenatus alive."

"That's not why," she insisted, following him across a street. With a strangled, mirthless laugh, she added, "And nothing about us has been easy."

"I admit it makes sense," he agreed as though he had not heard her. "We're both dovenatus. No one has to watch the other wither and die. We're the same species, for God's sake. But we shouldn't be together because it *makes sense*. I realize that now."

Coldness washed over her. Could he be saying he didn't *want* to be with her? "Of course not."

"But two people should decide to spend their lives together based on more than convenience. Not because I'm a dovenatu. Not because I turned you into one." He cut her a swift glance. "They should love one another."

She made a choking, strangling sound.

Didn't he know she loved him? Couldn't he look at her now and see it in her face? Feel it when she kissed him? Did she come across as a woman who didn't know her own mind? Who gave her heart so easily?

He shook his head, his voice final, dark as the night surrounding them. "Our lives are too long to suffer them with regrets."

"Our lives are too long not to give this a try. To give *us* a try."

The line of his jaw hardened. "You don't know what you're saying."

She worked to keep up with his fast pace. "I don't want to live without you, Rafe."

"You're just scared, Kit."

She let loose a laugh. "When have I ever been afraid?"

He halted before her, his gaze probing, searching. "Ever since I met you. Your tough-girl act never fooled me. You'll always be that little girl who watched her mother turn into a monster and devour her father."

Like salt to an open wound, she flinched.

She opened her mouth to hotly deny the charge, then swallowed hard. He was right. She had always been afraid. Afraid that revenge would consume her life. To the exclusion of all else. But not anymore.

"You're right. I'm still that little girl. I'm still afraid," she confessed with a lift of her chin. Heavy metal music played in the distance, a dull throb in the night. "More than I've ever been. But I'm not afraid of the same thing anymore." Thirst for revenge didn't poison her anymore.

He arched a dark brow, waiting.

She still had fears. But they had changed.

More terrifying than living out her life alone with only revenge as a companion, was living it without Rafe.

She exhaled through her nose, peering over the dark outline of Rafe's shoulder. The bar's yellow neon lights gleamed ahead of them. Would he leave her now, convinced she didn't love him?

Rafe was the one. She could not let him walk away.

"I'm scared of losing the man I love. You."

)) ) ● ( ( (

Now Rafe knew what he had craved through the long years. Without even knowing he craved *anything*, he had craved this: *Her.*

It was torture. She was saying everything he wanted to hear. That they could be together. Life mates in the truest sense. If only she meant it. If only he could buy into the dream of it all.

Because it was a dream. A dream that she could love him. After so many years, he had found a woman to love who loved him back. A woman who wouldn't age, sicken, and die in what amounted to only a blink of time for him. Someone who could live through the years by his side. Someone he had loved from almost the first moment he saw her. He couldn't be that fortunate.

He had deceived her, turned her against her will, trapped her. He would not trap her a second time. Would not let her settle for him because he was her only choice.

He recovered his voice, fought for the distance his heart screamed against. "I still wouldn't recommend you sticking around

Houston. You might be stronger than before, but you're not invincible. And everyone's after you—EFLA, NODEAL, the packs. Start over someplace else." He ignored the frustrated shaking of her head and continued, "Take a new identity—"

"Kit!"

They both swung around at the sound of her name. Rafe pulled her behind him, instinctively shielding her with his body at the approach of a scowling man.

"Gideon!" Kit rushed past Rafe and flung herself into her brother's arms. "I told you I would meet you—"

"I decided to come anyway. Kit, what's going on? I've been out of my mind." He glanced toward the bar. "What are you doing here? You can't be working."

"I'm planning to leave town, but . . ." Her voice faded and she looked to Rafe, uncertainty flickering in her green gaze.

Gideon followed her gaze. Even in the dark, Rafe easily noted the narrowing of his eyes, the tightening of his hand on his sister's shoulder. "Who is this?"

"This is Rafe. Rafe Santiago." She tugged her brother closer, her small hand disappearing inside his larger one as she led him toward Rafe.

Lean and tall, with Kit's same dark blond hair, Gideon March was a formidable man. He shifted a wary gaze from Rafe to his sister. "Who is this guy?"

Biting her lip, she sent Rafe a searching look, muttering, "It's complicated."

Rafe dragged a hand through his hair. Logic told him to leave, to let Kit explain everything to her brother. She didn't need him around to do that. Instead he heard himself say, "Let's go someplace and talk."

Kit nodded eagerly and looked back to Gideon. "Let's go to Grandmother's house."

Even as Gideon nodded, the expression he turned on Rafe was no less distrustful. "All right. Let's go."

The three departed, moving to their separate vehicles. Sitting behind the wheel of the car he had purchased outside Austin, Rafe flexed his hands over the leather and told himself he should just drive away, leave Kit for good no matter what he had just said. A clean break.

She would be fine now. And yet he found himself pulling out of the parking lot and falling behind the Hummer. Following her. Temporarily, he swore. Then he would leave.

Because it was the right thing to do. Even if his blood burned dark with the impulse to claim her, to keep her with him for all time. He would let her go.

The house was dark when they pulled up. From Kit's file, he knew her grandmother busied herself outside of the home—knitting circles, bunko, antiques collecting.

The three of them entered the house from the back door. Kit flipped on the lights, and Rafe followed the siblings into the living room.

Kit sat down on the sofa, rubbing her palms over the top of her thighs as if suddenly cold. "It's complicated, Gid."

"You said that already."

Rafe leaned against the arched doorjamb and crossed his arms. She glanced his way. He nodded encouragingly.

"I don't know where to begin." She pressed her fingers to her lips with a muttered curse.

"Start talking, Kit."

She shook her head, her words muffled against her fingers. Dropping her hand, she asked, "Did Cooper ever tell you about the Marshan Prophecy?"

Gideon shook his head, releasing a heavy sigh. "Look, I've just driven across the state without stopping because I was convinced you were in danger. I left my wife in a cabin by herself in the middle of nowhere. Start making some sense."

She nodded, suddenly looking pale—and Rafe understood. In that moment, it all became clear to him. She was worried about her brother's reaction, his acceptance of her. Would he look at her as she looked at herself—at *him*—when he first explained the truth to her?

She straightened her spine and clenched her hands together, looking so much like a soldier facing battle that his chest grew tight.

"Basically it boils down to one thing, Gid. I'm a hybrid lycan. A dovenatu." She gave a small, rolling nod. "We both descend from the world's first lycan . . . well, *before* he became a lycan. We descend from his son, Christophe Marshan."

Gideon stared at her in silence, still as stone.

"A dovenatu isn't anything like a full-fledged lycan," Rafe felt the need to volunteer. "They share many of the same powers, but bloodlust doesn't rule them. They're not evil. Or at least they don't have to be."

"Wait a minute." Gideon pressed his fingers to his temple as if suffering a sudden headache. He snapped his gaze to Rafe, his green eyes as hard as polished malachite. "First things first, who the hell are you?"

Rafe tightened his lips, knowing this wasn't going to go over well. If Kit were his sister, he sure as hell wouldn't like what he was hearing. Especially Rafe's role in it all.

Kit answered. "He's a dovenatu, too." She paused. Gideon pinned Rafe with a reproachful, suspicious stare. "He's the one that turned me."

Gideon's eyebrows winged higher. "That right?" He took a menacing step toward Rafe. "You turned my sister into some kind of half-breed lycan?"

Kit stepped forward, grabbing his arm. "He saved my life, Gid.

I was dying. If he hadn't turned me, I would be dead now. You should be thanking him."

Gideon looked down at his sister, an angry muscle rippling the skin of his jaw.

"Understand? He saved my life." Her throat worked as she swallowed. Green eyes scanning Gideon's face, she added. "And I love him."

Despite himself, something loosened inside Rafe at her words. He suspected he would never tire of hearing her say that. His chest expanded and he felt a great releasing of himself into the night, a sense of joy he had never known.

Suddenly the hairs on Rafe's neck prickled with awareness, ending his euphoria as effectively as a douse of cold water.

Uncrossing his arms, he spun around, muscles coiling tight in readiness. His nostrils flared, sensing the newcomer to their circle before he revealed himself.

An older, vaguely familiar man stepped into the room, a gun gripped in his hand. Easing away from the threshold, Rafe took several slow steps back, putting himself between the gun and Kit. Even if a bullet couldn't kill her, it would hurt. And he would save her from that pain.

"Jack," Kit exclaimed, trying to step around Rafe.

Rafe blocked her, his mind working, recalling from his review of her file that the grandmother had a boyfriend named Jack.

"Looks like I just hit the jackpot," Jack said. Nodding happily, he let his gaze fall on Kit. "The prophecy comes to life, eh?" He waved his gun up and down. "Good thing I'm packing silver."

*Silver.* Rafe's gaze narrowed on the gun's unwavering barrel, bitter rage rising high in his throat, threatening to choke him. He had no idea if silver could kill either one of them, if that was one characteristic he and Kit shared with their distant lycan brethren. He and Sebastian had never risked finding out.

Hoping to divert his attention, he asked, "So who are you, really?"

"My name is Jack. But Burnett's the last name. I used to work for NODEAL. Boston division. Years ago. Recently EFLA hired me as an undercover operative."

"What are you doing dating my grandmother?" Gideon asked, inching away from Kit and Rafe and closer to Jack.

"Stop," Jack barked. "Stay right there."

Gideon stopped.

Jack swept all of them with his gun. "Getting rid of you three should get me a nice promotion." A determined light gleamed in his eyes.

Gideon shook his head as if he could not believe it and began moving again, slowly. "But Grandma met you at that retirement community . . ."

"Do you know a better way to infiltrate? Dating that hag was genius on my part. No better way to learn about NODEAL's rogue lycan hunters." He took the last step toward Gideon, jabbing the gun close to his face.

Rafe tightened his hand on Kit. He had seen men on the edge before, in the First World War. Burnett had that same wild look about him.

Kit made a small sound of distress and tried to step around Rafe. He held her back.

"I can't believe you're still touted as NODEAL's best." Jack shook his head, glaring at Gideon. "Where's the sense in that? You're the traitor. You befriended one of the most monstrous lycans the world has ever known."

"Étienne Marshan was hunted down and destroyed years ago," Rafe inserted.

"Not him. Darius." Jack's lips curled as if he hurled an epithet.

A guarded look came over Gideon's face. "What are you talking about?"

"Don't deny it! I've learned a lot about you in the last year. I know you've allied yourselves with Darius." He buried the barrel of his gun into Gideon's cheek.

"It made more sense to let him live. He isn't a danger—"

"Are you listening to yourself?" Jack's face screwed tight with disgust. "Just shut the hell up."

"Jack," Kit spoke from behind Rafe, her voice soft and desperate. "Please put the gun down. You don't want to shoot us."

"On the contrary." He swung back around, and Rafe tensed, adrenaline spiking through him at the grinding click of the gun's hammer. "It's been a challenge this last year. EFLA ordered me to only gather information, but how I longed to put an end to all of you."

Rafe growled, the sound welling up from deep in the pit of his stomach. Kit squeezed his arm, staying his impulse to lunge at Jack. He glanced back at her, letting the sight of her face infuse him with calm.

"Jack," she continued, her hand stroking the necklace at her neck. "I know you cared about me—"

"Do you?" One corner of Jack's mouth lifted in a cruel smirk. "Gullible girl. That necklace there at your throat has allowed me to track you. Nothing more. You think I gave a shit about you? I needed to know what you were up to."

"What?" Angry fire lit her cheeks.

Rafe cursed under his breath. She was wearing the tracking device. Now he knew why every time they turned around some agent or lycan was in their faces. Jack had planted the device on Kit and fed the information to EFLA.

Kit snatched the necklace from her throat and flung it to the floor. "All the time I've been wearing this . . ."

"It was especially useful when you bailed town. I promised Laurent I would bring you down." His gaze slid to Rafe. "You're a bonus I

hadn't counted on. It seems his doubts about you were well founded."
He leveled the gun at Rafe's chest, eyes narrowing with deadly intent.
"They'll probably give me Cooper's job for killing you."

"Jack, no!"

Kit shoved Rafe hard, her newfound strength catching him off
guard.

He stumbled to the side, leaving her exposed, open for the shot
intended for him.

Everything slowed.

He watched the scene as though outside of himself. Saw himself stumbling, trying to right himself and turn. Trying to grab Kit
and pull her down. Heard the echo of his own cry.

The sound of the gun punched the air, an explosion in his head.
The force of the bullet propelled Kit back, knocking her off her
feet, launching her through the air. He groped wind, trying to grab
her, narrowly missing her arm.

He fell hard on his knees beside her. He caught her up in his
arms, clutching her tightly, pushing his palm at the gushing wound
on her shoulder. *No, no, no, no, no . . .*

The bullet hadn't struck a fatal area, but then it didn't have to.
Not if she possessed the same deadly allergy to silver that lycans did.

Blood, thick and warm, ran through his fingers, swift as water
spilling from a fountain. He pressed harder, determined to stop the
bleeding, determined that she live. Déjà vu washed over him. He'd
saved her before. He would again. He had to.

Gradually, another sound penetrated. Low and keening, persistent as the tolling of a death knell.

It was him, he realized. Mourning his life mate, the one intended for him. The only one there would ever be. All these years,
he had been waiting for her. Had found her, led by some strange
force. He saw that now. Understood. Kit was his destiny, and he'd
been foolish enough to think he could walk away from her.

"Why, Kit?" He smoothed a bloody hand over her forehead, rocking her in his arms.

He dimly registered the sounds of scuffling—splintering furniture and shouting. Another shot rang out.

Then Gideon was there, roaring in his face. "Let's go! C'mon! We have to get her help!"

He growled and swiped savagely at the hand trying to pull Kit from him.

"Listen, asshole, she's my sister! Let her go!"

His eyes clashed with Gideon March's hard, glittering gaze. Still he clung, physically unable to release her from his desperate hold. In some strange way, he felt releasing her would be tantamount to letting her die. As though he alone stood between her and death.

Kit's brother pointed a gun in his face. "Do you want to save her or not?"

Nodding, he snapped out of his stupor, even as he wondered how they could possibly help her. Last time, instinct had shown him what to do. Not now. Now . . .

Nothing. Nothing occurred to him.

Sweeping her up in his arms, he strode from the living room, without sparing a glance for the corpse he was stepping over. "Where are we taking her?"

Gideon, face drawn tight with anxiety, hurried past Rafe to get the door. "To the only one who may be able to help her."

◐ ◑ ◒ ● ◓ ◔ ◕

Voices ricocheted around Kit like flying bullets. Hard-edged, biting commands.

"Rafe," she whimpered, her blurred vision settling on a dark-haired hazy face above her. She inhaled, recognizing at once his musky scent, and tried to lift her hand.

Burning pain throbbed in her chest, spreading outward over her entire body. She cried out, dropping her arm.

She'd been shot. Jack had shot her. With a silver bullet.

Her veins constricted, seizing as though trying to stop the flow of poison through her blood.

"Kit! Stay with me!"

"Give her here," a voice snapped, for all its urgency still brisk and businesslike.

The warm arms surrounding her disappeared and she was placed on a hard table. Steel at her back. Coldness seeped through her clothes and into her bones. She shivered, her teeth chattering as she tried to lift her head, searching out Rafe's hazy face.

Pristine white surrounded her. The odor of ammonia stung her nose, and she wondered if she was in a hospital. What could they do for her?

She dimly heard fabric tear. A frigid breeze floated over her and she realized that someone had cut away her clothing.

Voices continued to buzz around her, congesting the air. She tried to form words, but her lips could not move. Suddenly a yellow, blinding light glared down at her. She jammed her eyes tightly shut.

The pain in her chest intensified. Exploded as poker-hot pincers dug through her flesh, striking bone in a grinding assault.

She lurched upright, screaming.

Hard hands grabbed her from all sides. She thrashed wildly, fighting them off, hissing at the agony of it.

She recognized Gideon's voice. "Dammit, hold her!"

"Did you get it out?"

Her face turned toward Rafe's voice, like a whispered balm to her heart. She whimpered to be near him, for him to make it stop. Take the pain away.

"It's wedged—I can't!"

"You have to get it out! We're losing . . ." The shout faded.

All the voices quieted to a hush, drifting away like insignificant smoke . . .

Darkness rolled in, a fog coming toward her, devouring the room's faultless white like a hungry beast.

She fell back, the slam of her head against cold steel just another sensation. The pain was fading, too. Like everything else.

Numbness set in.

She embraced the dark, where she felt nothing at all.

# 30

S trong, warm fingers flexed around her hand. "Kit. Wake up."
She moved her head, turning toward the sound of that beguiling voice, warm as fleece and spicy as rum swirling through her veins. A dull ache pervaded her body, and she moaned, longing for sleep again. She felt as though she'd been hit by a truck.

"Kit, can you hear me?

She opened her eyes. Rafe leaned over her, bright morning light haloing his dark head. His eyes gleamed down at her, burning obsidian, shining with something she had never seen before. The mattress dipped as he settled down on the bed beside her.

He lifted her hand and pressed a lingering kiss to the back of it. "God, thank you," he choked.

"Rafe." She lifted her free hand and dropped it to the back of his head, threading her fingers through his silky dark hair. "Are you all right?" she asked, remembering that Jack had tried to shoot him, remembering her agony in that moment, and remembering later, as they worked to dig the bullet from her body. Then nothing else. Everything went gray after that.

"Me?" Rafe lifted his head, his expression incredulous. "I'm fine. You're the one that jumped in front of me and took a bullet. A *silver* bullet." His eyes glinted with fury, the centers glowing like candlelight.

"Silver?"

"That's right. A memento." He held a small chunk of twisted silver between his thumb and forefinger. "We dug it out, but it was touch and go. Appears our allergy to silver won't necessarily kill us."

For the first time, she glanced around the room, eyeing the vaulted ceiling with its elaborate crown molding, the marble fireplace set in the wall across from the four-poster bed she occupied. The room was wallpapered in gentle stripes of blue and ivory. Not the clinical white she remembered.

"Where am I? I thought . . . I remember being in some sort of clinic?"

"That was downstairs, in Darius's lab. We moved you in here after you became stabilized. You should have mentioned him to me. Darius runs a hell of a facility." His mouth twisted. She followed his gaze to the IV attached to her arm that led to a bag of dripping fluid stationed beside the bed. "One of the scientists in his employ even went to med school."

She closed her eyes, relief sliding over her. She was alive. She was with Rafe. Her fingers tightened in the soft duvet cover. Life loomed ahead, full and bright with possibilities. If only she could convince Rafe that her feelings for him were genuine.

"Why? Why did you do it?" At the sound of his hoarsely muttered question, she opened her gaze to his face again. A suspicious gleam of moisture filled his eyes. She didn't need to ask to understand what he was asking.

Placing a palm against his cheek, she stared steadily into his eyes. "Because I love you."

He stared at her for a long, weightless moment. She held her breath, hoping he wouldn't deny her again. Hoping he would see that she'd risked her life for him out of love.

"I know," he whispered at last, as though reading her mind. "I know."

She watched him with hunger in her heart, waiting with more patience than she knew she possessed.

His throat worked through a swallow as he shook his head from side to side. "Call me a selfish bastard, but it wouldn't matter to me if you didn't love me. I got a taste of what it would feel like to lose you. I don't want to go through that again. You've got me, you're stuck with me. I love you, and I'm never letting you go." His expression hardened. "Now promise me you will never pull a stupid stunt like that again."

She smiled. "What? Take a silver bullet? Piece of cake."

With a growl, he slid his fingers behind her neck and kissed her. A hard, breath-robbing kiss that made her moan and clutch his shoulders.

"Rafe?"

"Hmm?"

She pulled back from his mouth. "Have you ever seen *The Waltons*?"

"*The Waltons*?" he echoed, dark eyes clouded with what she recognized as desire. Shaking his head, he fixed his dark eyes on her mouth intently. "Who are they?"

Smiling, she shrugged one shoulder and tugged him back down. "Never mind."

He lowered his head, reclaiming her mouth.

A moment passed, and she murmured against his lips again, realizing that as the first of their species, there were a few things yet to discover. "What about kids? Children? Can we have them?"

"We can try," he muttered, his hand sliding up her neck to tangle in her hair. "We can try a lot."

# EPILOGUE

"Mom! Amanda won't get out of the bathroom!"

"Shut up, tattletale!"

Kit smiled and shook her head as she added another pancake to the stack. The pile stood thirty high, and she was nowhere near finished. Three of her daughters buzzed around the kitchen setting the table, exchanging knowing looks.

At that moment, Rafe walked into the kitchen with their oldest son and daughter, all three still wearing their gear and carrying their weapons from the previous night's hunt. "Get changed," she greeted them. "Breakfast is almost ready."

A door slammed upstairs, followed by an indignant screech. Apparently Sam had forced his way into the bathroom.

Everyone in the kitchen lifted their eyes to the ceiling at the sudden eruption of shouts.

"My money's on Amanda," Hannah murmured as she laid out napkins.

Before Kit could reprimand her for betting on the likelihood of Sam getting pummeled by his sister, Rafe hugged her close, wrapping an arm around her waist and pressing a kiss to the side of her neck. She leaned into him, inhaling deeply, his scent as dear and familiar as her own.

"Is it my turn to break them up?"

Sighing with mock frustration, she handed him the spatula. "I'll go."

Turning, Kit headed for the stairs, her strides swift and purposeful. She called out over her shoulder, "Tomorrow night it's my turn to hunt."

Rafe's chuckle followed her. "How about we go out together?"

Stopping at the base of the stairs, she glanced over her shoulder, eyeing him standing in the cluttered kitchen amid five of their noisy children. Already, the oldest two were filling the younger ones in on the night's adventures. Future hunters all of them, they listened with rapt interest.

"And leave the kids at home?"

He nodded, and from the look in his dark eyes, she knew they might never make it to hunting lycans until *very* late in the night.

A contented smile curved her lips. "Perfect," she murmured.

And everything was.